five
KISSES

RACHAEL ANDERSON

HEA PUBLISHING

ISBN: 978-1-941363-29-4

Published by HEA Publishing

For my sister, Sarah,
who is the opposite of a shrew.
(Unless provoked.)

OTHER BOOKS BY RACHAEL ANDERSON

Regency Novels

My Sister's Intended
My Brother's Bride
The Solicitor's Son
The Fall of Lord Drayson
The Rise of Miss Notley
The Pursuit of Lady Harriett

Contemporary Novels

Prejudice Meets Pride
Rough Around the Edges Meets Refined
Stick in the Mud Meets Spontaneity
Not Always Happenstance
The Reluctant Bachelorette
Working it Out
Minor Adjustments
Luck of the Draw
Divinely Designed

Novellas

Righting a Wrong
Twist of Fate
The Meltdown Match

KISS ONE

1

Brighton, England
August 1814

ANTICIPATION SWIRLED AROUND Miss Sarah Meacham as she climbed from the carriage and lifted her gaze to the stunning neoclassical edifice before her. She had walked by the Marine Pavilion countless times during the past nine years, but until tonight, she'd never had the opportunity to enter its revered doors.

I'm here. I'm actually here. She struggled against the urge to fidget and squirm.

She paused next to her chaperone for the evening and glanced from the tall and elegant woman to her taller, almost-as-elegant husband.

It was an awkward situation to be sure, but it was either come with Mr. and Mrs. Winters or not come at all. Having lost her mother a little over a year ago, Sarah had no proper chaperone of her own. Her father, still mourning the loss of his wife, seemed to have forgotten he had two daughters to look after.

Most girls Sarah's age had been presented two summers prior, but her seventeenth year had passed without incident, along with her eighteenth. She should have been a seasoned veteran of balls and dinner parties by now. Instead, here she was at nineteen, still a novice—with a chaperone she had met only yesterday.

At least you are here now, she told herself firmly. *At least you have Peter.*

Only a fortnight prior, Mr. Peter Hatch had burst into her life like a knight intent on rescue, sweeping her out of obscurity. He'd showered her with pretty posies, invited her on numerous walks, drives, and rides, and tonight, he'd seen to it that she'd received an invitation to one of the Prince Regent's famed soirées. Peter had even convinced his aunt to act as her chaperone.

He was sent straight from heaven, Sarah had told her thirteen-year-old sister earlier that day.

Her thoughts must have conjured him up because Peter's exuberant voice came from behind.

"Hello Aunt, Uncle, and of course, the lovely Miss Meacham. It seems I couldn't have timed my arrival more perfectly." He took Sarah's hand and pressed a kiss to her glove, sending happy shivers up her arms.

She grinned at the man who'd taken her heart captive only weeks before. How handsome he looked in his navy jacket and buff-colored breeches.

"Mr. Hatch." She nodded in greeting, trying not to sound as breathless and giddy as she felt.

Peter held out his arm, but as much as Sarah ached to take it, she hesitated. Would it be proper to walk in with him, or should she remain at his aunt's side? Her schoolmistress had always said that if a woman wanted to be respected, she must behave circumspectly.

Oh, how Sarah wanted to be respected, especially by Peter and his aunt.

"This isn't London, Miss Meacham," Mrs. Winters finally said as she tugged her gloves higher on her arms. "Proprieties are not as strictly observed here. Peter can escort you inside and dance the first set with you. After that, and between partners, your place will be with me."

Relieved, Sarah slipped her arm through Peter's. How good it felt to be near him, like walking through the gardens on a refreshingly warm afternoon. In contrast, the carriage ride with his aunt and uncle had been more akin to a chilly, drizzly evening. They'd been courteous, but also frigid, barely talking to Sarah at all.

Mr. and Mrs. Winters preceded the pair into the pavilion, and Sarah took a deep breath. Her skirts swished against her legs, her slippers scuffed at the stone path, and her smile widened.

Peter gave her hand a pat and leaned in close. "Are you happy, my sweet?"

He'd started using that endearment only last week, which had made her *most* happy. Butterflies twirled a waltz in her stomach.

"What if I trip?"

"You'd never."

"Spill punch on my dress?"

"Highly unlikely."

"Say something ridiculous?"

"Impossible."

She grinned at him, admiring his handsome profile and his perfectly-coiffed hair. Mostly blond, it flowed across his head in elegant waves, never a single hair out of place.

Peter was the epitome of many youthful fantasies. He may not be as tall as she'd once envisioned, and his jackets

3

hung a smidge loose about his shoulders, but none of that mattered. The moment his sapphire blue eyes had locked on hers that afternoon across the Steine, Sarah had felt an inkling. A few days later, when he'd finagled an introduction to her father and begged her to accompany him on a drive, she'd known.

One day, she would marry Mr. Peter Hatch.

Her body trembled with excitement as they paused in the middle of the great hall, waiting in a small line for their names to be announced. Unable to stop herself, Sarah looked around, soaking in the ambiance. She'd heard the prince had a penchant for Chinese decor, but she'd still envisioned a room bedecked in cream with pale-blue accents—the colors one would see in a neo-classical building. Instead, she was met with brightly painted murals, bamboo furniture, and the colors of gold, red, and black.

She tilted her head towards Peter and lowered her voice. "It's interesting, isn't it? The room, I mean."

"I suppose," he said, glancing about. "Truth be told, I hardly notice it anymore."

Of course he didn't. Peter had been a regular at the prince's parties for years. Sarah should have known better than to make such a comment.

A novice indeed.

"Peter," she tried again, "I want to thank you for tonight, and well, the past fortnight, really. You have been . . ." Her voice drifted off as she looked into his eyes. What words could possibly convey the depth of her gratitude and love for this man? Amazing, fabulous, or marvelous sounded trite, yet they were all true.

"Beastly?" he guessed with a smile. "Arrogant? Supercilious? Cantankerous?"

Sarah laughed. "You've been none of those things, as you well know. You've been wonderful."

His smile widened, and he patted her hand. "I'll take that over beastly any day." His attention drifted past his aunt and uncle to a tall and slender woman standing in front of them. Not much older than Sarah, her dark eyes settled on Peter for a moment before sliding to Sarah. After a quick appraisal, she turned around, giving Sarah a view of an intricate and unique chignon. Rich, brown hair twisted at the sides, then crisscrossed down into a lovely U-shaped knot.

However had her maid managed that? It was really quite stunning.

Peter cleared his throat and shuffled his feet as though uncomfortable, and Sarah turned her attention back to him. His lips were drawn into a troubled frown, his brow furrowed.

She opened her mouth to inquire if something was the matter when an unruly curl pulled free from her own knot and bounced to her cheek in an act of rebellion.

Peter must have caught the movement because his brow cleared, and his smile returned. "You and your curls. What are we to do with them?"

"I'm beginning to think I should cut them off," Sarah teased, tucking the ringlet back into a pin and silently pleading for it to stay put. No matter how much she pinned, twisted, or attempted to tame her curly, red hair, ringlets were continually popping free. It was maddening.

"It would be a travesty," said Peter gallantly.

"Mr. and Mrs. Gregory Winters, Mr. Peter Hatch, and Miss Meacham," boomed a voice that startled Sarah. Only then did she realize they had at last entered the salon.

As she studied the new room, her gaze rose to the towering, domed ceiling and large bow windows that peered out across the Steine. The view was stunning, especially in this particular light, with the sun on its way down.

5

"Peter, I could live in this room."

He chuckled.

Music met her ears, coming from a large ballroom to the left. Throngs of people filed about, and the room appeared to be like everything else she'd seen—ornate and lovely. Through the open doors to the right, Sarah was able to see far into the distance. There was an anteroom, followed by a library, and beyond that—she squinted—hmm . . . was that a conservatory? How delightful.

"Are we allowed to venture that way?" she asked Peter, pointing through the doors. "I would very much like to see the conservatory at some point."

He leaned down and whispered in her ear. "If you'll be my partner for the dinner dance, I'll take you on a private tour after we eat."

Anticipation encircled her again as she nodded her agreement. This night may very well become a fairytale. She pictured Peter pulling her into a darkened corner of the room and stealing a kiss—or rather, *attempting* to steal a kiss. Sarah hadn't decided if she would allow such a thing to happen.

Peter guided her into the ballroom. A new set was forming, and he tugged her onto the floor.

Only after they'd taken their place did he ask with a cheeky grin, "You'll dance with me, my sweet, won't you?"

"You'd be wiser to ask whether or not I know *how* to dance," she responded.

"Gads. Never say you do not."

"Hush," she said. "I must concentrate or make a fool of us both."

He chuckled as he took his place. "My lips are sealed."

Thankfully, he was a man of his word.

Sarah thought back to the steps a friend had taught her

the summer before—steps Sarah had rehearsed numerous times over the past week while her younger sister plunked away on the pianoforte. But it had been one thing to dance with an imaginary suitor in the quiet of her own home, another to stand in the middle of a crowded ballroom, face to face with the most distracting of men.

It took all of Sarah's focus to keep count. *1-2-3-4-5-6, 1-2-3-4-5-6.* She repeated the numbers over and over in her mind, stumbling here and there and nearly plowing into a woman at some point, but in the end, she made it through her first real dance—at Brighton's famed Marine Pavilion, no less.

"You were magnificent," Peter said as he led her to his aunt.

Sarah laughed. "You exaggerate, sir, but I thank you nonetheless. Hello again, Mrs. Winters."

Peter bowed low over her hand and murmured. "I shall return for that dinner dance." With the grace of a true gentleman, he rose and strode away.

Sarah's eyes lingered on him until he disappeared into the crowd. Only then did she notice Mrs. Winters's look of disapproval.

"I see you haven't had much experience dancing, Miss Meacham."

Sarah had no excuse, other than the fact that this was the first time she'd ever danced in public. *I am what I am,* she thought. If Mrs. Winters found fault with that, so be it.

"Was it that obvious?"

To Sarah's surprise, the woman seemed to soften a little. She shrugged. "Only to a trained eye. But not to worry, by the evening's end you will feel more experienced."

Sarah had her doubts. Her unfashionable red hair woven into an unremarkable coiffure and simple white gown made her a daisy in a room filled with exotic orchids. She'd likely not draw the notice of any man but Peter. "You're assuming other men will ask me to dance."

"Why wouldn't they?" Mrs. Winters asked. "You are a pretty thing. You need only lift your chin and look a man in the eye to attract his notice. Ah, here comes Mr. Bledsoe now. Quick, look up and smile."

Sarah did as instructed, and to her surprise, the wiry, nervous-looking fellow caught her eye and slowed his steps. After a brief exchange with Mrs. Winters, Sarah found herself a partner for the next dance.

So that's how it's done, she thought as she was led onto the dance floor. She glanced back at Mrs. Winters, wondering at her motivation for helping Sarah. Perhaps she was trying to make Sarah into the woman her nephew deserved, or—more likely—she hoped to turn Sarah's head away from Peter and towards another young buck.

If that was the case, it would never work. Every man in the room paled in comparison to Peter.

Sarah dropped into a curtsy. "You'll have to forgive me if I accidentally tread on your shoes, Mr. Bledsoe. I'm still a bit rusty at the cotillion."

"Oh, no. I mean, you couldn't. Or wouldn't. Or—" He clenched his jaw and shook his head before trying again. "That is to say, it's all right if you do."

The poor man looked ready to faint. Perhaps it was his first dinner party as well.

Sarah arched an eyebrow, hoping to set him at ease. "Gallant words, sir, but you can't possibly mean that."

"Oh, but I do," he insisted. "These boots are the sturdiest I own. A horse stepped on them once, and I hardly felt a thing."

"Indeed?" Left with no other recourse than to examine

his boots, Sarah dropped her gaze. Though not high fashion, his boots did appear quite sturdy. "Perhaps I should be hoping you won't tread on *my* slippers then."

He must have missed the teasing in her tone because his cheeks became ruddy—not the best look on him.

"I was only jesting, sir. I'm certain you are a fine dancer."

"I'll do my best," he promised.

To her relief, the music began. Sarah curtsied, smiled, counted steps, and somehow made it through another dance without too many mishaps. Overall, she considered it a success.

Once returned to Mrs. Winters's side, Sarah made sure to lift her chin, smile, and catch the eye of every young man walking past. As if by magic, one after another stopped, begged an introduction, and asked her to dance. It was nothing short of miraculous.

When the dinner dance was finally announced, Sarah excitedly searched the room for the only man she cared to dance with, but Peter was nowhere to be seen. Where had he gone? Only moments ago, she'd spied him dancing with a pretty, blue-eyed blonde. A prick of jealousy had accompanied the sight, but Sarah pushed it aside, reminding herself that Peter was only doing what was expected of him. His heart belonged to her.

Couples began to take their place in line, and Sarah rose on her tiptoes to see over the white feathers sprouting from a woman's coiffure.

"For goodness sake, child, come down off your toes," hissed Mrs. Winters, fanning her face with rigorous movements. "You have the appearance of an eager puppy. Who are you searching for?"

Sarah's heels reconnected with the floor. "Peter—er, I

mean, Mr. Hatch. He requested my hand for the dinner dance."

Mrs. Winters's lips pressed into a grim line. "Did he now."

Sarah nodded absentmindedly, looking around once more. "Something must have detained him. Perhaps he spilled his drink or twisted his ankle? I do hope he is all right. He promised me a tour of the conservatory as well."

"You give him too much credit, my dear," Mrs. Winters murmured under her breath.

Sarah paused in her search of the room to stare at her chaperone, sure she'd misheard. "Pardon?"

Mrs. Winters straightened. "You'd do well to look in another direction, Miss Meacham. Ah, here comes a woman who knows my nephew well. Perhaps she can open your eyes. Miss Ellington, how are you this evening?"

Sarah blinked, trying to make sense of her chaperone's strange words, only to realize that the woman called Miss Ellington appeared equally surprised, as though she hadn't expected Mrs. Winters to speak to her. Even more strange was the fact that Miss Ellington happened to be the same woman Sarah had noticed in the great hall earlier—with the unique chignon—and neither Peter nor his aunt had acknowledged her then.

"Miss Ellington, I'd like you to meet my guest for the evening. This is Miss Meacham."

"How do you do?" Miss Ellington politely curtsied in Sarah's direction, though her words were stiff and somewhat cold.

Before Sarah could respond in kind, Mrs. Winters said, "My nephew has offered to take Miss Meacham to dinner, then on a tour of the conservatory, but he seems to have disappeared. As has *Miss Tillis*." Mrs. Winters directed a knowing look at Miss Ellington before continuing. "Perhaps you would be so kind as to show Miss Meacham the conservatory in his stead? I believe you are more familiar with that room than I."

Sarah's mouth fell open as she stared at the two women. Whoever this Miss Ellington was, she was *not* an acceptable substitute for Peter. Besides, he'd promised to show her the room *after* dinner, not before.

Oh, Peter, where are you?

Miss Ellington hesitated before accepting her fate. "I would be glad to show you the conservatory, Miss Meacham. Shall we go now?"

Sarah began to shake her head, but Mrs. Winters gave her a gentle nudge, saying firmly, "You should go, child."

"But—"

"Now."

Sarah clamped her mouth closed and finally nodded, even though the whole situation seemed completely nonsensical. Perhaps Mrs. Winters had imbibed too much or suffered some sort of apoplexy.

Sarah quickened her steps to keep up with the taller woman. "Miss Ellington, you needn't show me the conservatory. Peter has already promised to take me after dinner."

"How good of him." She used the same tone as Mrs. Winters. Sardonic. Cold. Disbelieving. Miss Ellington put a hand on Sarah's arm, prodding her past a group of women giggling in the salon, and guided her into the anteroom.

"Tell me, Miss Meacham, how well do you know Mr. Hatch?"

Sarah didn't care for the other woman's tone and responded stiffly. "We've grown quite close these past few weeks. He's been most attentive."

"I have no doubt."

They moved on to the library, where they happened upon the Prince Regent lifting his glass to some cronies. My, he was a large man. Boisterous too, from the sound of his voice echoing through the room. Both women dropped into a quick curtsy before Miss Ellington pulled Sarah across the room and to the conservatory doors.

Only then did she stop to face Sarah. "There are certain things you must see to believe, however painful the sight might be."

Sarah had no response to this, other than to think everyone around her had gone mad. Perhaps it was the food, the drinks, or the unusual décor. It did seem to cast a spell on the place.

Miss Ellington finally sighed and gestured for Sarah to precede her into the conservatory.

Sarah frowned as a strange sort of dread pressed down on her, making her wonder briefly if Peter was not the man she'd believed him to be.

No, she thought fiercely. *This is ludicrous. He would never do anything to harm me.*

Moonlight cast a soft glow across the ornamental trees, plants, and flowers, creating a magical, ethereal effect. *See?* she thought. *There is nothing to be afraid of in here. It's peaceful and romantic.*

Sarah opened her mouth to tell Miss Ellington that she would prefer to finish the tour with Mr. Hatch when a soft murmur caught her attention. It came from a darkened corner of the room, where a couple stood, locked in a passionate embrace.

Sarah's body stiffened.

Her breath hitched.

Her eyes widened.

It can't be, she thought. Sarah would recognize that ill-fitting jacket and buff-colored breeches anywhere.

Peter.

No.

He blocked all but the woman's arms and hands, but her fingers wound around Peter's neck and raked through his once-immaculate hair. She moaned some more as his kisses moved from her mouth to her neck, revealing a mass of blonde curls.

"I could never care for another woman, my sweet," came Peter's voice. "'Tis you, and you alone, who has my heart."

My sweet. The words rang through Sarah's head like a bull on a rampage, igniting all sorts of angry thoughts and feelings. That was *her* endearment. Her man. Her room.

Only he wasn't her man. Not any longer.

The swine.

Unable to pry her eyes away from the scene, Sarah drew in several deep breaths. But it was no use. The more she watched the couple devour one another, the more incensed she became. Her jaw clenched, and her fingers curled into fists. *How dare you, Mr. Peter Hatch!*

"You have my heart as well, my love," came the woman's breathless voice. Sarah could only assume it was the blue-eyed girl she'd seen Peter dancing with not ten minutes before. What had Mrs. Winters called her? Miss Tillis?

"Tell me she means nothing to you. Tell me she is a plain, empty-headed widgeon."

"Miss Meacham is all of those things and more," he murmured, his mouth claiming Miss Tillis's once more.

Sarah's jaw fell open. They were speaking of *her?*

Her blood heated to a boil, threatening to spew from her body. Every part of her wanted to attack the man and pummel him senseless. Her body trembled as she fought against the urge, the voice of her schoolmistress resounding in her ears.

Never let your temper control you. You must be better than that.

Sarah *was* better. Better than Mr. Peter Hatch and certainly better than the strumpet he continued to kiss. A woman of good breeding would never attack a man, no matter how much he deserved it. Instead, she would walk away, calm herself, and find another, more dignified way to enact revenge.

Miss Tillis giggled breathlessly. "It was most unkind of you to leave her without a partner for the dinner dance."

"Most unkind," he repeated like a lovesick idiot.

"What would she think, I wonder, if you were to walk into dinner with me on your arm?" Another giggle.

"I wouldn't care," he murmured.

Miss Tillis's fingers ran up his arms and wound around his neck once more. She rose to her tiptoes, revealing a pretty pair of blue eyes darkened by the shadows. "Shall we go in then? I'm ravenous."

The moment her gaze locked with Sarah's, Miss Tillis froze, and her grating, high-pitched voice squeaked, "Peter. Miss Meacham is—"

"Miss Meacham be hanged," Peter growled as he tried to capture the woman's mouth once more.

In that instant, something snapped inside of Sarah— something that made her forget all about her school-mistress's instructions and counsel. She strode forward with only one thought in her head: *Proper young ladies be hanged.*

Mr. Hatch seemed to realize something was amiss because he finally looked over his shoulder. His eyes caught hold of Sarah's just as she pulled her arm back to launch the hardest punch she had ever thrown. Actually, it was the *only* punch she had ever thrown, but she put her whole soul into it. Her fist connected hard with his face as pain ignited in her fingers.

Peter groaned and reeled back in shock, his hand flying to his nose as blood came spurting out. Miss Tillis screamed and backed into a corner like a spineless jellyfish.

Sarah stepped forward to throw another punch, thought better of it, and delivered a solid kick to his shin instead. When that didn't produce another groan, she hitched up her skirts a little and aimed higher. Her father's stablehand had once taught her where to kick a boy if she wanted to bring him to his knees.

It worked admirably.

Peter moaned and doubled over, one hand leaving his bloody nose to cup his nether regions. Miss Tillis screamed again until Sarah's venomous glare quieted her.

"Have you gone mad?" Peter finally found his voice.

"Yes." Surprisingly, Sarah's voice sounded more controlled than she felt. She elevated her chin and stared daggers at him. "You are nothing more than a slimy, sniveling, toad-eating buzzard, Mr. Peter Hatch. If I never lay eyes on you again, it will be too soon."

With those parting words, she spun on her heel, ready to be done with Mr. Peter Hatch, the conservatory, and the entire soirée.

What she discovered, however, was an audience. A large group of people now surrounded them, with Prinny standing next to Miss Ellington at its center.

·· 2 ··

A NORMAL, LEVEL-HEADED woman would have come to her senses at the sight of so many horrified expressions. She would have begged the prince's apologies and quickly excused herself before he summoned his servants to have her forcefully removed.

It's what Sarah *should* have done.

Unfortunately, the feeling of rebellion still roared within.

Why should I care about their opinions? They don't care about mine, and they certainly don't care about me. They are only here to gawk, judge, and gather ammunition for gossip.

Driven by this devil-may-care attitude, Sarah strode to the prince, curtsied, and asked if she could borrow his half-filled goblet of wine. Politely, of course. He was, after all, the Prince of Wales.

With a quirk of his lips and a gleam in his eyes, he held out his drink.

"Thank you, Your Highness." Sarah accepted the glass.

The prince probably expected her to gulp down the

17

contents to fortify her spirits, but she didn't. Instead, she approached the horrid Mr. Hatch one last time. It was a satisfying sight to see his blond locks unattractively disheveled and blood smeared across his lying mouth. He required only one last touch.

His eyes widened, and his hands flew forward as she tossed the wine square in his face with a satisfied smirk.

"You are nothing more than a shrew!" he roared.

Sarah acknowledged the insult with a cheeky curtsy and said, "That's Miss Meacham to you, sir. Good evening."

With as much dignity as possible, Sarah returned the goblet to the prince. "You have a beautiful home, Your Highness. It has been a pleasure."

He chortled, his large belly shaking as he did so. "No, no, the pleasure is all mine, *mademoiselle*."

Sarah quickly examined the room for an exit, but the doorway was blocked with an ever-increasing flock of onlookers, and she wasn't about to battle her way through them. She'd done enough damage already. Instead, her gaze landed on a large open window overlooking the Steine.

Did she dare?

The shadows beckoned, offering to swallow her up and hide her away from all the prying eyes. Sarah couldn't resist. With as much decorum as she could, she strode across the room, slipped through the opening, and escaped into the night.

· · • · ·

THE MORE DISTANCE Sarah placed between herself and the pavilion, the worse she felt. Snippets of scenes flashed through her mind.

The punch to his nose.

The hard kick to his groin—with her skirts hiked up, no less.

Her frenzied diatribe.

The borrowed glass of wine. And not just anyone's glass—the *prince's* glass, ruler of England and Sarah's future king.

The full weight of her actions came barreling down at her like a guillotine. Her first day out in society, and she'd ensured her own social execution. Possibly her father and sister's as well.

Heaven help her. What had she done?

Sarah gulped in deep breaths of air and tried to calm herself.

At least I know the truth now.

At least I made Peter look the fool as well.

At least . . . Sarah tried to think of other positives, but they eluded her.

At least I didn't cry, she finally thought, even as tears sprang to her eyes.

How could she have been so blind? She'd been so certain that Peter's attentions had been genuine, so sure her hunt for a husband had ended before it had really begun. She'd even contemplated a few names for their future children: William Peter and Charity Bethia. Sarah had always liked the name Charity.

A shame she didn't have an ounce of that particular trait within her at the moment.

I hate you, Peter Hatch. I hate you.

She brushed angrily at her tears, despising them almost as much as she despised the man who'd caused them. What would become of her now? What would become of her father and sister? They would inevitably be shunned as well.

Bethia still had five years before she would be of age. Perhaps by then, this wretched night would be forgotten.

Who was she kidding? It was a useless hope. If Sarah's

schoolmistress could be believed, the ton never forgot anything. They held on to scandal like a priceless family heirloom, always anxious to cut, snub, and ostracize.

Sarah glared into the darkness, feeling wretched all over again. Her only hope was that her father would someday remarry a respected gentlewoman, and her new stepmother would properly introduce Bethia into society.

It could happen.

It *had* to happen.

A carriage rattled up behind her, and Sarah stepped out of the way, landing her foot in a chilly puddle.

She muttered an unladylike curse and glared at the coachman.

To her chagrin, he pulled the carriage to a stop next to her and tipped his hat. The door opened with a squeak, and Miss Ellington's face peered out.

"Hello, Miss Meacham. Would you care for a ride? It appears we are going in the same direction."

Sarah rubbed her arms, wishing she hadn't taken the cowardly way out of the pavilion. If she'd ducked through the crowd and exited normally, she could have collected her wrap. Her face and arms had long since capitulated to the cold, and the toes of her left foot, now wet, were beginning to prickle.

As much as she'd love to accept the offer of a ride, however, Sarah had no intention of stepping into any equipage with the likes of Miss Ellington. The woman was not her friend. A friend would have told Sarah what they'd find in the conservatory. She would have warned or prepared her in some way.

Instead, Miss Ellington had tossed Sarah into a churning sea without even asking if she could swim.

Sarah hadn't swum. She hadn't even kept her head

afloat. She'd plummeted straight to the bottom and drowned while Miss Ellington stood by and watched.

"No, thank you," said Sarah before picking up her skirts and moving forward once more. Her home wasn't much farther. Another twenty minutes or so, and she could warm herself by the fire.

"No, Chelle, you mustn't," cried an unfamiliar female voice from inside the carriage.

"I'll return in just a moment."

Sarah looked back to see Miss Ellington climb down the steps. When her coachman saw what she intended to do, he leapt from his perch. "Please, Miss, allow me."

But Miss Ellington was already on the ground, her azure skirts glowing faintly in the moonlight.

"Roddy, I'm perfectly capable of climbing down from a carriage without assistance, and Susan, please remain in the coach. I mean to walk with Miss Meacham for a few moments."

Her coachman frowned his disapproval but tipped his hat just the same. "Very well, Miss. I'll follow with the coach."

Sarah scowled and continued walking, further annoyed when Miss Ellington fell into step next to her. Curse the woman's longer stride.

"You will have to run if you wish to outdistance me," she said.

"Ladies don't run," Sarah snapped.

"They don't punch, kick, or toss wine at men either."

"No need to tell me what I already know," came Sarah's angry response.

"Then perhaps I'll tell you what you do not know. After your, er . . . interesting departure, Prinny informed Mr. Hatch that he ought to do the honorable thing and wed Miss Tillis without further ado."

How wonderful, Sarah thought derisively. The man who'd only just crushed her dreams would get exactly what he wanted—a blissful union with the woman he professed to love. "I'll have to remember to congratulate the happy couple."

Miss Ellington hopped over a puddle. "Oh, they will not be happy for long. Loyalty and commitment are required for that."

Sarah frowned, not understanding.

"That sorry pair has been playing a recurring game of cat and mouse for over two years now—one that relies on unsuspecting people like you to keep things interesting. It's cyclical, you see. They are mad for each other for a time, but one eventually tires of the other or their eye is caught by someone new. They part ways until the one inevitably grows jealous and uses some poor innocent to win the other back. Somehow, it always seems to work, likely because they are both nitwits."

"How kind of you to inform me about this *now.*" Sarah quickened her steps, wishing Miss Ellington would climb back into her carriage and leave her be. Instead, the woman grabbed hold of Sarah's arm and pulled her to a stop.

"You're freezing," she said. "Even through my gloves, I feel it."

Sarah pulled her arm free. "I don't care."

Miss Ellington looked heavenward for a moment and may have even rolled her eyes. Sarah wasn't sure.

With a sigh, the taller woman said, "I am sorry, Miss Meacham. Truly, I am. I should not have let you walk into that room without warning you first. It was unfeeling of me, I know. But before you judge me too harshly, please understand that last summer my younger sister was in your very shoes. She came to visit me for the summer, and Mr.

22

Hatch flirted and charmed and stole her heart. She was certain an offer of marriage was forthcoming, and I championed the cause as well. He seemed a perfect match for her at the time. It wasn't until I stumbled upon him and Miss Tillis at a garden party that I realized how naive and foolish we'd both been."

Sarah shivered as she looked Miss Ellington in the eye. If that was true, how had Sarah not heard talk of Mr. Hatch's rakish ways before now? For nine years, Sarah had called Brighton her home. She may not be officially out in society, but she wasn't completely oblivious of news or gossip. One afternoon spent in the lending library informed her of a great many things.

Or so she'd thought.

"I didn't see the point in trying to warn you," Miss Ellington continued. "Mr. Hatch plays a very convincing suitor, and from the way you were looking at him all evening, I could tell you'd been caught in his snare. Why would you believe a complete stranger when I wouldn't have thought it possible either? I decided it was best to avoid an argument and let you see the truth for yourself."

Sarah had to concede that she probably wouldn't have believed Mr. Hatch capable of such deceit. Like Miss Ellington, Sarah had been sure it was only a matter of time before he asked for her hand.

Nearly twenty years of age and still so naive. Ugh.

"Mark my words," said Miss Ellington, "A union between that pair will only bring misery."

Misery. Sarah had to admit she liked the sound of that. She shouldn't, of course. She should want to turn the other cheek, forgive and forget. But in her current state of mind, she couldn't bring herself to do either—not when misery would bring about justice.

Perhaps she should stop thinking ill of Miss Ellington.

"Mrs. Winters asked you to show me," Sarah said, realizing that her chaperone—Peter's *aunt*, of all people—had tried to warn her in some way.

Miss Ellington nodded. "I suppose she was attempting to correct past grievances. Once I'd put my heartbroken sister on a stagecoach bound for our childhood home, I called upon Mrs. Winters and gave her quite the tongue lashing. She and my sister had become fairly close, you see, and I was angry that she allowed her to walk into Mr. Hatch's snare unaware. It was Mrs. Winters who should have warned her, and I told her as much. Then I stormed out and haven't spoken to her since—until tonight, that is. I believe she was trying to help you the way she hadn't helped my sister."

A breeze pulled several ringlets free from Sarah's knot and whipped them around her face. She wrapped her arms around herself, thoroughly chilled. "I see."

"Do you, truly? Honestly, Miss Meacham, had I known how spectacularly you'd react, I wouldn't have taken you into the conservatory. I would have dragged you into a closet and held you captive until you promised to believe me."

Sarah snickered, though it was anything but humorous. "Had you done that, it might have been you who'd been punched and kicked."

Miss Ellington giggled. "I think you broke his nose and very possibly have taken away his ability to reproduce. The world is in your debt."

Sarah groaned and buried her face in her hands. "I'll never be able to show my face in public again, will I?"

"Oh, it's not as bad as that," said Miss Ellington. "In fact, it may not be bad at all."

Sarah slowly lowered her hands, not daring to hope. "What do you mean?"

"After Prinny scolded Mr. Hatch, he tried to drink from his goblet, only to recall it had been emptied. Then he laughed and laughed, saying he'd have to invite the beautiful Miss Shrew to all of his parties from that point forward. He'd never been more diverted in his life."

"Miss . . . Shrew?" Sarah squeaked.

Miss Ellington slipped her arm through Sarah's and tugged her towards the carriage. "There are worse names to be called."

"Name one," challenged Sarah.

"Oh, I don't know. Perhaps a slimy, sniveling, toad-eating buzzard," quipped Miss Ellington with a grin.

Sarah smiled a little, and for a brief moment she felt the weight of her mistakes lighten. But it didn't last long. In the end, she needed to accept her fate.

"As soon as morning comes, and the effects of his drink wear off, the prince will come to his senses."

"Perhaps," said Miss Ellington as her coachman leapt down to assist them into the carriage. "Or perhaps you will suddenly find yourself quite popular, in that notorious sort of way. I'm wagering on the latter."

Sarah ducked inside the carriage and nodded at the other woman. Miss Ellington's companion, she presumed.

"Miss Meacham, allow me to introduce you to Mrs. Brommely, the headmistress of the school for young ladies where I teach. Mrs. Brommely, this is Miss Meacham."

The two women only had the chance to greet each other briefly before Miss Ellington returned to the subject at hand. "I believe you are about to become quite the sensation, Miss Meacham, which leads us to another matter—your hair. Forgive me for being so blunt, but would you be open to a change?"

Sarah's hands flew to her ringlets, only to realize that

many of them had escaped and were now jutting out at various angles. Merciful heavens, when had that happened? Hopefully not before she'd left the pavilion.

"I'm afraid there's nothing to change. My curls have a mind of their own."

"They certainly do," agreed Miss Ellington. "Which is why you mustn't try to tame them."

"I . . . I don't understand."

"You will tomorrow morning when I call on you, at which time I will show you how to turn them into an asset. When the prince sees his fiery and diverting Miss Shrew again, he'll want to make you his next conquest."

Sarah shuddered at the thought. The prince might be rich and royal, but he was old enough to be her father, portly, and not even remotely attractive.

But if Miss Ellington was correct, and they could somehow turn potential ostracism into notoriety, Sarah would gladly accept whatever help her new friend could offer.

"You'll soon be the talk of the ton and will have men lining up to court you," promised Miss Ellington.

The Sarah from an hour or two earlier might have loved the idea of men lining up for her. Now, however, she wanted nothing to do with it. After this evening, she would never trust another man again. No matter how handsome or charming a future suitor might be, he wouldn't be handsome or charming enough to tempt her.

From this point forward, her head would rule her emotions. She would face the coming scrutiny with a stiff upper lip, embrace her new reputation as Miss Shrew, and live the remainder of her life free from the snares of men.

No one would ever pull the wool over her eyes again.

KISS TWO

·· 3 ··

Brighton, England
Five years later, August 1819

Sign and be done with it, man, thought Mr. Ian Collum as he watched the young, pale-faced man hold the quill over the contract, ready to scrawl out his name, only to set it down with a sigh.

Jibes and crivens, now what?

A fortnight prior, Ian had made inquiries about a certain property located just west of Brighton in Hove. Quaintly situated on a small rise, the brown, brick home, with its host of white-paned windows, matching corbels, and steeply-pitched roof, looked out across the English Channel. On a clear day, and with the help of a looking glass, Ian might be able to see all the way to France.

The second he'd laid eyes on Ivy Cottage, he'd wanted it. He'd wanted it for the large elm that draped majestically over top, the perfectly-sized stables it housed, and the meadows that encircled it. The fact that it was in fairly close proximity to the newly improved Shoreham Harbour was an additional perk. Having recently relocated his shipping business from the overcrowded and foul-smelling town of Portsmouth, all Ian needed was a place to call home.

"Is there a problem?" Ian asked, purposefully sounding more Scottish than English. It could be an effective intimidation tactic, as Scots were known for having fiery tempers.

"No and yes," Mr. Gyles said smoothly, running a finger along the feather of the quill. "I just have one additional condition that must be met before I add my signature to the contract."

Ian's frown deepened. They had already discussed everything that needed discussing. They'd already agreed on a price, and Mr. Gyles had made it clear he had no use for the property. He'd inherited it only months before, and it had been sitting empty for several years prior to that.

"Condition?"

Mr. Gyles cleared his throat and shifted in his seat, but to his credit, his green eyes stayed locked on Ian. "It's more of a favor, really."

"Explain."

Mr. Gyles cleared his throat again, and his gaze snapped nervously to the side before returning to Ian. "I require your assistance with a . . . delicate matter."

Not one to beat around the bush, Ian rolled his eyes. "Out with it, Mr. Gyles."

"Very well. I would like you to court a certain woman in town."

Ian blinked once, twice, and then a third time. That was the last thing he'd expected to hear. He'd come here to purchase a house, not discuss courting or women.

Mr. Gyles let out a breath and combed his fingers

through his hair, disrupting a few brown curls in the process. "I have fallen in love with a woman named Miss Bethia Meacham. She has an older sister, Miss Sarah Meacham. Have you heard of her? The family lives in Brighton."

"Nae," said Ian stiffly.

"She's quite lovely. Quick-witted. Well-spoken. Good natured, despite what the gossips might say."

Before this point, Ian would have described Mr. Gyles as an intelligent man of sound mind. Now, however, he wondered if the man had gone daft. "Are you referring to your bride-to-be or her sister?"

"The sister. She's quite talented in a myriad of things as well, including . . ." He cleared his throat and mumbled something that sounded like, "fisticuffs."

"Fisticuffs?"

"Er . . . yes."

Ian rubbed his temples using the thumb and third finger of the same hand. How was it that a conversation about a house had transitioned into talk of a woman engaging in fisticuffs? Who was this woman?

"Forgive me, Mr. Gyles, but will you, or will you not, sell me the property in question?"

"Hear me out, Mr. Collum. I wish to wed Miss Bethia, but her father refuses to give his consent until her older sister is engaged. I simply need you to, er . . . engage her. The older sister, I mean."

"You want me to make an offer of marriage to some lass?" Ian didn't think his eyes could grow any larger. How the devil did that amount to a small favor?

"No, no, of course not. But it is my belief that her father will relent if Miss Meacham were to show an interest in a suitor. She has sworn off all men, you see, ever since . . . well, never mind that. I simply need you to become her beau for a time. That is all."

All? Ian couldn't believe what he was hearing. "Absolutely not."

"In that case . . ." Mr. Gyles picked up the contract as though he meant to rip it down the middle.

Ian's chair squeaked as he stood and planted his palms on the desk, using his towering height and solid build to his advantage. "We had an agreement."

Mr. Gyles set the contract back on the desk and met Ian's gaze. "We still do, assuming you'll agree to my condition."

"Condition," Ian scoffed, pushing himself upright. "You're talking about preying on the emotions of an innocent lass—your future sister-in-law, if it comes to that. Do you really think it a good idea?"

"I'll admit, it's not ideal. But I'm desperate enough to try anything."

That much was obvious. Ian could see the determination in the younger man's eyes. Trouble was, Ian didn't have the same amount of leverage. Mr. Gyles had already shown he wasn't as anxious to sell as Ian was to buy.

"What will happen should her father not consent to your marriage without an actual engagement on our part?"

"I will be forced to wait for Miss Bethia to reach her majority. Or elope, though I'd rather it not come to that."

"That's not what I was referring to," said Ian.

"Oh, yes, the house. Of course. In that case, you will be off the hook, and I will sign the property over to you immediately."

"Before or after you run off with Miss Bethia?"

"Before. You have my word."

Ian took a few steps around the room and rubbed his forehead. "This is madness."

"Agreed."

"Why me?"

Mr. Gyles turned his palms up as though he couldn't say for sure. "Because no other man has been able to turn her head. Because you have that mysterious look about you that women swoon over. And because I'm fairly certain you want that house as much as I want Bethia."

In other words, Ian was the only man Mr. Gyles could bribe—or rather, manipulate. Och, if only he'd feigned a minor interest in the property instead of shown his hand.

Perhaps he could find another. Or build something similar.

Nae, 'twould never do. That elm reminded him too much of his favorite climbing tree as a lad. The moment he'd seen it, a feeling of nostalgia had assaulted him. Ian knew what he wanted, and he wanted that house.

He dropped down on the chair and drummed his fingers against his leg as he considered his options. "You said she was lovely."

"She is."

"Quick-witted too?"

"Yes."

"You also mentioned the gossips and . . . fisticuffs?"

Mr. Gyles grimaced as though berating himself for letting those things slip. "She has a bit of a reputation—Miss Shrew, they call her. Apparently, she struck a man once. Years ago. Broke his nose, I believe, at least that's what they say. Bethia swears it's an exaggeration, that her sister wouldn't harm an ant."

Ian stared at the younger man, his mouth agape. "*She broke a man's nose?*"

Mr. Gyles shrugged. "I can't say for certain as I wasn't there. I only know what's been said. It's my understanding that Prinny was particularly fond of her, at least before he left Brighton."

"Prinny, as in the Prince of Wales?"

"Yes. They were said to be great friends."

Ian tried to connect the pieces in his head, but no matter which way he turned them, they didn't seem to fit. "Does she not have suitors already?"

"According to Bethia, many have tried over the years but failed. She's spurned them all and is now considered something of a spinster."

"How old is she, exactly?"

"Four and twenty, I believe."

The more Ian learned about Miss Meacham the more curious he became. She sounded like a complete paradox. A bonnie lass who broke noses, shunned men, and claimed the titles of Miss Shrew *and* Prinny's friend. Whoever she was, she certainly wouldn't be interested in the likes of Ian. He may have been blessed with good looks and a charming manner, but he didn't exactly run in exalted circles. One would never find *his* name on the prince's invitation list.

"You've chosen the wrong man, Mr. Gyles. I am the last person anyone should recommend to a gentlewoman. Or are you forgetting that I'm a tradesman?"

Mr. Gyles hesitated, then shrugged again. "She needn't know that."

Ian chuckled derisively as he returned to his seat and folded his hands behind his neck. "You want me to lie?"

"Only avoid certain subjects."

"How do you propose we meet?"

"I can introduce you as an old friend from Scotland. It would explain your slight burr."

"One would think a man from Scotland would have a strong burr," Ian said dryly.

"Hmm, good point." Mr. Gyles thrummed his fingers against the top of his desk. "How did you come by your accent, exactly? You are obviously well educated and have spent time on both continents."

"That's not important." Ian wasn't about to make Mr. Gyles his confidant any more than he was ready to agree to this so-called condition. Though really, what other choice did he have. It didn't help that the fascinating Miss Shrew had piqued his curiosity.

"There is an intimate dinner party on Friday next that the Meachams are planning to attend. I can introduce you then."

Ian grimaced. Hobnobbing was not his style. He enjoyed the occasional dinner party with close friends or business acquaintances, but when it came to attending a function only to see or be seen, he'd rather not be seen. While in the East Indies, Ian had learned to politic well—it had been a necessity for those wanting to advance—but he'd never cared for the practice. It was one of the many reasons he finally took the plunge, left India behind, and ventured out on his own.

Now *he* was the one in control, and he intended to keep it that way.

"This plan is ludicrous," Ian said. He didn't have time to court some woman, at least not at present. Someday, he held hopes of finding a good woman and settling down, but that day was not today.

Mr. Gyles leaned forward, his brown curls swaying. "It may be a ludicrous plan, Mr. Collum, but it's my *only* plan. If you want that house, you'll do as I ask."

Ian clenched his jaw, thinking he should walk away from Mr. Gyles, his mad proposition, *and* the house. Perhaps if he gave it some time, that man would come to his senses. Or perhaps he'd find another buyer.

Ian realized he'd been tapping his knee, so he fisted his

hand and forced it to be still. Would it be so difficult to take a bonnie lass driving a few times? Send her some flowers, a note or two, and attempt to woo her a bit? From what Mr. Gyles said, she certainly wouldn't bore him. Besides, once she realized how unfit he truly was, she'd dismiss him and that would be that. The man would have no other choice but to sell.

Before he agreed, however, Ian had some terms of his own.

"If I am to do this—or rather, *attempt* to do this—I will go about it in my own way. You will not introduce me into local society, nor will I play the part of an old, family friend."

"But how will you—"

"I require only that you point out the lass in question and provide me with a list of the places she frequents, along with the times she usually frequents them."

"But—"

"Trust me, Mr. Gyles. I will meet Miss Shrew—

"Miss Meacham."

"And I will do everything in my power to engage her interest, as you put it. But should she reject me as she's done with all the others, you must agree there's nothing more to be done and sign over the property."

Mr. Gyles studied Ian a moment before shaking his head. "I need more from you than a valiant attempt. I *need* you to win her over, and I have every confidence you're up to the challenge. It may take time and a few failed attempts, but with your looks, confidence, Scottish charm, and determination, she'll come around. If not, I've heard rumors that Mr. Kemp might be interested in the property."

Ian narrowed his eyes. "Sell Ivy House to someone else, Mr. Gyles, and I'll personally see to it that you never wed Miss Bethia."

Mr. Gyles didn't appear phased. "See that I do, and the house is yours."

Ian sighed, knowing he'd been defeated, at least for now. "Are you certain there isn't another lass who could capture your fancy? Preferably one without an overbearing father and a shrewish sister?"

"It's Miss Bethia or no one."

Of course it is. Which left Ian with only two choices: walk away from that house or refocus his energies on courting a woman who didn't want to be courted.

"Very well. I'll do what I can to woo Miss Shrew."

"Miss Meacham."

"Miss Meacham, then."

Mr. Gyles grinned in approval. "That's the spirit. I'll get you the information you've requested as soon as I am able."

"Any idea as to why Miss Meacham has been so difficult for men to woo?"

Mr. Gyles shrugged. "She supposedly broke the bloke's nose because he broke her heart, and she has sworn off men ever since."

If that was the case, Ian's job just became much more difficult. A lass who placed all men in the vile, untrustworthy category was a force to be reckoned with. He'd known someone like that in India. It had taken five years just to earn her friendship, and that was all she'd ever given.

He wasn't about to spend an additional five years on Miss Shrew.

"You're that anxious to saddle yourself with Miss Bethia?"

"Yes."

Ian sighed. There was nothing for it. The poor sop was besotted, and now Ian would have to feign the same afflicttion in order to close the deal. He could only pray the woman was as lovely and engaging as Mr. Gyles made her out to be.

He did have one last thing to say, however. "If I actually succeed in gaining Miss Meacham's affections, am I to break her heart as well? I've already felt the pain of a broken nose twice in my life. I don't fancy feeling it again." Nor did he fancy hurting the lass, even a shrewish one.

Mr. Gyles pushed his chair back and stood. "We'll cross that bridge when we get to it. In the meantime, do we have an accord?" He held out his hand, watching Ian expectantly.

Ian hesitated, thinking about Miss Shrew, the house, and the determined man before him. He'd always hated the feeling of being cornered, and that's precisely how he felt now. Outmaneuvered and trapped. He could only hope he would eventually find a way out.

·· 4 ··

SARAH ROSE TO her tiptoes, reaching, stretching, and straining for all she was worth, but her fingers could only brush the spine of *Frankenstein, vol I.*

Drat.

Not long after its 1818 publication, the circulating library in Brighton had purchased only one copy of the three-volume set. Even though the story had become wildly popular, the stingy proprietress, Mrs. Wright, refused to purchase another. Stories about monsters were not in good taste, she'd once said, and Sarah ought to be grateful she'd made an exception for the one copy.

To further frustrate matters, Mrs. Wright didn't keep any sort of waiting list for popular titles, nor would she divulge the identity of the current borrower of a book. If a patron could locate a book on her shelves, he or she could borrow said book. If there was no book to be found, "Perhaps next time," was always said with a smile.

Sarah had come to despise that woman's smile. Because of her stubbornness, over a year had gone by, and Sarah had yet to see the first volume of *Frankenstein* on the library's shelf.

Until today.

If only she could reach it.

She pushed her toes to their limits and strained one last time, but it was no use. The book was just out of reach, and the sliding ladder was currently being used by a gangly-looking boy who'd been given the task of shelving a large basket of books. Sarah wasn't about to interrupt him. She'd likely startle him and cause him to fall.

Instead, she scanned the room for a chair, but it was a busy afternoon in Brighton, and they were all occupied—mostly by people who cared more about socializing than reading.

Annoyed, she turned back to the bookshelf, wondering if one of the lower shelves would support her weight. She only needed a little more height. The span of her hand would suffice, or . . . Her gaze fell on the bottom shelf where several sturdy-looking editions of *The Holy Bible* had been placed.

Yes, those could work nicely.

Sarah crouched down and tugged one of the books from its place on the shelf. A shameful amount of dust coated the top, so she tried to blow it off before tipping the book on its side. Dust floated in the air around her as she pulled a second bible from the shelf, and then a third. She wrinkled her nose against the temptation to sneeze, thinking someone should at least dust them off every once in a while.

After making sure the books were as secure as she could make them, Sarah brushed the dust from her hands and climbed on top, proud of her ingenuity. Now, she would finally, *finally* get to read—

She frowned at the hole where the first volume of *Frankenstein* had stood only moments before. Where had it gone? She quickly scanned the rest of the books on the shelf, only to be disappointed. Had she imagined it? No, the book *had* been there. She was certain of it. Someone must have stolen it while she was building her stack of books.

An unfamiliar man stood within an arm's reach of her. With his back against the bookcase, he was looking down at a book—*her* book—and flipping through the first few pages. Dark, almost black hair fell forward, landing just below his eyes. His skin was dark too, as though he'd spent a great deal of time in the sun.

Sarah pressed her lips together in consternation. Why couldn't he be out in the sun now and away from this library? No matter how imposing he might look, she wasn't about to let him walk away with *Frankenstein*. She'd waited too long.

"I wouldn't waste your time with that one," she said, hoping to persuade him to put the book back. It wasn't the thing to speak to a person without a proper introduction, but she wanted the book badly enough to make an exception.

He didn't appear to have heard her, so she tapped him lightly on the shoulder and raised her voice a little. "I hear it's an incredibly dull story."

He looked up in confusion only to follow her gaze back to the book in his hands. He closed the cover and lifted it up for her inspection.

"Are you referring to this?" Almost black eyes peered at her. She might have thought he hailed from Spain if not for the Scottish lilt she detected in his voice.

Sarah cleared her throat and nodded. "From what I understand, it leaves much to be desired."

He twisted to face her, leaning one shoulder against the bookcase. She couldn't help but notice how well his shoulders filled out his coat. He was also tall. Even on her pile of books, her eyes were only level with his slightly bent nose, as though he'd broken it a time or two.

"I've heard the opposite." One of his thick eyebrows quirked as though he'd only just noticed something strange. He glanced down at her feet before meeting her gaze once more.

"Is there a reason you're standing on a stack of bibles?"

"I, er . . ." Sarah scrambled for something to say, not wanting to admit she'd been trying to reach the very book he now held—the book she'd only just described as lacking.

"It's a known fact that the Bible can bring one closer to God so . . . I, er, thought I'd give it a try. What do you think? Do I look more holy to you?"

She had to stop herself from cringing. Of all the ridiculous things to say. She sounded idiotic—or worse, blasphemous. She could only pray that lightning wouldn't come through the ceiling and strike her down.

He studied her a moment, undoubtedly trying to gauge her level of seriousness. "Considering I have no idea what you looked like before your . . . angelic ascent, I can't say. But yer a bonnie lass, I'll grant ye that." His accent became more pronounced, and he grinned, obviously teasing her.

She didn't return the smile.

He pushed away from the bookcase and pointed to the shelf above her head. "I'm guessing you used the bibles as a stool to reach this shelf here." He patted the place where *Frankenstein* once stood. "Is there a book I can get for you so you can climb down from your perch? People are beginning to stare, and I doubt the proprietress would appreciate seeing any book, especially a bible, being used as a stool."

Knowing he was probably right, Sarah ignored his proffered hand and stepped down on her own. She glared at the few people she caught looking their way before returning her attention to the mysterious stranger.

Goodness, he was tall. The top of her head barely reached his shoulders.

His lips quirked into a half smile. "Feeling a wee less holy now?"

Blast his charming accent. "Perhaps. But I'm not sure if my decreased proximity to God is to blame or someone else."

He chuckled, then folded his arms, still clutching the book, and propped a shoulder against the shelf once more. "You should probably try reading the bible instead of standing atop it," he suggested. "In fact, there's a story in Genesis—that's the first book, you see—"

"I've heard of it," she said testily.

"About a civilization who tried to build a tower to Heaven, as you have done, and had their languages confounded as a result."

Sarah cocked her head. "Your point, sir?"

"'Tis a good thing we can still understand one another."

"I might prefer it if we couldn't."

He grinned, not seeming the least bit put out. "In that case, you should have built a taller tower."

Sarah eyed the book tucked under his arm, wondering if she dared to snatch it away and make a run for it. Surely, he wouldn't make a scene by chasing after her. Though the scene she'd make would be something for the gossips.

"You keep eyeing this book, which leads us back to where we began. How can a story about a monster be, how did you put it? Incredibly dull?"

Sarah had to concede it hadn't been the wisest thing to say. She should have said it was disturbing and caused the worst sorts of nightmares. That would have been more plausible.

"I haven't the faintest notion. Perhaps the plot is tiresome and uninteresting."

"Then I shall like it all the more. I prefer tales that play out at a more deliberate and leisurely pace, especially when monsters are involved. Now, is there a book I can procure for you, or were you really trying to gain some ground with God?"

Though he didn't smile, his eyes gleamed, and his lips twitched in the most irritating manner. He was laughing at her. In fact, he'd probably been laughing the entire time. Argh. Had he seen her reach for that book and had taken it on purpose? The gleam in his eyes told her that could easily be the case.

Abominable man.

Sarah folded her arms, ready to be done with this silly charade. "If you must know, I have been on the hunt for that book for over a year now and was in the process of finally obtaining it when you stole it out from under me. Should you insist on borrowing it first, I would be most appreciative if you would tell me when you plan to return it so that I can borrow it next."

He looked down at the book and examined it a moment. "Why didn't you say as much to begin with? Had I known this was the book you were after, I would have done the gentlemanly thing and allowed you to have it first."

She eyed the book, still in his hands, not quite trusting him or his handsome face. "*Are* you a gentleman, sir?"

"Nae," he said with a grin. "Just a man who spied a bonnie lass and couldn't resist teasing her a little. I hope you'll forgive me, just as I hope you'll sleep more soundly than I did after reading that book."

He took hold of her hand, and his gaze locked on hers. Ever so slowly, he lifted her fingers to his lips and pressed a deliberate, almost seductive, kiss to her knuckles.

She inhaled sharply as the heat from his lips burned

through her hand, igniting something within. A strange sort of fire sparked to life, surging through her body and evoking a myriad of sensations—both thrilling and terrifying.

Sarah had been kissed on her hand before, but never like this—or rather, it had never affected her like this. She stiffened, staring at him as though he were the devil himself. Perhaps he was. Come to taunt and tempt and wreak havoc on her senses.

She opened her mouth to say something, but nothing came out. All coherent thoughts fled, and, like a dimwit, she merely stood there, wondering what in the world had come over her.

He smiled in a knowing, self-satisfied way before turning her now-shaky hand over and setting the book on top. When she didn't immediately grip it, he cupped her fingers and curled them around the spine.

"A pleasure," he said. Then he released her hand, bowed, and made his way out of the library.

Sarah's eyes followed him until he'd disappeared from sight. Only when her head began to spin did she realize she'd been holding her breath.

She grabbed a nearby shelf for support as she tried to regulate her breathing. Who was that man and where had he come from? She had never laid eyes on him before. He hadn't even asked for her name, not that she would have given it to him if he had. But why go to all that trouble to steal her book if not to gain an introduction? Perhaps he'd been put off by her ridiculous talk of God and holiness. Or perhaps he was merely a tease.

She transferred the book to her right hand and shook her left, hoping to rid it of the warmth and pressure that still lingered. He might as well have branded her knuckles with that kiss, the way it refused to subside.

Drat it all. She ought to know better than to let a man unsettle her. It didn't matter that he'd been interesting and charming, or that she'd found much to like in the confident way he walked, his disarming smile, and how he'd spoken as an Englishman one moment and a Scot the next. She refused to dwell on him a moment longer.

She'd come here for a book, and now that she finally had it in her possession, she would return home and begin reading it at once. The story of a murderous monster would certainly drive out any remaining thoughts of dark eyes and a flirtatious grin. By tomorrow, she'll have forgotten all about the mysterious man she'd encountered in the library.

Yes, that was precisely how it would go. She hugged the copy of *Frankenstein* to her chest as though it could save her, then forced her feet to move in the direction of the pro-prietor's desk.

May we never meet again, Mr. Scottish Lilt.

KISS THREE

5

SARAH MOVED AWAY from the window in her family's cheerful salon and peered over her friend's shoulder to examine her latest sketch. Miss Michelle Ellington, or Chelle, as she was known to her friends, had a knack for designing hairstyles—first on paper and then on a person. Had she been born into a lower class, she would have been the perfect lady's maid. Instead, Chelle was the granddaughter of a duke, and not just any duke—His Grace the Duke of Chester, a former chum of the late-King George III.

Beautiful, well-connected, and wealthy, few could understand why Chelle had taken a teaching position at Miss Addison's School for Young Ladies. Only those who really knew her understood, Sarah being one of them.

Following Sarah's accidental rise to notoriety five years prior, Chelle convinced her to take on a new look—one befitting a shrew, she'd teased. Since that time, Sarah stopped trying to tame her wayward curls. Instead, she did as Chelle suggested and piled them high, letting them spill out around her head. The effect was bolder than current fashion dictated, but it was also more flattering.

In the end, the new look, along with Prinny's seal of approval, had made Sarah an original, at least for a while.

No doubt about it, Chelle was a genius in matters of hair. Her pretty brown tresses—always twisted or braided into a unique knot—attested to the fact. People who didn't know Chelle likely credited a maid for the creations, but that wasn't the case. Her friend worked the magic all on her own.

"It's lovely," Sarah said about Chelle's latest sketch. A loose braid flowed from the crown of the woman's head to the middle of her back, with several tendrils escaping along the way. Lately, Chelle's designs were becoming daring in the extreme.

"Should I wear my hair like that to the soirée tomorrow evening?" It was a question Sarah often asked Chelle. A test, so to speak. If Chelle couldn't condone a hairstyle on Sarah or Bethia, the sketch would be relegated to her ever-increasing pile of discarded ideas.

"We both know it's a style more suited to a bedchamber than a party," Chelle said. "But I grow weary of thinking up new chignons. Why can't women let their hair down every once in a while? It would open up a whole new realm of possibilities."

"Perhaps you should compile all of your discarded sketches and publish them into a book. You could call it *Styles for the Boudoir*. Or better yet, *Braids for the Bedchamber*. Alliteration can be your friend."

Chelle laughed. "Brilliant. I shall do it. Don't think that I won't."

"I will purchase the first copy printed," Sarah promised.

"This coming from the woman who waited over a year to read *Frankenstein* because she refused to purchase a copy of her own."

"Touché," Sarah said, "Though I would part with my coin for you."

Chelle curled up on the sofa and tucked her legs beneath her. It was a position also more suited to the bedchamber, but Chelle never worried about etiquette when it was just Sarah about.

"Speaking of *Frankenstein*, have you finished the first volume yet? I'm dying to discuss it with you."

Sarah dropped down beside her friend and stole a biscuit from the tea tray. "I've been trying to pace myself, hoping I'll find the second volume at the library soon, but it's been annoyingly elusive. I'm going to finish the first one in a day or two and be on pins and needles until I can get my hands on the second. Why won't that stubborn woman just tell me who borrowed it?"

Sarah had returned to the library every day since she'd borrowed the first book, and every day, the shelf remained devoid of the second or even third volume. Also gone was the mysterious man who'd teased and charmed and continued to pester her thoughts despite her determination to forget him. She'd looked for him everywhere—the library, the beach, the Steine—but no luck. He'd vanished the way the volumes of *Frankenstein* had done after they'd first arrived in Brighton.

It was most irritating.

Not that Sarah truly wished to see him again. She didn't.

"Perhaps luck will be with you tomorrow," Chelle said, referring to the book.

"Perhaps," Sarah agreed, though she wouldn't wager a farthing on it.

The front door burst open, and Bethia's breathless voice called out, "Sarah, where are you? I must speak with you at once."

"In the salon, Beth," Sarah answered with a smile. Bethia had always been the dramatic sort. What felt like life or death to her was usually just a misunderstanding or a minor disappointment. Only a few months prior, Bethia had rushed to Sarah's side, certain she'd contracted smallpox. It had been a mosquito bite.

Bethia breezed into the salon wearing a grin the size of the English Channel. Dressed in her favorite yellow frock, with her blonde curls framing her flushed face, she looked like sunshine itself.

"Oh good, you're here too, Chelle. I have such news for you both."

Chelle set her drawing aside and clasped her hands on her lap. "You look ready to burst. Do tell."

Bethia bounced up and down a few times, wringing her hands until she did burst. "He wishes to marry me!" A squeal erupted from her mouth. "Can you believe it? He loves me!"

"Who?" teased Sarah, even though she knew the answer.

"Mr. Gyles, of course." Bethia plopped down on the chair across from them, still bouncing about. "He's to leave for London on the morrow and wanted me to be certain of his feelings before he left. Said I'm not to look at another man until he has returned." She giggled. "As if I ever would."

Sarah caught Chelle's gaze for a moment before cautiously smoothing out her skirts. Ever since Sarah and Chelle had introduced Bethia into society six weeks before, Mr. Gyles had made his intentions clear. He called almost daily and showered her with flowers, sweet notes, and invitations to drive or walk. The only maid the family employed was growing weary of accompanying Bethia on her many outings.

But marriage? So soon?

Thankfully, Sarah wasn't the only person who stood in her sister's way. "Has he spoken with Papa?"

It was the wrong question to ask. Bethia's smile became a frown, and a pouty one at that. "They spoke over a week ago, but of course it didn't go well. Anthony said Papa had his reasons for not consenting at this time, but he wouldn't tell me anymore than that. Which is why I came to you. Papa will listen to you, Sarah. I know he will. Please, you must convince him to let me marry Anthony. If not, I'll surely expire."

Sarah barely refrained from rolling her eyes. "Don't be dramatic, Beth. A person does not expire from a wounded heart." Sarah was living proof of that.

"Oh, but *I* will," Bethia insisted. "I love him as I have never loved another."

Sarah was again tempted to roll her eyes, then reminded herself about a time when she'd had similar thoughts—a time when she'd been young, naive, and besotted.

Thankfully she was older now and much, much wiser.

"You have only just entered society, dearest," Chelle said, providing another voice of reason. "You can't possibly know that yet."

"I can and I do," Bethia insisted. "Please, Sarah, say you'll speak with Papa."

Bethia was nothing if not persistent, and Sarah wouldn't hear the end of it until she agreed. With a noncommittal shrug, she said, "I will try, but I make no promises. You know how stubborn Papa can be."

"I also know how persuasive *you* can be." Bethia clapped her hands together in a dreamy sort of delight. "Oh, thank you, dearest of sisters. I can't believe I will soon be Mrs. Anthony Gyles. It's too wonderful for words. Oh, I almost forgot. This came for you." She pulled a note from her reticule and passed it to Sarah. "The boy who delivered said he would wait for a response."

Sarah twisted around to look out the window. Sure enough, a boy of no more than twelve or thirteen stood next to a horse, frowning at the house and tapping his foot impatiently.

Sarah shot her sister a look of frustration, to which she gave an apologetic shrug.

Chelle scooted closer, eying the note curiously. "What sort of message requires an immediate response?"

Sarah had the same thought as she examined the note. *Miss Sarah Meacham* was written across one side in a bold script, and a melted blob of burgundy wax sealed the back. There was no official seal. No return direction. Only her name.

She cracked it open.

For the bonnie lass, Miss Sarah Meacham,

I have in my possession vols 2 and 3 of Frankenstein should you wish to read them. (Nae, I am not holding the library's copies captive, lest you leap to that conclusion.) I require only one small favor in return for the loan: That you grant me the pleasure of your company on a ride tomorrow afternoon at one o'clock. Please send your answer by way of my young charge.

Your servant,

The Scot from the library who's not a gentleman and ought to be ashamed of himself for taking such liberties.

Sarah's lips twitched and her heart skipped about like an excited puppy. Why, she couldn't say for sure. She didn't want it to skip. She didn't want her mouth to smile either. And she certainly didn't want to look forward to seeing him again.

But she did.

Sadly, emphatically, stupidly.

So much for being older and wiser.

He's not a gentleman, she told herself firmly. *You don't even know his name.*

What sort of man wouldn't at least give a name? Perhaps her heart was only drawn to the objectionable sort.

"Well?" Bethia's voice intruded. "What does it say?"

"Er . . ." Sarah looked from her sister to her friend, not sure how to explain. She hadn't told them about her encounter with the mysterious man in the library and didn't want to now.

Chelle snatched the note from Sarah's fingers and read the words, only to arch an eyebrow in a look that said, *You've been keeping something from us, you naughty girl.*

Bethia grabbed the letter next and read it greedily. When she lowered it back to her lap, she was beaming.

"Crags, Sarah. You've a new admirer," she cried. As a child, Bethia had learned an unsavory word that she'd often blurt out at the most inconvenient moments. It would always horrify their mother. Begging, lecturing, and sending Bethia to her room did nothing to dissuade her, so their mother had done the only thing she could think of. She'd taught her daughter a new word to say instead: Crags.

It had worked like a charm. Bethia had laughed when she'd heard it. She'd also delighted in the laughter the word evoked in others whenever she blurted it out. It had become Bethia's word—a word she carried with her into adulthood.

Chelle, however, looked more concerned than pleased by the note. "A man who's not a gentleman? What does that mean?"

"I haven't the faintest idea. As you can see by the letter, he hasn't mentioned his name. We spoke briefly in the library the other day. He retrieved *Frankenstein* before I could get to it, and I begged him to let me have it first. He conceded, and I left with the book. That was the extent of it."

Chelle looked like she didn't believe Sarah, while Bethia declared, "You must accept at once."

This time, Sarah did roll her eyes. "Honestly, Beth, you cannot be serious. I would never agree to go driving with a man with whom I haven't been properly introduced."

Bethia appeared ready to argue, then slumped back in her chair and sighed. "Crags, I suppose you're right. But oh, how I wish he would sweep you off your feet and steal your heart. Then you could be as happy as I am."

Sarah wanted to say that she was perfectly happy in her current, unmarried state, but she held her tongue and went to the sideboard to retrieve a pencil and paper instead.

> *Dear Mr. Not-a-gentleman,*
> *I am flattered by your invitation, but I do not know your name, nor have we been properly intro-duced. Pity. I would like to borrow those books.*
> *—The woman who slept soundly after reading vol I*

The last line was an outright lie. Not only had she not finished the book, but every creak of her floorboards or scrape of a branch against the window pane had set her heart to skittering and her mind to conjuring up a massive creature with a grotesque face lurking in the shadows. Oddly enough, she couldn't wait to get her hands on the remaining two volumes. There was something exhilarating about being frightened out of one's wits.

Sarah folded her note, not bothering to seal it, and walked outside to where the boy stood by his horse. He had olive skin, black hair, and almost black eyes.

"I apologize for keeping you waiting," Sarah said. The boy looked even younger than she'd first thought. He couldn't be more than nine or ten.

"Are you Miss Meacham?" he asked, jerking his head back to whip his untidy hair away from his eyes. His accent was similar to a man she'd once met from India. He sounded as though he'd pulled his tongue to the back of his mouth, giving his voice a darker, interesting sound with an upward inflection at the end.

"I am," Sarah said.

"I was about to knock on your door. Took you a bit to answer this." He held up the note she'd just given him. Though small and gangly, Sarah found his boldness endearing. She also liked the way he spoke.

"Do you have a name?" she asked.

"Banjeet, at your service, Miss." He made an awkward attempt at a bow, and Sarah stifled a smile.

"Does your employer have a name as well, Banjeet?"

"Employer?" The boy looked confused for a moment before brightening. "You must mean *Pita*."

"Was, er . . . *Pita* the one who wrote me this note?"

"Yes, yes, though he's only *Pita* to me. Mr. Ian Collum's his true name, though he's usually called Cole."

Ah, Sarah thought, *so the mysterious man does have a name—or rather three names.*

Most interesting.

"How long have you been in his employ?" she questioned, wondering how much information she could gather from the young Banjeet.

"Years. I'm only an apprentice now but will someday become a great shipmaster, just see if I don't." Banjeet held himself up tall and proud. The boy had pluck, that much was certain.

"I've no doubt that you will."

The cheeky grin returned. "The finest in all the seas, even finer than Captain James."

Sarah had to smile at that even though she had no idea who Captain James could be. "Mr. Collum owns ships, you say?"

"Three for now and more to come. A lot more."

"What does he do with all those ships?"

The question seemed to annoy the young Banjeet because his brow puckered, as though Sarah should already know the answer to this. "Imports supplies, of course."

Of course, Sarah thought wryly. "What kind of supplies?"

The sun peeked through the clouds, causing Banjeet to squint up at her. "You ask a lot of questions."

"I have a lot of questions."

He shoved the note she'd given him into the pocket of his shirt and scrambled onto his horse. "*Pita* can answer the rest. Already been gone too long as it is. Good day, Miss."

After a quick nod, he galloped off, leaving Sarah staring after him. Apparently, Mr. Collum owned ships and took in young Indian refugees, or was Banjeet the only one? The more she learned about the mysterious Scotsman, the more mystified she became.

Perhaps if she'd agreed to the drive—

No, that was out of the question. He'd made it clear he wasn't a gentleman, and the young Banjeet had confirmed as much. For all Sarah knew, Mr. Collum was a smuggler.

··6··

SARAH LEANED ACROSS the counter in Mrs. Wright's Circulating Library, desperate for any information the proprietress could give her.

"Mrs. Wright, I have been here every morning for the past fortnight, and I have yet to see either the second or third volume of *Frankenstein* on your shelves. I finished the first book last evening and am on pins and needles to learn what happens next. Can you please tell me when you might expect them back?"

"Not everyone returns books in a timely fashion, Miss Meacham. Yourself included." Short and stout, with frizzy, gray hair, Mrs. Wright added a few books to a large basket and slung it over her arm, signaling she had other duties to attend to and couldn't be bothered by Sarah's pleas any longer.

Oh no you don't, Sarah thought. *I will follow you around all day, if I must.* "Will you at least send me a message when—"

A large crate of books landed on the counter next to

Sarah, and the woman's usually stern face brightened as she took in the newcomer. "Why, Mr. Collum, how nice to see you again. What do you have there?"

Sarah slowly turned her head to see the tall and handsome Mr. Collum grinning at the proprietress, sparing Sarah barely a glance. He smelled of leather and some sort of exotic spice—a scent he might have smuggled from India.

"Forgive me, Mrs. Wright. I didn't mean to intrude," came his deep, faint brogue.

Normally, Sarah didn't care much for the Scottish accent, but spoken in that way, with just a hint of it—well, it was like a dusting of sugar on a biscuit.

He looked at Sarah, his eyes filled with humor and mischief. "I rudely cut you off just now. Please, continue what you were saying, Miss . . . ?"

Sarah's eyes widened at his blatant ploy. He expected her to introduce herself, did he? Honestly. An honorable man would have approached her father or a close acquaintance and sought an introduction that way, but not Mr. Collum.

Sarah ignored him and turned back to the proprietress. "As I was saying, Mrs. Wright, once the books are returned, would you kindly send a note around? I'll be forever in your debt."

The woman gave Sarah a look meant to whither even the most robust flower, then smiled disarmingly at Mr. Collum. "Sir, you must forgive Miss Meacham. She's a bit preoccupied at the moment and meant no slight, I assure you. Miss Meacham, I'd like you to meet Mr. Collum. He's new to Brighton."

The aggravating man tipped his hat in her direction, his expression triumphant. "A pleasure, *Miss Meacham*," he said.

"Likewise," Sarah answered dryly.

"Now," Mrs. Wright continued, "What can I do for you, Mr. Collum?"

How the man had weaseled himself into the proprietress's good graces so quickly was anyone's guess. Sarah had kept an account at the circulating library for over six years now, and to her recollection, she hadn't once been met with such a cheerful welcome. Granted, she'd probably made a nuisance of herself during the past year or so, but a kindhearted proprietress would have been sympathetic to Sarah's plight, not irritated by it.

For pity's sake, why couldn't she just keep a list of those waiting for popular titles? Surely, Sarah wasn't the only one with this frustration.

"I've come bearing gifts for your library," Mr. Collum said, tapping the crate. "Just some *auld* books I discovered in my new place of business. They've been gathering dust for years, and I've no use for them at present. These flowers are for you as well. Thought they'd brighten your library."

One would think he'd given Mrs. Wright a crate of gold pieces instead of books and flowers, the way she set her basket aside and beamed at him. "How thoughtful you are, sir. Most people only want things from me, but you always come bearing a gift of some sort."

As she set the small posy aside and excitedly lifted books from the crate, Sarah felt abashed. How often had she made demands of the woman? Apparently too much. In fact, she was probably at the very top of *that* particular list, not that Mrs. Wright kept lists—at least not written ones.

Sarah made a mental note to be a little more gracious and a little less difficult in the future, at least once she'd finally satisfied her curiosity about *Frankenstein*.

A certain book caught her eye, and Sarah rose to her

tiptoes to get a better look at the contents in the crate. In the center, three black and rust-colored spines sported the word, *Frankenstein*. As if by magic, volumes I, II, and III were all there, right in front of her.

Mrs. Wright must have caught sight of them as well because she met Sarah's gaze with a stern look of her own. "I must catalogue them first."

"How long will that take? I can wait." Sarah glanced out the window to see her family's maid calmly waiting on a bench. Poor Suzy. She probably had a long list of things needing to be done back at home and was anxious to return.

"A few weeks at the soonest."

"A few weeks!" Sarah exclaimed, certain that couldn't be the case. The woman was probably punishing her, doing everything in her power to keep Sarah from finishing that story.

"Each book that comes to this library must be examined, cleaned, recorded, and properly labeled before we can add it to our shelves. It's a lengthy process, and I've just gotten a new shipment from London that must come first."

One breath, two breaths, three. "Would you allow me to borrow them before they are recorded?" she asked.

"Oh no, I could never do that. If I made an exception for you, I'd have to make them for all of my patrons, and that would never do. You understand." So patronizing, so stubborn, so . . .

Completely out of patience, Sarah said, "Very well, but if you lend those to someone else first, I'll . . . I'll . . ." Sarah nearly said she'd cancel her subscription, but she couldn't make herself say the words. She loved the library too much to ever do such a thing.

The woman's eyes widened and her hand flew to cover her nose in a protective gesture. "You'll what?" she asked worriedly.

Good heavens, does she truly think I'd strike her? Sarah had delivered only one jab in her entire life—five years ago to a swine of a man who'd deserved far worse. From Mrs. Wright's fearful expression, one would think Sarah went around beating every soul who irritated her.

Honestly.

"I'll be very disheartened," Sarah finished lamely.

"Oh." The woman lowered her hands, appearing relieved.

Mr. Collum seemed to notice something in the crate and leaned over to examine the contents. "How did these end up in here?" He withdrew the three *Frankenstein* books and dusted off one of the covers with his leather-clad fingers. "I beg your pardon, Mrs. Wright. I meant to set these aside for someone else and must now rescind my gift of these books. How deplorable of me."

"Perfectly understandable, Mr. Collum," Mrs. Wright answered, not the least bit put out. In fact, she sounded pleased, as though he'd just solved a problem. "I already have that particular set of books anyway."

"I wouldn't be too sure of that," muttered Sarah. "They've been absent from your shelves for quite some time now. Perhaps they've gone missing."

"That is assuredly not the case, Miss Meacham. I know precisely who has them."

"Who might that be?" Sarah held her breath, hoping against hope the woman would at last reveal a name. Any name. *Please give me a name.*

Mrs. Wright wagged a chubby finger. "You know very well I can't divulge the names of my patrons. Mr. Collum, thank you for your many contributions this day. They are most appreciated." She replaced the remaining books and hefted the crate to her hip, practically scuttling away and leaving Sarah to face the mysterious Scotsman alone.

Her gaze slid to him and the books he'd tucked beneath his arm. He was so tall, so handsome, so completely unpredictable.

He was also smirking at her.

"I wish I could be of assistance to you, Miss Meacham, but these books have already been promised to a new acquaintance of mine."

"Indeed."

"Aye, a bonnie, spirited lass who has captured my interest. She is planning to take them off my hands tomorrow morning at—say, eleven? When I collect her for a long-awaited drive?"

Sarah had to smile at his words, high handed though they were.

How easy it would be to nod, accept the books, and join the dratted man on a drive. She wanted to agree. She wanted to pepper him with questions about his young, Indian charge, his shipping business, his accent, and where life had taken him. He would certainly prove to be both entertaining and charming.

Her heart urged her to accept.

But that was precisely the problem. Sarah didn't trust charming. She trusted only her instincts, and right now, her instincts were telling her to run away.

"I hope your new acquaintance enjoys the books," she finally said. "I, on the other hand, will continue to wait for the return of Mrs. Wright's copies. Good day, sir."

Back straight, head held high, Sarah walked out of the library empty handed, all the while wishing the publisher of *Frankenstein* to the devil. The story should have been published as one volume, not three.

She could only hope the rest of the tale would be worth the trouble.

· . ● ● . ·

As SARAH SAUNTERED up the path to her house, anguished sobs came from the direction of the garden. A knowing look passed between her and her maid.

Bethia, they silently agreed.

"Go on in, Suzy. I'll be along momentarily. I haven't forgotten my promise to help you with the dusting."

"Oh, Miss, there's really no need."

"There is every need. I'll not have you work yourself into the ground because you're obligated to join me on my outings to town. Tomorrow, I'll wake Bethia and take her with me instead. Now off you go."

The maid nodded gratefully and quickened her steps towards the house while Sarah headed to the garden. She walked around a tall hedge and through an iron gate, finally stopping when she spied her sister kneeling next to a stone bench, her head buried in her arms with her pretty pink gown flowing about her. If Mr. Gyles were here now, he'd undoubtedly be smitten all over again by the picturesque sight she made.

Sarah approached gingerly, taking a seat on the bench next to her sister's head and wondering what had happened. Only last evening after dinner, Mr. Gyles, now in London, had arranged for a large bouquet of pink lilies to arrive at Bethia's door. She'd twirled around the house in a state of bliss.

Sarah had to give Mr. Gyles some credit. He certainly knew how to woo her sister.

Looking at Bethia now, however, one would think he'd given her a heap of rotten apples instead.

Sarah gently touched her sister's shoulder. "Beth, what has happened?"

Golden locks lifted, and bright blue, tear-filled eyes met Sarah's as Bethia hiccupped her way through an explanation. "Oh, S-Sarah, the most d-dreadful thing. I d-decided it was unfair t-to ask that you s-speak to Papa on my b-behalf. So I w-went to him." Fresh tears welled. "H-he wouldn't listen."

"Now, Beth, this will never do." Sarah grasped her sister's arms and pulled her up to the bench next to her. When her sister's shoulders continued to shake mournfully, Sarah gave her back a gentle rub. "Calm yourself, my dear. Nothing ever gets sorted while one is in hysterics."

"Crags, Sarah, h-he raised his v-voice at me!" Bethia exclaimed. "S-said I'm n-not to m-marry until you d-do. P-Papa never r-raises his voice."

Sarah had to agree. Their father was the gentlest person she knew, especially when it came to his youngest daughter. Something had obviously upset him.

"I will speak to him," Sarah said.

That didn't seem to give her sister much hope, but she wiped away her tears nonetheless—a sign that she had calmed a little. Bethia was good in that respect. Her histrionics didn't usually last long. She fell out of her moods almost as quickly as she fell into them.

"H-he seemed most determined." She sniffled.

Sarah nudged her sister's arm and smiled. "A quality he passed along to me, as you well know. Not to worry, my dear. Tomorrow, I will go to him and discover exactly why he is so set on this course. Once we understand his reasons, we can form a plan of attack. For now, however, I wish to understand *your* reasons. What is it you like so much about Mr. Gyles? Is it the blackness of his clothes? He does seem to like that color, doesn't he? Or is it the fastidious way he ties his cravats? Perhaps it is the length of his side whiskers. They are most distinguished."

A snicker sounded, and Bethia gave Sarah a nudge to her ribs. "Don't be silly. I'm not as shallow as that. While I do think him more handsome than any other man, my feelings go beyond that. He's so good to me, he makes me laugh, and he values my opinions. It's the reason he's in London now, you know."

"What do you mean?" Sarah asked.

Her sister's expression glowed with pride as she nodded. "He was approached about an investment opportunity and couldn't decide if he should take the gamble. I encouraged him to go to London and speak to those involved face-to-face so that he might get a better feel for things. He agreed that would be best. He just didn't want to leave before our betrothal was announced. He worried some young buck would try to steal me away while he was gone. As if that could ever happen."

"Definitely not likely," Sarah agreed.

Bethia smiled wistfully. "I finally convinced him to go, and in his letter to me last evening, he mentioned that his future wife was wise indeed. Said he's learned more in the few days he's been in London than in all the months he's been exchanging communications."

Sarah listened thoughtfully. It seemed she hadn't given Mr. Gyles—or her sister—much credit. Very few men took women into their confidence when it came to matters of business. Sarah's own father refused to confide in her, even when it was apparent something was amiss.

"I'm glad to hear he discusses such things with you," said Sarah.

"As am I," Bethia agreed. "He likes to talk through things that trouble him. Mostly, I just listen, but when I have something worthwhile to contribute, I say it. If he thinks me silly, he never says so, and I love that I can always speak my mind. Honestly, we can talk for hours and hours and never run out of things to say."

Bethia looked down at her lap and played with the folds of her pink muslin skirts. "I realize you think me young and naive, Sarah, but I know my own mind. Anthony is a good man, and we are a good match."

Sarah had to admit, her sister didn't sound the least bit young or naive in that moment. Rather, she sounded wiser than Sarah had been at her age. Perhaps it was more than infatuation her sister felt. Perhaps the pair truly did love each other. Sarah really had no way of knowing as she'd never experienced true love herself. After all, she'd once considered the dashing and handsome Mr. Hatch a worthy contender for her heart.

What rot.

"The more you speak of this Mr. Gyles, the more I like him," Sarah confided.

Her sister smiled and tilted her head. "Six weeks ago, if someone had told me I could form such a strong attachment in so little time, I wouldn't have believed it. But then I met Anthony, and—" She sighed. "Oh, how I miss him."

There were times when Bethia needed a mother more than a sister, and though Sarah tried to play both parts, she often fell short of the mark. What Bethia needed now was their mother's guidance and steadying influence. She would have known how to best handle this situation, what to say to Bethia now.

Unfortunately, it was up to Sarah to make sure everything turned out for the best. Trouble was, she had no idea what that would be.

7

SARAH PLOPPED DOWN on the settee opposite her father in the study and folded her arms. "Papa, I need to speak with you."

Seated in his favorite chair by the fire, one leg crossed over the other, he didn't acknowledge her. Instead, he continued to peer through his spectacles at the book he held, probably hoping his eldest daughter would leave him be.

Unfortunately for him, Sarah was not easily dissuaded.

"I found Beth sobbing in the garden yesterday afternoon."

No response. Not even a glance in her direction.

"She said you wouldn't allow her to marry before I do, which I'm sure we can both agree is completely ridiculous."

Still nothing.

"She said you yelled at her."

As Sarah hoped would be the case, her father at last closed his book and removed his spectacles. "I did not yell. I raised my voice a little. She wouldn't hear me otherwise."

"You made her cry."

He leaned his head back and stretched his neck before giving her a weary look. "For that, I am sorry."

Something troubled him. Sarah could see it in the lines around his eyes and mouth. She also noticed that his brown hair was beginning to gray at the temples. He suddenly looked ten years older than he had the day before. Or perhaps Sarah was just paying closer attention.

If only he'd talk to her.

She leaned forward to rest her elbows on her knees and interlocked her fingers. "I know that Beth is young and shouldn't rush into marriage. But she seems to know her own mind, and Mr. Gyles has not given us any reason not to like him, has he? If given the chance, they could suit each other very well."

Her father closed his eyes and rubbed his temples— something he did whenever his patience was being tried.

"Despite what you might think," he said at last. "I haven't completely shirked my duties as a father. I have done my research and have learned that Mr. Gyles will make an admirable husband for Bethia. A few weeks ago, he came to me, asking for Bethia's hand. We spoke at length on this subject and came to an understanding. The problem isn't with him or your sister. It's with you, my dear."

Sarah straightened with a frown. "Me?"

She was the last person her father worried about—or should worry about. After all, she'd found a way to enter society on her own, and, thanks to Prinny, she'd once been invited to every party and had been welcomed in every home. Her popularity had diminished since he'd left town while renovations took place on the pavilion, but Sarah had still managed to give Bethia a proper comeout.

"You've become too set in your ways, Sarah. You won't give even the most decent of men half a chance."

"That isn't true," she argued. "I give everyone a chance."

Her father cast her a look of disbelief, and Sarah's gaze dropped guiltily to her lap. Her blue cotton dress appeared almost violet in the light coming through the window.

"Not all men deserve your ill opinion," her father said gently.

For some reason, the face of Mr. Collum appeared in Sarah's mind, but she was quick to remind herself that just because he'd taken on the care of a young Indian boy didn't mean he was a good man. For all Sarah knew, he could be raising the boy up to be a smuggler. Besides, wouldn't a decent sort of man have given her the books instead of using them to bait her?

It was probably not the fairest assessment, but she wasn't ready to give anyone the benefit of the doubt, least of all a man.

Which was exactly the point her father was trying to make, she supposed.

"We should be discussing Bethia, not me," said Sarah.

Her father picked a piece of lint from his breeches and flicked it away. "You want what's best for your sister, do you not?"

"Yes."

"Because you care about her."

"Yes."

"Well, I care about *both* of my daughters, and it is my intention to see you each happily settled."

"Then why not let Beth marry Mr. Gyles?"

He seemed to consider his words before responding. "Two reasons. The first being that once your sister marries, your position in society will change from a feisty original to an overlooked spinster."

"I am four and twenty, Papa. I am already an over-looked spinster. I became as much the moment Prinny left town."

"Your mother was four and twenty when we married."

Sarah looked at him in surprise. Her father rarely spoke of his late wife and never without a great deal of prodding.

"Is that true?" *Please tell me more.*

He grunted. "You have a reputation as being unobtain-able, that is all. You are not on the shelf just yet. You need only offer some encouragement, and you'll have suitors aplenty."

Sarah disagreed. Aside from Mr. Collum, it had been some time since a man had requested her company for more than just a dance.

"You said there were two reasons. What's the second?"

"If I allow Beth to marry, you will have no reason to change your ways. You will continue on as you are and will eventually become a spinster aunt to your sister's children. I want more for you than that."

Sarah stared at her father as the full meaning of his words registered. Did he truly intend to hold Beth's hap-piness hostage until Sarah changed her ways? Good grief, if he did that, neither of them would marry.

"I have no wish to wed, Papa," she said firmly. "I'm happy as I am."

"A sentiment I hope to change."

This wouldn't do at all, and Sarah refused to budge until she'd made her father see the error of his ways. "What you are doing is not fair to Beth or Mr. Gyles. Or me, for that matter. Nor is it right."

"Nor is it fair—or right—that you lump every interested man into the same category as Mr. Hatch."

"That is my choice," said Sarah.

"And this is mine."

They stared at each other in a silent standoff for what felt like hours. There was a determined set to her father's jaw, unlike any she'd ever seen. He wasn't going to change his mind.

Sarah leaned forward, imploring him. "This is ridiculous, Papa. You are punishing us both, and for what purpose? By allowing Bethia to marry and me to continue as I am, you will be pleasing us both."

"Marriage is not a punishment, child."

"I am not a child." She scowled, then winced at the petulant way her words had sounded.

Her father's raised brow agreed.

Sarah bit her lip in consternation. She despised being manipulated, and by her own father no less. Who was he to decide what would make her happy?

"I'm not saying you *must* marry," he said, as though reading her thoughts. "I only want you to be open to the possibility should a worthy man earn your regard."

"But if I do not marry, then Beth cannot," said Sarah, testing the waters to see how far his determination went.

Her father dragged a finger across his lips in a contemplative gesture before responding. "If I see some changes in you, I might reconsider."

Ah, thought Sarah. Perhaps the situation was not as dire as it had first seemed. All she needed to do was show an interest in a man for an acceptable amount of time, and Bethia would be allowed to marry. She could do that.

Perhaps the dull but handsome Mr. Finlay would suffice. Or even the more entertaining Mr. Carter. They had both asked for a dance at last Friday's soirée. With a little encouragement, she could turn one of their heads, for a while at least.

"I mean some *real* changes," her father added, giving her a look that said he knew exactly what she was thinking. "I'll know sincerity when I see it."

Blast his perception, Sarah thought sourly. The only man who seemed sincerely interested in her at the moment was Mr. Collum—a man her father would never deem suitable.

Although . . .

Perhaps that could work nicely in her favor. If her father's plan were to backfire, and his eldest daughter began falling for an unsuitable tradesman, he may come to regret his machinations. After all, no husband would be preferable to an unworthy one.

Yes, that *could* work out nicely.

Sarah tried to ignore the thrill of anticipation that accompanied thoughts of Mr. Collum. She would only encourage him as long as it took to change her father's mind.

Before her father could perceive her new plan of action, she stood and nodded her agreement. "I understand, Papa. I will see what I can do."

That seemed a satisfactory answer. He slipped his spectacles back on and picked up his book, no doubt congratulating himself for his handling of a delicate situation. "See that you do."

As Sarah walked from the room, she wondered if he'd still be congratulating himself in a few weeks' time.

· . • . • . ·

"THERE YOU ARE, Miss," Suzy's breathless voice called out. "I've found you at last."

Sarah looked up from where she'd been conversing with Bethia under the shade of the large oak tree behind their house. Thirty minutes prior, she'd found her sister sprawled out on a blanket, blowing fluff from dandelions.

"I hadn't meant to hide," Sarah told Suzy. "I hope you haven't been searching long."

Suzy carried what appeared to be a package under one arm. "Not too long, Miss. This came for you about ten minutes ago."

Suzy held out the package, which Sarah examined curiously. She hadn't been expecting anything, although the moment she'd accepted it, she knew exactly what it contained. Books.

Her heart gave a little lurch, and her mouth widened into a smile. She ripped back the paper, revealing all three volumes of the coveted *Frankenstein*. Tucked into the first volume was a note, which she quickly pulled free.

> *Dear Frankenstein Enthusiast,*
>
> *I could not, in good conscience, keep these from you any longer. Feel free to add them to your collection or, when done, donate them to Mrs. Wright's fine establishment. I will leave that up to your discretion.*
>
> *Your servant,*
> *Mr. Collum*

Sarah's smile dwindled as she read his words. It was a perplexing reaction, considering she'd just gotten exactly what she'd wanted—the second two volumes of *Frankenstein* with no strings attached. But his note sounded so final, as though he'd given up on her.

Oh dear. That wouldn't do at all, especially now that her situation had changed. After speaking with her father, Sarah now *wanted* strings attached. At least one string. A little one.

"Are the books from that mysterious man in the library?" Bethia asked with a teasing grin. She sat up and leaned over her sister's lap, trying to read the words for herself, but Sarah was quick to refold the paper.

"Did he ask if he could call on you?" Bethia asked.

"Er . . . no."

"Another drive then?"

"No."

"A stroll?"

"Beth, honestly."

"Some other sort of outing?"

Sarah shook her head, causing her sister to frown.

"Did he at least say he hopes to see you again?"

Sarah felt her spirits dip even lower. Bethia could be annoyingly relentless at times. "He said I can either keep the books or give them to the lending library once I have finished."

"Oh."

Sarah's sentiments exactly. So much for her plans to engage his interest with the hope of foiling her father's schemes. Now it was *her* plans that had been foiled. She'd have to resort to Mr. Finlay or Mr. Carter and pray she'd be able to convince her father she was in earnest.

Blast.

"It's for the best, Beth," said Sarah. "He's not a gentleman."

Bethia tugged another dandelion from the grass and rolled to her stomach. "Gentleman or not, he was refreshingly original."

Sarah had to agree. His notice of her, however short lived, *had* been refreshing. But it was over now. Like every other man who had looked her way, Mr. Collum had come to realize she wasn't worth the trouble.

Sarah tried not to sound too glum when she said, "His interest has obviously waned."

Bethia sighed. "Pity that. Now you will have to choose a less interesting man to fall in love with." Sarah had told Bethia about the so-called bargain she'd made with their father.

"I don't intend to fall in love with any man."

"More's the pity." Bethia blew the fluff from the dandelion, and Sarah watched it float away on the breeze.

Her fingers brushed the stack of books in her lap, and she gritted her teeth, trying to focus on the positives. At least she could finish her story now. She should be happy about that. And she *was* happy for the most part. But there was still a bothersome feeling lurking at the back of her mind, or perhaps in her heart, telling her she'd missed out on something.

Despite everything, she had wanted to see Mr. Collum again. She had wanted to talk with him, laugh with him, and bask in the warmth of his gaze.

A drive with him would have been lovely.

· · · · ·

Dear Mr. Collum,

Thank you for the books. They are greatly appreciated, especially without any added contingencies. However, if the invitation for a drive has not yet expired, I have been considering reconsidering.
—Miss M

Candlelight flickered across the small wooden desk in Sarah's bedchamber. She looked over the note before crumpling it into a ball and tossing it on to the empty grate in her fireplace. It had been a silly note to write, especially since she didn't even have the man's direction. What did she hope to do? Extract the information from Mrs. Wright at the lending library, assuming he'd signed up for a subscription? Sarah knew from experience how fruitless that endeavor would be. If she truly wanted to speak with him again—and she did—her only option was to frequent the library, and perhaps the other shops as well, with the hope of running into him.

Sarah blew out her candle and crawled into bed. As she pulled the blanket up to her neck, she watched various shadows dance across her ceiling. Only a few nights previously, she had seen a huge, disfigured monster in those shadows. Now all she could spot was a slightly crooked nose, long side whiskers, and rich, dark hair that tossed to and fro.

When she finally drifted off to sleep, the three volumes of *Frankenstein* remained all but forgotten on her bedside table.

· · 8 · ·

SARAH SMILED AT Mrs. Wright as she slid all three copies of *Frankenstein* across the desk at the lending library. She'd had the books for exactly one week and could finally say she'd read the tale in its entirety.

"I would like to donate these to your fine establishment," she said.

Mrs. Wright raised a questioning eyebrow. "Mr. Collum gave them to *you*, I see."

"He did. And now I am giving them to you. I'm sure there are other patrons who would like to read these books as well. Frankly, I am ready to forget all about the murderous monster."

To Sarah's surprise, the woman leaned forward in a conspiratorial way and lowered her voice. "I had the same thought. Couldn't sleep for weeks after reading those books. The author who contrived such a tale ought to be ashamed of himself."

Sarah nodded slowly, not sure how to respond. The story had been unsettling, to be sure, but she'd found it more thrilling than upsetting.

"Would you rather I find a different benefactor for these books?" Sarah asked, not wanting to upset the woman further.

Mrs. Wright hesitated before shaking her head. "No. They are still, as you know, quite popular. Though I can't understand the draw, I'd best keep them."

Sarah refrained from pointing out that Mrs. Wright had read them as well, but thought better of it and nodded instead. "You are good to put the desires of your patrons ahead of your own."

The woman actually smiled at Sarah. *Smiled.* "That is kind of you to say, Miss Meacham. I do try when I can. Now, is there anything I can help you find while you are here?"

Sarah had to tighten her jaw to keep it from dropping. Mrs. Wright had never been this willing to help. Apparently, all she'd needed was a little kindness.

Isn't that what we all need? Sarah thought to herself, feeling humbled. How many times during the past several years had she put her own interests ahead of Mrs. Wright's? Too many to count. The woman worked hard to provide a valuable service to the town. Perhaps Sarah should focus more on that and less on her perceived injustices.

She had Mr. Collum to thank for that lesson, among a few other things.

"Thank you for the offer, but I came only to pass along these books. I'd also like to apologize for my, er . . . excessive persistence. I must have been a sore trial to you, and I'm sorry for it."

Apologies were amazing things. When spoken sincerely, they had the power to mend wounds, soften hearts, and bridge gaps. Sarah could see evidence of that in the broadening of Mrs. Wright's smile. Perhaps someday, if Sarah behaved better, they might even become friends.

"Apology accepted," said Mrs. Wright.

Her task complete, Sarah smiled as well. "If you happen to see Mr. Collum, will you extend my thanks to him? I haven't had the opportunity."

A twinkle appeared in the woman's eyes, and she nodded in the direction of the large window that looked out onto the cobblestone street. "You can thank him yourself. If I'm not mistaken, that phaeton belongs to him."

Sarah spun around. Sure enough, a phaeton pulled by two matching gray horses stopped across the street. A tall man sat on the high perch and tipped his beaver at a passerby. The two began conversing.

"Some say he's a nabob," whispered Mrs. Wright. "Others speculate he's a smuggler, which is utterly ridiculous if you ask me."

Sarah turned back to the proprietress. "I learned long ago that people aren't always what they seem. Do you know him well?"

The proprietress shook her head. "No, but you can tell a lot about a person by observing them from afar. He's frequented my library often during the past fortnight, and he's always had a kind word to say to me and any other person he encounters. I've noticed him assisting my young apprentice several times, and he's returned books to the shelves that others have left strewn about. He also brings me a pretty posy most days, which he purchases from that young girl on the corner who sells flowers. When he walks away, she looks down at the coins in her hand and grins, as though he paid her more than expected. Now you tell me, Miss Meacham. Does that sound like a wicked man to you?"

"No," Sarah answered, looking back to the street, where Mr. Collum was now speaking with the young flower girl. He dropped a handful of coins in her palm, and she rewarded him with a broad smile. Then he tipped his beaver and walked away with not one, but two posies.

The moment Sarah realized he was headed towards the library, her pulse quickened, and her mind emptied of every thought except how handsome and elegant he looked. If she didn't know any better, she'd think him the perfect gentleman.

The door opened, and he caught her gaze as he stepped inside. A small smile appeared, along with a twinkle in his dark eyes.

"I had a feeling I'd encounter two bonnie lasses this morning." He held out a small bundle of yellow and white wildflowers to Sarah and another to Mrs. Wright. They looked a little mashed and were crudely tied with twine, but knowing where they'd come from, Sarah had never seen anything lovelier.

"You always know just how to brighten my library, Mr. Collum," said the proprietress. "Thank you."

"Yes, thank you," Sarah added lamely, unable to think of anything original to say. All week, she had been searching the town for him, but now that he stood before her, her mind was a blank.

Say something, anything, she thought, and fingered the flowers instead.

Mrs. Wright gave Sarah an odd look. "This is a happy coincidence, sir. We were only just talking about you."

"Is that so?" he said, raising an eyebrow at Sarah.

Mrs. Wright looked pointedly Sarah's way, silently prodding her to speak.

In that moment, she wanted to slink away, regroup, and not return until her head had cleared and her heart had ceased its infernal pounding.

"Er . . . yes," she finally blurted. "I wanted to thank you for the, er . . . books as well. So . . . er . . . thank you."

She cringed inwardly at her own stupidity. One would think she couldn't string two sentences together. It didn't help that Mr. Collum looked ready to laugh.

"I see you are donating *Frankenstein* to the library. Does that mean you have finally finished the tale, or did you find it too disturbing to read through to the end?"

"I finished it," she said, somewhat proud of herself for completing a full sentence without blubbering.

Mrs. Wright chimed in, "She was just as disturbed as we were."

His mouth widened into a smile, and he leaned an arm on the counter, looking down at Sarah. "How very interesting. I take it you did not sleep as soundly after the second two volumes?"

Sarah squirmed under his gaze. She must be a constant source of amusement for him. If not for the fact she'd only just connected with the proprietress over this very issue, it would be an easy thing to deny.

She opted to change the direction of the conversation instead. "Do you think the author led a disturbing life, or does he—or perhaps she—just dream of science and murder?"

"Oh, the author is surely a man," Mrs. Wright was quick to say. "No woman could have written such horrors."

Sarah and Mr. Collum exchanged a look, but it was the latter who said, "You never know, Mrs. Wright. Both men and women are capable of dark thoughts. All it would take is an overactive imagination and a talent for words."

"I refuse to even contemplate the possibility," said the woman, for once not smiling at Mr. Collum.

Ha, thought Sarah with delight. It seemed even the great Mr. Collom could cause offence every now and again.

He seemed to realize as much, but to his credit, he didn't try to take back his words or apologize for them. Instead, he gave the older woman a disarming smile.

"Come now, Mrs. Wright. Surely even you have had some dark thoughts on occasion. Perhaps you've hoped that a difficult or cantankerous customer might meet with a timely demise?"

Sarah leaned forward as well, joining in the fun. "Never say you've had such thoughts about me, Mrs. Wright."

The woman winked playfully at Sarah before picking up the three books. "I might wish a person to the devil every now and again, but that is the extent of it. Now, if you'll excuse me, I've some work to do."

She bustled away, her plump body bouncing as she walked. When Sarah's attention returned to Mr. Collum, she found him leaning one hip against the counter, studying her. "Tell me, Miss Meacham, which category do you fall under— difficult or cantankerous?"

Sarah looked around her. Two older gentlemen sat conversing at a table near the door, and a young boy swept the floor not far from them.

Her fingers fiddled with the small posy before she finally conceded, "Probably both. But in my defense, she was just as difficult."

That seemed to amuse him. "You appear to be on good terms today."

"Only because I have at last satisfied my curiosity of *Frankenstein*. I assured her I would not be pestering her over books in the future and even apologized for past wrongs."

He gave her a look of triumph. "So my gift of the books has served you well, first by assuaging a long-held curiosity and, as a result, improving your relations with Mrs. Wright.

If I didn't know any better, Miss Meacham, I'd say you are in my debt."

This was the perfect opportunity for Sarah to say, *You're right. I am. However can I repay you, sir?* Or better yet, *Perhaps that offer of a drive is still on the table?*

But when she opened her mouth to say as much, her thoughts went awry, and her stomach began fluttering.

In the end, all that came out was a pitiful and cowardly, "I must go."

She walked quickly towards the door, needing to get away from him and the disturbing effect he was having on her. The story of Frankenstein's monster may have frightened her, but the fear she'd felt in the wee hours of the morning after reading the story didn't hold a candle to the fear she felt now.

For five long years, Sarah had distanced her heart from men. The idea of reopening it, even just a little, sent waves of panic through her. What had she been thinking to contemplate something more than an acquaintance with Mr. Collum? She'd be far better off mastering whatever acting skills she possessed and trying her luck with Mr. Finlay or Mr. Carter.

"Miss Meacham."

Mr. Collum had apparently followed her outside. The sound of his voice caused her steps to falter, but she didn't turn around. Instead, she waited in suspense as horses whinnied, carriage wheels scraped the ground, and people shuffled past. The street was filled with life, but the sound that rose above all the rest were Mr. Collum's footsteps as he came around to face her.

His beaver was still tucked under one arm, and he squinted as he watched her with a perplexed expression.

"You seem to be in a wee hurry. Might I offer you a ride

somewhere?" Then he looked around as if searching for something. "Did you come to town alone?"

"Er . . . not exactly," Sarah admitted. "Our maid accompanied me, but it is her day off, so she continued on to the home of her family. I had planned to walk back alone."

He brightened. "Och, so you *are* in need of a ride. How fortuitous I came along when I did. Will you allow me to see you home safely?"

"I, er . . ." What was it about this man that discomfited her so? Why couldn't she just say, *That would be lovely, sir. Thank you,* and climb into his phaeton? Wasn't this precisely the opportunity she'd been wishing for all week?

Say yes, you ninnyhammer, she thought.

"Your note did say you've been considering reconsidering," he added.

The flutters in her stomach took a turn for the worse, and her gaze snapped to his.

"What note?" she managed to squeak.

He pulled a wrinkled paper from his pocket and unfolded it, showing her the same message she'd crushed into a ball and tossed onto her grate days before. She'd meant it to serve as kindling for the next cold night. How the devil had it come to be in his possession?

"Where did you get that?" she asked sharply.

"It arrived at my place of business yesterday afternoon, which makes me wonder how you knew where to send it. I don't believe I ever gave you that direction."

"I didn't send it," she said, her mind whirling at the strangeness of it all. Even if Suzy had removed it from the grate, she never would've sent it without asking permission. She was too loyal for that.

Bethia, on the other hand . . . Sarah had caught her sister sneaking out of her room just the other day. Had she taken it? But how could she have known where to send it? Bethia knew even less about the man than Sarah did.

"How very perplexing," said Mr. Collum. "Am I to understand you did not write this?"

At his stare, Sarah's confusion gave way to embarrassment. As much as she wanted to deny having written the note, her conscience wouldn't allow it.

"I did write it," she confessed, her cheeks warm. "But as you can see by its shriveled state, it was not meant to be sent. It was bound for the fire. I can only assume my sister discovered it and somehow learned of your direction. That is the only explanation."

"Or a mystical force is at play," he said, grinning.

Goodness, he had a nice smile. It softened his features and added to his handsomeness. Why couldn't he be hideous to look upon or merely unlikable? It would certainly ease the strain on her nerves.

"You think it floated up my chimney and somehow came to land on your doorstep?" she asked.

"I think"—He took her arm and tucked it through his own—"that you should take a ride with me, Miss Meacham."

"And *I* think that you are being too presumptuous, sir." Sarah let her arm fall free, suddenly overwhelmed. Lowering her pride had never been an easy thing for her, especially when accompanied by the paralyzing fear that she'd grow to like him even more than she already did.

It was only a drive.

Only a drive.

He stepped to the side to let a woman pass before folding his arms. "You are an enigma, Miss Meacham. You write that you have changed your mind and would like to drive with me after all, yet you continue to resist. Would it help to know that it was your father who told me where I might find you this morning?"

Sarah could scarce believe it. Mr. Collum had been to her home? "You spoke to my father?"

"Aye. He gave me quite the interview. Turns out I knew a cousin of yours in India. Your late mother's nephew, I believe."

"He mentioned my mother?" Sarah was beginning to feel as though a mystical force *was* at play.

"Only a wee bit," he said cautiously, as though worried he'd introduced a tender subject. "I was sorry to learn of her passing."

Sarah pressed her lips together as a tumult of thoughts and feelings pressed down on her. Was Mr. Collum really as sensitive and kind as he came across? Could she trust his motives? Could she trust *him*? He'd somehow charmed Mrs. Wright, her father, and even Bethia, who hadn't yet met him.

Sarah didn't know what to think anymore, not that she ever did, but everything felt even more confusing now.

"Who are you?" she finally blurted, unable to keep the question inside any longer. "You say you are no gentleman, but . . ."

Her voice trailed off as a worrisome thought entered her mind. Was her father so desperate to marry her off, that he'd settle for anyone, even this stranger, a potential smuggler?

No, that wasn't fair. Sarah had to agree with Mrs. Wright on that score. Mr. Collum couldn't possibly be a smuggler. He was, however, a tradesman, and therefore beneath her. Did her father not care about that?

Do you? came an internal voice.

"Drive with me and learn for yourself who I am," said Mr. Collum. "I have an open carriage, and I promise not to abscond with your virtue. You may ask as many questions as you like, I will answer as many as I like, and you need not make the walk home alone."

Left with no more excuses, Sarah finally forced herself to nod.

The smile he rewarded her with had a weakening effect on her knees.

Good heavens. What am I doing?

You're doing this for Bethia, she told herself firmly. *All for Bethia.*

· · 9 · · ·

"A smuggler?" Mr. Collum chuckled as he guided his horses around a tight turn. "How did anyone come by that notion?"

Sarah found it interesting that he didn't also scoff at the word nabob. Perhaps there was some truth to that rumor?

"You have that aura of mystery about you," she said as she gripped the seat of the phaeton to keep from sliding into him, "and your Scottish accent comes and goes, as though you play different roles."

"Those two things make me a smuggler?"

"The fact that you own a shipping company plays a part as well."

He didn't laugh this time, but his lips were still quirked in amusement. "Are you asking if I am a smuggler, Miss Meacham, or are you only telling me what the gossips are saying?"

Sarah didn't know what she was saying exactly. Her father seemed to think she judged men too quickly and unfairly, but better that than trust too easily. While she didn't believe Mr. Collum to be the dishonest sort, she still didn't know him, and she wasn't about to trust a man with so little to go on.

"I don't believe you to be a smuggler, sir," she said at last.

"How can you be sure?" he asked. "I do, as you pointed out, own a small fleet of ships, and England's steep tariffs are a bothersome business. Perhaps I *am* a smuggler. Or a pirate, for that matter."

Sarah cocked her head and gave him a smug smile. "You wouldn't think tariffs bothersome unless you bothered to pay them."

He chuckled again. "In other words, you think me a law-abiding tradesman. How very dull. I'd prefer to be thought of as a pirate. Any chance you can feed the gossips that particular rumor? I'd love to see people shrink away in fear when I approach."

"How very morbid of you. Are you certain you didn't enjoy *Frankenstein* at least a little?"

He made a face. "Not even a little."

"Perhaps you really are dull then."

He laughed and guided his horses down a road that ran parallel to the sea. The strong breeze lifted the brim of Sarah's straw bonnet and batted her loose curls around her face. She breathed in the fresh, late-August air and looked out across the ocean. She'd only ever walked along this path. It felt like a treat to be in a high-perched phaeton, rumbling along at a more exhilarating pace.

"The sea, on the other hand, is never dull, is it?" she said.

"Not in the least," he agreed. "Have you ever sailed, Miss Meacham?"

"No."

"Would you like to?"

"Yes."

"Would you like to sail with me?"

Sarah's gaze strayed from the sea to his handsome profile. She had always wondered what it would feel like to float across the English Channel. What would Brighton look like from that perspective? Would she be able to see France? Would the sea smell different than it did on shore, and would the waters look as dark as they appeared from the shore?

"Your father and sister would be welcome as well," Mr. Collum added. "I'm not suggesting you join me unattended."

The way he ducked his head and fiddled with the reins, not glancing her way, made Sarah wonder if he actually felt nervous. Was he worried about another rejection? How endearing.

"I will have to check with Papa and Beth, but I'm certain they'll be thrilled at the prospect of such an adventure. I know I am. It's something I have only ever dreamed of doing."

He seemed to relax a little, and a smile lifted his lips. "Sunday then? Five o'clock?"

"Only if you're referring to the evening hour," she said, causing him to chuckle.

"Aye, although if you were to see the sun rise from the middle of the Channel, you would be glad to rise early. But not to worry, the sunset will be magnificent as well."

"It sounds heavenly," said Sarah.

He smiled. "Dress warm. It is breezy on the waters."

"We will, and . . . thank you. The closest I have ever come to sailing is bathing in the sea."

The carriage hit a large rut, and Sarah was jostled to the side, her shoulder slamming into Mr. Collum's.

"Pardon me," she quickly said, sliding back into place and righting her bonnet.

"'Tis the horses and carriage that should beg *your* pardon," he said.

"Not the driver?" She smirked, and he shook his head.

"My horses have a mind of their own, and the carriage is content to follow. I'm merely another rider."

"In that case, I'd like to disembark. I have no wish to be carried off somewhere by mischievous beasts."

"Have no fear, Miss Meacham. They have yet to abduct me or my passengers. I'm certain they will eventually return you to your home. Likely, when they grow hungry."

She giggled and shook her head. "You, sir, are ridiculous."

"And you, Miss Meacham, should laugh more often. It suits you."

He cocked his head to look at her, and Sarah colored under the warmth of his gaze. But she couldn't wipe the smile from her face. It had been a long time since she'd felt so . . . happy. Refreshed. Invigorated. Renewed. Ready to let those lovely gray horses carry her wherever they pleased. To think she'd almost turned down the ride. What a mistake that would have been.

"Do you bathe in the sea often, Miss Meacham?" he asked.

Sarah thought wistfully of the hours she'd spent with her mother floating in the frigid waters of the Channel. "Not anymore."

"You've outgrown the pastime?"

Is that what had happened? Sarah couldn't be sure. She just remembered spending hours in the waters and then . . . none at all. "Mama fell ill when I was young, not long after Bethia was born. When she didn't recover, my father moved our family to Brighton, hoping the health benefits of the sea would heal her. She bathed often, and once I reached the age of twelve, Papa allowed me to join her. We spent many happy hours frolicking in the waters, but after she passed, I suppose it lost its appeal."

He nodded as though he understood. "Years ago, I was offered a writership position with the East India Company. My mother urged me to accept and make something of myself, and so I did. I was there a little over a year when I received word of her death. She's buried in a small church-yard not far from my childhood home in Scotland, but I can't bring myself to return. It would feel too empty without her there."

Sarah wasn't sure which would be worse, having to watch a loved one wither slowly away as she had done with her mother, or have her taken in an instant, with no warning. At least Sarah had been able to say goodbye and make the most of what time she'd had left. Mr. Collum had not been as lucky.

"What about your father?" Sarah asked.

His brow furrowed, and he shook his head as though he didn't wish to speak of the man. Sarah wasn't sure what to make of that. Had his father died as well, or was it something else? She didn't feel comfortable inquiring further.

A familiar tree came into view, and Sarah touched his arm. "Would your horses be willing to stop here for a moment, do you think?"

"I could talk them into it." He tugged on the reins, and they began to slow.

"How very accommodating they are." Sarah pointed. "See that lovely elm there? On the other side, there is something of a path that leads to a spectacular viewpoint. Would you like to see it?"

"Aye." He jumped from the phaeton and came around to assist her.

As she met his gaze, it struck her how much she wanted to trust this man. He may not claim to be a gentleman, but everything she'd learned about his character had attested to the contrary. He was kind, well spoken, and everything about him felt . . . safe. But hadn't she once thought the same of Mr. Hatch?

If only she could trust her instincts.

She began to slide from the seat and grab hold of his shoulders for support, but her boot became caught in something, and she fell, or rather, lunged at him instead. With a squeal, her hands flailed in the air as she pitched forward. The brim of her bonnet knocked against his beaver, and her nose and mouth connected with his face in a hard smack.

"Och," he grunted at the same time she did, her top teeth smarting from the impact.

Thankfully, his strong arms kept her from falling all the way to the ground. For a moment, he struggled to keep them both upright before he finally regained his balance and steadied her.

Still in his arms, Sarah focused her eyes on his cravat. One would think she was adept at making a fool of herself around him. Actually, according to the rumors that never seemed to expire, she was adept at making a fool of herself everywhere she went. Always the unstable Miss Shrew.

The scent of leather and spice filled her senses, and she felt herself tipping toward him just a little.

She cleared her throat, but somehow dared to peek up at him. He was so close she could see the short stubble on his chin and found herself wondering what it would feel like to touch it. "I'm dreadfully sorry, Mr. Collum."

"We can move beyond formalities now, can we not? You did just kiss me, after all. My name is Ian."

Sarah immediately pushed free from his hold, her cheeks burning. What a thing to say. "I did no such thing, Mr. *Collum*." Why did her voice have to sound so breathless, so . . . affected?

He chuckled as he bent to retrieve his hat and made a show of dusting it off before tucking it under one arm. "Were you attempting to maim me, then? I've heard rumors that you are handy with your fists, but no one mentioned you could use your mouth as a weapon as well."

Sarah's jaw clenched. Apparently, Mr. Collum had made other friends as well—those who'd seen fit to enlighten him about her past. How very kind of them.

"You've done your research, I see. I'm surprised you haven't called me Miss Shrew as of yet," she said stiffly.

He reached for her bonnet and shifted it to the left before tucking a few of her curls back in place. Sarah stood rooted to the spot, torn between wanting to lean into him again or step back. She decided on the latter.

"*Are* you a shrew?" he asked.

"Only when provoked."

He chuckled. "Am I provoking you now, Miss . . . Shrew?" He sounded hesitant, as though he was testing the waters. Strange how the epithet didn't irritate her as much coming from him. Instead, he made it sound flirtatious.

Too bad she wasn't in the mood to flirt. Her emotions were too unstable to do anything but sigh and shake her head. "You have nothing to fear, sir. I have no intention of breaking your nose at present. Tell anyone I kissed you, however, and that might change."

He grinned and nodded. "Duly noted, but to be fair, it did sort of feel like a kiss—a bungled attempt at one, but a kiss nonetheless."

Sarah frowned at him for a moment before spinning on her heel. "The viewpoint is this way."

Without another word, she slipped around the tree and through some tall grasses, where she found the overgrown path she and her mother had once taken. A short walk brought her to a lovely rise overlooking the outstretched beach and sea. Really, the view wasn't any more spectacular than many other spots along the road, but Sarah had fond memories of this place.

A swift breeze whipped at her loosened tendrils and bonnet ribbons, stirring up memories. Sarah closed her eyes and tilted her face into the obscured sun, enjoying the smell of earth and seawater and the distant sound of waves lapping against the beach.

I miss you Mama, she thought. They'd once walked for hours along the road overlooking the sea, eventually coming to this exact spot, where they'd spent more hours talking about everything and nothing. Sarah remembered one particular conversation with a pang.

Why do I have red hair, Mama? No boy will ever love me.
The right boy will. He'll think it enchanting.

Sarah had loved the sound of that word even though she'd doubted any man would think such a thing. Actually, what Sarah had loved most was her mother. Some mothers tried to change their daughters, but not hers. Hers had been accepting, loving, and perfect.

"Penny for your thoughts," came his deep, Scottish lilt as he stepped next to her.

Sarah blinked and shook her head. "I was merely thinking of my mother."

"Did you come here with her?"

She nodded, appreciating his perception and the kindness in his tone. "Only once. It's a long way from home, but I'll never forget that day. She loved the color of my hair." What an absurd thing to say, but out it came anyway.

He playfully tugged on a stray tendril, his fingers brushing the spot below her ear and sending a thrill down her spine. "I'd have to agree. It's an enchanting color."

Sarah's gaze flew to his, her heart leaping about like a newborn kitten. "Pardon?"

His hand fell away, and he shuffled his feet as though embarrassed for taking such liberties. "Forgive me. I only meant that I can see why your mother liked it so much. It's a bonnie shade. Not quite red, but not brown either. It's . . . unusual, like you."

"Thank you," she murmured, knowing he'd meant it as a compliment.

"And thank *you* for introducing me to this view. It's a bonnie sight as well."

She tilted her head at him, suddenly remembering that she was at liberty to ask any question she wanted. "You say you come from Scotland, but your accent is often faint. Why is that?"

He stiffened and looked away, as though the question bothered him. But he eventually answered her. "I was schooled in England. At Shrewsbury."

Sarah tried to mask her surprise, but it was a difficult thing to do. Shrewsbury was a school for gentlemen—not men who claimed to be something else.

"Shrewsbury is a long way from Scotland," she said when he said nothing more.

"Yes." Again, the set of his jaw told her he didn't care for this line of questioning. Yet he didn't try to dissuade her or change the subject, probably because he'd told her she could ask him anything. She appreciated his willingness to honor that promise.

Out of respect for him, however, she opted to move on to another, hopefully less sensitive topic.

"Banjeet is quite the character, isn't he?"

That did the trick. His expression softened. "That's one way of putting it. He spoke to you?"

"For quite some time, actually. He was most informative."

Mr. Collum snickered. "I can only imagine what he must have said, all of it worrisome."

Sarah tucked her hands behind her back, taking note of some dark clouds coming their way. The wind seemed to be picking up as well. "He introduced himself, which was more than you ever did, and he told me your name as well. He also mentioned you import a great many things but was very elusive about what those things are."

She cocked her head to shoot him a questioning look.

"Probably because it's uninteresting cargo. I have two coasters used to bring in lumber and coal, and I've recently invested in a smaller ship to travel between here and France, importing commodities like wine, cheese, and butter. Brighton is a booming place at the moment, and trade is good. I hope to be able to purchase another ship within the year."

"I see." Mr. Collum had led an interesting life, to be sure. Scotland, England, India, and probably other places in between.

"What is Banjeet's story? How did he come to be here with you?"

Mr. Collum appeared hesitant to answer, scraping at the grasses beneath his boot. "'Tis a sad tale. Are you certain you wish to hear it?"

Sarah glanced around for a suitable place for them to sit and decided on a large boulder a few steps away. She sat first then gave the spot next to her a pat.

"I would very much like to hear it," she said, ignoring the hard, uneven surface beneath her.

He smiled and dropped down next to her, leaning forward to rest his elbows on his knees.

"Banjeet's mother was a beautiful, vivacious Indian woman who caught the eye of many British soldiers. But it was a man I once thought of as a friend who captured *her* eye—and heart. Unfortunately, he considered the attachment a mere diversion. Once he learned he'd fathered a child, he requested a transfer and fled."

From his tone, it was obvious he was still angered by the other man's actions. "He left her ruined, without any offer of support or hope. Her family disowned her and many of her friends left her to bear the burden alone. Only a few of us stood by her throughout the ordeal, not that she accepted much help. At one point I tried to convince her to marry me, thinking to shield her with my name, but she refused. She was stubborn and determined to suffer the consequences of her choices alone. In the end, it was her undoing."

Sarah drew in a quick breath, her heart aching for the woman, her son, and Mr. Collum. "What happened to her?"

"I watched her whither from a confident woman into a waif of a thing, sewing her fingers to the bone just to keep her son fed. On her deathbed, she begged me to take Banjeet, even though he was barely eight at the time. We had a special bond, he and I, and she knew I would care for him as if he were my own. It was the only thing she had ever asked me, and I could not deny her. Not long after her passing, Banjeet and I sailed for England."

Sarah wasn't sure how to respond. To some extent, she could empathize with Banjeet's mother, as she, too, had once entrusted her heart to the wrong man. But she hadn't been ostracized from her family as Banjeet's mother had been. She hadn't been forgotten by friends or left to fend for herself.

Suddenly, the epithet that had haunted Sarah all these

years no longer seemed like much of a trial. She still had her father, sister, and Chelle, along with some family friends. She was still accepted among her peers, even though her welcome had waned over the years.

"I'm sorry for your loss," Sarah said. "And Banjeet's as well. She sounds like someone I would have liked."

"You would have had something in common. She, too, was slow to trust." Mr. Collum smiled a little, and that twinkle she was beginning to like appeared in his eyes. He nudged her shoulder with his own. "Although she would never have thrown herself in my arms as you just did."

Sarah attempted a glare, but her twitching lips took all the effrontery out of it. "One of these days, you may come to regret toying with me, Mr. Collum. I have friends in high places, you know."

He chuckled as he watched her. "Do you mean the prince? What do you intend to do, have him spread vicious rumors about me being a smuggler or a nabob, because that's already been done. From what I understand, he isn't even in Brighton and likely won't return until the pavilion's renovations are complete. Perhaps you'll convince him to cease purchasing lumber from me."

Sarah rolled her eyes, realizing she hadn't intimidated him in the least. "You'd think my threats would have more power to sway, considering my reputation. Are you not worried I'll blacken your eye or break your nose?"

"You did attempt to fatten my lip earlier."

"I thought I tried to kiss you," she retorted, only to regret her words the moment his grin widened.

"The bonnie lass admits it at last," he teased.

"You, sir, are a toad."

"And you, Miss, are a delight."

She wasn't sure what to say to this, but her cheeks grew

warm and her stomach tied itself into knots. But for once, she basked in the feeling instead of trying to squelch it.

"I've put you to the blush," he said. "Are you so unused to compliments?"

"I . . ." Sarah's voice trailed off, making her sound like a dunderhead. It wasn't that she was unused to compliments—she'd heard many during her years of popularity—it was more that she was unused to the sincerity that seemed to accompany Mr. Collum's compliments.

A strong wind whipped around them, setting her bonnet askew. Sarah clamped her hand over the top of it and glanced to the side. The dark clouds that had loomed before now surged in their direction. "That storm is coming in fast."

As another gust of wind assailed them, Mr. Collum followed her gaze, then leapt to his feet and held out a hand. "Let's get you home, Miss Meacham. The sooner the better."

Gone was his playful teasing. He looked worried.

As he rushed her back to the carriage, Sarah said, "This isn't the first time I've been caught in a storm, sir. A little rain won't be the death of me."

"I fear it'll be more than a wee bit, and I'll not be responsible should you take a chill."

He helped her into the phaeton, jumped up next to her, and urged his horses along. Sarah lifted her gaze to the skies, and a raindrop splattered against her cheek. Followed by another and another. She quickly ducked her head.

Mr. Collum shrugged out of his jacket and draped it around her, telling her to button it up. She was grateful for the offer. Within minutes, sheets of rain descended on them. While his coat kept her somewhat dry, he was getting soaked to the bone. Poor man.

"Only a gentleman would offer his coat to a woman during a rainstorm," she called out loudly, trying to lighten the mood.

"It was a demand, not an offer," he returned.

"Thank you nonetheless," she said, happy to see a bit of a smile lift his lips, if only for a moment.

"My place of business is closer than your house. Would you mind if we stopped there to wait out the rain?"

"Not at all." Her bonnet and Mr. Collum's coat were doing a decent job protecting her face and upper body from the onslaught, but her skirts were now quite wet, sending chills up and down her legs. She could only imagine how cold Mr. Collum felt at the moment.

The sooner they could get out of the rain the better.

$\cdot\cdot$ 10 $\cdot\cdot$

THEY ARRIVED IN front of a tall, narrow, nondescript building on a grimy, water-sodden street. Through the rain, Sarah could make out the Shoreham Port in the distance. It wasn't the prettiest of sights, but from what Sarah had heard of other port towns, she wasn't too surprised. They were a place for sea-roughened men. Thankfully, the rain had washed away most of the foul smells.

Mr. Collum ushered her inside before returning to tend to his horses and carriage. Alone and dripping on the rough, wooden floor, Sarah looked around at the dim interior. Several chairs were strewn about, and two mismatched desks stood on either side of the room, piled high with papers, ledgers, and books. One had been pushed against the wall while the other faced the room's center. A large, wooden bookcase stood not far away, in no better state of organization than the rest of the room. Fifty or so books sat on its shelves, tilted this way and that. Many of them even had their spines facing inward, hiding all but the rough-cut pages.

Good grief. Did the man not know how to organize?

How could a person operate a successful business in this manner?

Sarah shivered and pulled Mr. Collum's jacket tighter about her, realizing that he was still out in the rain without it. Drat. She should have given it back the moment she'd stepped inside. Although two windows peered out across the street, the cloud-encrusted skies, mixed with the clutter, made the room feel dark, cold, and bleak.

The brim of her blue linen bonnet sank low over her eye, weighed down by the added water it carried. Sarah tugged the pins that secured it to her head and removed it, then attempted to pat down her damp and frizzy hair. With no mirror to assist her, she shoved the few pins back in, hoping she didn't look too much like a wild animal.

A large fireplace beckoned her from across the room, and she noticed a basket of coal and a pile of lumber adjacent to it. If she and Mr. Collum were to ever dry out, they'd need the warmth it offered. Sarah strode forward, grabbed the tinderbox from the mantle, and set to work. Over the years, she'd gotten fairly good at building fires. Suzy couldn't be expected to do everything, after all.

As she fanned the flames to get the logs burning, the door flew open, allowing the wind and cold to blast through the room.

Assuming Mr. Collum had returned, Sarah continued to prod the flames without glancing his way. "This fire will do us no good if you insist on keeping that door open," she said at last.

"Who might you be?" came an unfamiliar, gravelly voice.

Sarah twisted around on her heels, then stood, taking note of a small, burly man standing just inside the door. He closed it slowly, watching her with suspicion. Sarah swallowed, noting his unfriendly expression and rugged appearance. Was he in Mr. Collum's employ?

She forced a smile. "Forgive me, sir. I am Miss Sarah Meacham, a friend of Mr. Collum's. We were out driving not far from here when the storm came upon us. He brought me here to wait it out and is now tending to his phaeton and horses. He should be along momentarily."

The man removed his hat and scratched what remained of his damp, brown hair. The gesture made him look a little less intimidating. "Cole brought you 'ere, did 'e?"

"My home is on the other side of Brighton. Please forgive the intrusion. It is a great inconvenience to be caught unaware."

"No trouble at all, Miss . . . Meacham, did you say?"

"Yes, and you are?"

"Miles Davies, but most call me Davie."

"Pleasure to meet you, Mr. Davies. And thank you for not giving me the boot."

"Davie," he corrected. "Mr. Davies is my father." He shuffled his feet in an awkward move before gesturing to the fireplace behind her. "Is that your doin'?"

She glanced over her shoulder, happy to see large flames dance around the logs. "Yes. I hope it's all right. It's cold in here, and Mr. Collum and I are very wet, him especially." She bent to retrieve the tinderbox from the floor and returned it to the mantle.

"'Course it's all right," he grumbled, scratching his head again looking for all the world as though he'd rather be anywhere but alone with her. He likely had no idea how to converse with a woman like Sarah.

She was about to ask how he knew Mr. Collum when the door opened, and a large gust of wind swept in, sending several papers flying off the desks. Rain splattered across the floor as Mr. Collum slammed the door closed.

"It's getting worse," he said, glancing at Sarah. "I asked a stable boy to take word to your father, but my conscience wouldn't allow me to send him out in this. I told him to wait until the worst of the storm had passed."

Sarah nodded. "My father will think I took refuge in town, as I have done in the past. He will not worry for a while yet."

The fire crackled and snapped, drawing Mr. Collum's attention. He strode towards Sarah and stopped at her side, rubbing his hands for warmth. "Did you actually start a fire, Davie?"

"Not me," came the gravelly response. "She did."

Mr. Collum's look of surprise caused Sarah to lift her chin. "I'm not completely useless, sir."

He chuckled. "Any woman who can light a fire and break a man's nose is certainly not useless, Miss Shrew." He lowered his voice and added, "Though your kissing skills could use some work."

Sarah playfully slapped his arm only to grab hold of it seconds later. It was ice cold.

"You're freezing!" she cried, feeling guilt at keeping his coat. She quickly shrugged out of it. "You must remove that wet shirt at once and put this on. The inside is still dry and will warm you."

His eyes crinkled with amusement, but he didn't reach for his coat. "You're asking me to disrobe? Now?"

Sarah refused to let him embarrass her. "Once my back is turned, yes. I'm sure Davie can assist you if needs be."

Mr. Collum snickered. "I am not completely useless either, Miss Meacham. Believe it or not, I am capable of changing my shirt without assistance, though I wouldn't mind your help."

Her pulse quickened at the insinuation and a fresh blush heated her cheeks. She glared at him and shoved the coat into his grasp.

Davie began chuckling until Sarah glared at him as well. The chuckle quickly became a cough.

"Change. Now," Sarah said to Mr. Collum. Then she turned her back to him, folded her arms, and waited for him to obey.

To her consternation, he placed the coat back on her shoulders and took hold of her upper arms. As he leaned in from behind, the warmth of his breath sent a slew of chills down her back. Wonderful chills. The desire to turn around and slide her arms around him waged an internal battle.

"If it's all the same to you, bonnie lass, I'd prefer to change into dry clothes."

You cannot fall for him. You cannot, she thought.

The warm of his breath left her neck, and the legs of a chair scraped the ground. She looked back to see that Mr. Collum had placed a chair in front of the fire. "Do sit down and dry your skirts, Miss Meacham."

He collected a kettle from the top of the bookcase and disappeared through a door at the side of the room. The sound of footsteps ascending stairs caused Sarah to look up with a curious frown.

"'Is livin' quarters," Davie supplied.

"Ah." The news surprised her. From the way he dressed, his lovely matching grays, and the well-equipped phaeton he drove, she'd pictured him living in a large home with servants aplenty. Did he even employ servants? Who cooked his meals, cleaned his quarters, and laundered his clothes? Where did Banjeet sleep? She assumed upstairs as well.

What a strange but interesting life.

Davie gathered the papers that had blown to the floor, then took a seat at the desk facing the wall and began thumbing through them, apparently intent on getting back to work.

Sarah shoved her arms through the coat and took a seat by the fire, but she soon grew cold anyway. She needed to occupy herself. Moving would keep her warmer and give her something to think about besides the man who was causing all those creaks overhead.

Her gaze landed on the disorganized bookcase. Perhaps she could do something about that. She wandered over and examined the four shelves, trying to understand Mr. Collum's method of organization. The spines facing out were not alphabetized, and judging by the small amount of dust on many of the covers, he made use of the books fairly often. Surely, he'd appreciate a little organization. Not only would it look tidier, but his books would be much easier to find.

Unable to talk herself out of it, Sarah knelt on the floor and began straightening and alphabetizing. If Davie noticed, he didn't say anything. She forged on, turning all the spines outward, brushing dust off some, and alphabetizing them in the way books were organized in the lending library.

"What is it you do for Mr. Collum, Davie?" Sarah asked, hoping to start some conversation. The only sounds in the room came from the creaks overhead, the crackling fire, and the rain splattering against the windows.

Davie didn't even glance up from the ledger on his desk. With his back to her, he muttered, "What I don't do 'twould be a shorter answer."

"I know you don't help him dress," Sarah tried for a lighthearted tone, hoping to make the situation a little less awkward.

He harrumphed and turned the page of his ledger. "Don't cook for him neither."

Sarah took his curt answers as a sign to leave him be and continued tidying the bookshelf. As she slid the last book into place, she rose and stepped back, admiring her handiwork.

Much better, she thought. Organized, clean, and even pleasing to the eye. Mr. Collum couldn't be anything but grateful.

She looked around the room and spotted one more book on the fireplace mantle. *Recreations in Science and Natural Philosophy* by Edward Goulde. Hmm . . . It belonged on the third shelf near the beginning. Several books would need to be moved to the lowest shelf to make room, but that was easily done.

Sarah was in the process of reconfiguring the two lowest shelves when the sound of footsteps clomping down the stairs reached her. It was a blessed sound. Just as she pushed the science book into its rightful place, Mr. Collum's voice reached her.

"What are you doing?"

Sarah rose from her knees and brushed her hands together, pleased with her efforts and hopeful he would be as well. She turned to face him. "How you managed to find anything on those shelves is beyond me. Ah, you've brought tea and muffins. Bless you." She was starving.

He set the tray down and frowned at the bookcase. "The muffins are a few days old and probably stale, but the tea is fresh. Where did my copy of *The Wealth of Nations* go? It was on the upper shelf this morning."

"Now it's on the lowest shelf, here." Sarah tapped the spine of the book. "You probably don't recognize the cover, considering its spine was hidden."

"Actually, it was turned on its side on the top of the bookcase, the place where I store the books I'm currently reading. The ones with spines hidden, as you say, are those I've already read. And the books that used to be on the bottom right are those I haven't yet had a chance to peruse."

"Oh." Apparently, the man *had* employed some method of organization, albeit an odd one. The pride Sarah had felt moments earlier became something more like misgiving.

She gingerly slid out *The Wealth of Nations* and set it on the top of the bookshelf with a pat. She wished she could restore all of the others to their rightful places, but she'd never remember where they'd been.

Blast.

She clasped her fingers together and gave him a placating look. "They are now alphabetized by title and appear more orderly, do they not?"

"Appearances can be deceiving."

"Yes, well, I did say you'd come to regret toying with me. Have I managed to achieve that already?"

"Not in the least, Miss Shrew." He chuckled and began pouring tea into three cups. He gave one to her, set another on the desk next to Davie, and took the third for himself.

She was sipping her tea and basking in the warmth it offered when he said, "The bookcase does look more orderly. I thank you."

What tea remained in Sarah's mouth went spewing back into her cup as she snickered. She closed her eyes and shook her head. "I'm sorry, sir. Truly, I am. I thought I was being helpful."

"Just promise you'll leave my files and ledgers alone."

"Done." She tried to look out the front window, but the many drops scattered across it made it difficult to see much. "Has the rain let up yet? I believe I have already overstayed my welcome."

A crash of thunder startled Sarah, answering her question.

Mr. Collum stiffened and frowned, lines of worry creasing his brow. "Any word, Davie?"

The older man shook his head. "Nothin' yet."

"Good. That should mean they diverted to Portsmouth."

Davie turned to face the window as well, his expression skeptical. After a moment, he shoved his chair back and stood. "Think I'll take another gander."

Mr. Collum nodded. "Take my umbrella."

"Nah. My 'at'll do me fine." Davie shrugged into a worn greatcoat and snatched a black, wide-brimmed hat from a rack near the door before disappearing outside.

Sarah continued to peer out the window, wondering what they'd been talking about. Was one of Mr. Collum's ships out in this weather? Perhaps all three? Goodness, she hoped not.

"I wish you'd sit by the fire," he said. "Your skirts are still quite damp, and you must be freezing. I'm sorry I don't have a dry gown lying around for you to change into."

"It would be an odd thing if you did," she said before returning to the chair, which had warmed in her absence. She leaned forward and held out her hands.

When Mr. Collum slid a chair next to hers, she cocked her head at him. "Do your ships divert to Portsmouth often?"

"Only when the weather requires it. I used to operate my business there, but it is a filthy, overcrowded port. Once I'd learned Shoreham had undergone some improvements, I jumped at the chance to relocate. No port town could ever be called beautiful, but it's a great deal cleaner here. I still have friends there, however, who allow us to rent space in their warehouses when needed. It's an added expense I'm never thrilled to pay, but better that than putting my men and my ship at the mercy of the dreaded Shoreham piers. They are set too close together for my liking."

He spoke to her freely, as he would to another man, and she appreciated it. Her father always seemed to worry and fret about something, but Sarah rarely knew what that something was. Whenever she'd ask, he'd merely pat her hand or give her a weak smile, saying it was nothing to bother about.

"You're worried," she said.

He studied her a moment before nodding. "Aye, mostly because I can't be sure they went to Portsmouth. With any other shipmaster, I could, but Captain James is as skilled as he is arrogant. I wouldn't be surprised if he attempted to bring the ship into Shoreham."

"Has he tried before?"

"Aye, but not in conditions as stormy as these." Worried lines furrowed his brow as firelight danced across his face. "I shouldn't have allowed Banjeet to go with them."

Sarah's breath caught in her throat. Banjeet was on board that ship. Though they'd only spoken once, the thought of him coming to harm concerned her as well. She could only imagine the extent of fear Mr. Collum was experiencing. Banjeet, his men, the ship, his cargo—they were all at risk. And what had she done to ease his concerns? Take his coat and wreak havoc on his bookcase.

"It was to be a quick trip to France and back, and he begged and begged." The way Mr. Collum spoke the words, in that quiet, contemplative way, made it sound like he was talking more to himself than to her. "The lad was born with an excess of persistence, along with the heart, soul, and legs of a seaman. It's an everyday battle to keep him away from the docks and ships."

"He mentioned he was apprenticing to become a shipmaster."

Mr. Collum barked a laugh. "Aye, and I'm apprenticing to become an architect."

He smoothed back some hair that had fallen forward into his eyes and continued. "The only thing I'm trying to teach the lad at present is reading, mathematics, science, and how to speak and behave properly. I've even employed various tutors, but the only thing Banjeet excels at is the art of diversion. Only last week I found him with his latest tutor, Mr. Gains, dickering with a merchant over the price of a shawl. Banjeet had learned Mr. Gains was sweet on a lass, so he convinced the poor man to buy her a shawl as a token of his appreciation. They tried to tell me it was a lesson in mathematics, but any fool could see Banjeet had preyed on Mr. Gain's sympathies to escape his studies in lieu of the docks."

Sarah smiled. "Banjeet is no fool."

"Nae, he's a conniving, manipulative rapscallion who will do whatever it takes to get his way."

"Some would call that driven and resourceful."

"I call it irritating."

Sarah laughed. "At least he knows what he wants."

"Aye, that he does. It's one of the reasons I'm determined to see him well educated. If he wants to become a shipmaster, I'll see to it he's the b—"

The door burst open and the object of their discussion ran in, dripping, shivering, and grinning widely. "You should have seen it, *Pita*! The ship nearly hit a pier, and Captain—"

The rest of his words were muffled as Mr. Collum leapt from his chair and pulled the boy into a fierce hug. Sarah was happy to see the lines of worry fade into an expression of relief. He obviously cared a great deal for Banjeet.

You, Mr. Collum, are a good man, Sarah thought.

Mr. Collum pulled back, keeping Banjeet at arm's length. "You're well? My men? The ship?"

Banjeet extracted himself. "Never say you were worried, *Pita*. I was with Captain James."

"That's precisely why I *was* worried," said Mr. Collum. "You should have sailed to Portsmouth."

"Portsmouth," Banjeet scoffed. "We couldn't go so far out of our way, not when there's a cricket game tomorrow. You need Captain James, Higgins, and Leo. They're the best chance we've got."

"We could have rescheduled, Banjeet."

The door opened again, and Davie reentered, along with another man Sarah assumed was Captain James. Tall and well built, the man carried himself with a great deal of arrogance, as though he'd just accomplished an impossible feat. He was younger than Sarah had pictured but older than Mr. Collum by five or six years. Late-thirties, she'd say.

"Banjeet, you must be frozen," said Mr. Collum. "Run upstairs and change into dry clothes."

Banjeet looked ready to argue until his gaze landed on Sarah, who was now standing by the fire. Recognition sparked in his eyes. "You're the woman with all the questions."

"The very same." Sarah smiled. "It's a pleasure to see you again, Banjeet."

"It's her all right." He grinned at Mr. Collum. "I couldn't be sure at first. Her hair is different. More wild."

"Banjeet. Upstairs. Now."

"Aye, sir." A cheeky grin accompanied Banjeet's salute, then he raced for the side door, leaving a small puddle behind.

The moment Mr. Collum's attention diverted to the men, Sarah patted her hair self-consciously, cringing at all the frizz and disarray she felt. Enchanting? Hardly. Why did her hair have to be so blasted curly? As much as she'd loved her mother, Sarah didn't care for some of the traits she'd passed on, such as her curly, untamable hair. At least her mother's had been a lovely, golden yellow.

"Cole, before you rake me over the coals, you should know I was in complete control of the ship at all times," Captain James said.

Mr. Collum didn't appear appeased. "Such as the moment you nearly collided with a pier? Yes, Banjeet already told us about that particular incident."

James shook his head. "You know how Banjeet exaggerates. I promise you, we didn't come within ten meters of any pier."

Mr. Collum glanced in Sarah's direction and replied curtly, "Now is not the time for this. We'll talk later."

"Very well," the shipmaster said.

Davie wasn't as cooperative. He wagged his fist at the shipmaster and growled, "Tell me you didn't risk the men and the ship for a blasted game of cricket."

"Davie, we will discuss this later," Mr. Collum repeated, giving a stern look to his employee.

If Sarah could have made her excuses and left right then, she would have. Mr. Collum had business matters to attend to, and she was in the way. Thankfully, the rain appeared to be letting up. The only problem remaining was the large puddles strewn about, turning a once sturdy road into a myriad of sink holes for carriage wheels.

It must be late afternoon by now. What would she do if the roads were now impassable? Had word of her situation even reached her father yet?

"We'll likely have to travel by way of horseback, Miss Meacham, but I will get you home," Mr. Collum promised, somehow reading her mind.

While she appreciated his determination, it had been

ages since Sarah had been on the back of a horse. Their father had sold their horses and cart years earlier, explaining they no longer had need of them. *Everything is but a short walk away,* he'd assured her.

Sarah had agreed at the time, but the port of Shoreham was not a short walk away. Even if her father had learned of her predicament, he wouldn't be able to fetch her.

"I'm not certain I remember how to ride," she confessed, despising herself for adding another complication to the day.

"I have a gentle mare you can ride. You need only hold on."

"That I can do," Sarah said, hoping that was indeed the case.

"I'll get two 'orses saddled right away and ask a groom to see Miss Meacham home," Davie interjected. "We should look over the cargo and make sure there's no damage."

"Thank you, Davie, but my inspection can wait. I will accompany Miss Meacham."

From Davie's frown, Sarah assumed he didn't care for that answer, but he stalked out the door without argument.

Sarah stood awkwardly by the window, hating that she was keeping Mr. Collum from his duties. What had begun as a pleasurable ride had culminated into a situation where she was decidedly in the way. There was also the fact that she had to look quite haggard. What she wouldn't give for a hot bath, a hearty meal, and home.

The shipmaster cleared his throat. "I should make sure everything has been offloaded and is now secure."

Mr. Collum nodded as he glanced at the ceiling, which was no longer creaking from footsteps. "Banjeet has un-doubtedly escaped down the back ladder and has returned to the ship. Will you keep an eye on him until I return?"

"Of course."

The captain left, leaving Sarah alone with her guilt and Mr. Collum.

She clasped her hands nervously in front of her. "Sir, if you need to attend to your business, I can—"

His answering chuckle cut her off. "You can what, Miss Meacham? Walk? Ride home alone?" He took both of her hands in his and began rubbing them between his own. Oddly enough, the warmth from his hands caused goosebumps to erupt across her arms. She liked his touch, and, drat it all, she liked him.

Her gaze traveled up to his face, taking him all in. There was that stubble again, so masculine. His strong jawline, imperfect nose, and creases around his brow and at the corners of his mouth that told of worry, frustration, and laughter. In that moment, he became very human to her.

"For weeks now, I have done everything I could think of to finagle some time with you," he said. "What you probably see as a day of misadventures, I see as good luck. My inspection can wait. I *want* to accompany you home."

"I . . ." Her head felt foggy all of a sudden, and her breath skidded about in her chest.

"You are still cold and probably starving," he said, continuing to rub her hands.

Cold? Sarah thought dumbly. How could she be cold when a fire raged inside of her? No, she wasn't the least bit cold, and the only hunger she felt was the desire for him to take her into his arms and hold her close.

What a turn this day had taken.

"I . . ." Her voice faltered again, her tumultuous thoughts refusing to give her something intelligible to say.

Mr. Collum smiled, as though he knew the effect he was having on her. "I have a greatcoat you can borrow. It'll be too large, but it will keep you warm."

Sarah pulled her hands free and took a step back. It helped. Her mind cleared and the air became easier to breathe.

"Do you think the horses are ready?" she asked.

He continued to study her, looking as though he wanted to say something else, but his attention was soon drawn to the window.

"Aye. Here comes Davie now. It appears as though he's even found you a side saddle. How fortuitous. I'll run up-stairs to collect my extra greatcoat, and we can be off."

Sarah bit down on her lower lip. The approaching horses were tall, black, and intimidating. What Mr. Collum called fortuitous Sarah called terrifying.

·· 11 ··

IAN GLANCED AT Miss Meacham and fought back a grin. Her droopy bonnet, oversized coat, and untamed hair made her appear as though she'd been dragged from the sea. She clung to the pommel with one hand while attempting to keep the greatcoat closed with the other. Her once-lovely afternoon dress, now smudged and creased, was not meant for riding. As she bounced along, her skirts continually flew up, revealing some bonnie ankles.

He'd suggested they circumvent the busier areas of town and take a lesser-used route instead, even though it meant crossing through some untamed fields. From a distance, it was highly unlikely anyone would recognize the disheveled, greatcoat-clad person as the intriguing Miss Shrew, and Ian intended to keep it that way. Her reputation would not receive further injury at his hand.

As much as he needed to return to the docks, Ian had been truthful about wanting to accompany her home. He only wished she would speak. Typically, her thoughts were written across her face, but there were times, such as now, when it was anyone's guess.

Was she regretting her decision to join him today? She had handled everything with poise, a sense of humor, and—what surprised him the most—acceptance. She hadn't turned up her nose at his unconventional living situation, hadn't looked down at Davie, despite his bad manners, and hadn't muttered one word of complaint even though she'd undoubtedly been cold, hungry, and uncomfortable. He admired that.

"Well, Miss Meacham," Ian finally said, hoping to get her talking. "Have you learned not to drive with the likes of me again?"

Her mouth quirked up a bit. Despite her dishevelment, her smile still transfixed him. "I don't know, sir. Have you learned not to ask?"

She hadn't said no, and he counted that as a win. "I would ask if you'd like to go again tomorrow if I thought you'd accept."

"Your cricket game is tomorrow," she countered.

"Aye," he said, "and what a muddy debacle it will be. Friday then?"

Miss Meacham laughed—a delightful sound that cheered his soul. "You cannot be serious. It'll likely take you days to recover from the disruption of today's events. There is your bookcase to reorganize, your shipmaster to speak with, your latest shipment to inventory, your larder to re-stock, and who knows what else. Not to mention the fact that I must be the most unsightly woman you've ever accompanied."

"You haven't met Davie's wife."

"Davie is married?"

"Aye. To a cantankerous old bat, poor man. Even in your current state, she still has you beat."

"Ha. My current state indeed. You certainly know how to flatter a woman. Have you been taking lessons from Banjeet?"

Ian chuckled. "'Twould seem so. I would beg your pardon for such ungentlemanly behavior, but—"

"Yes, yes. You are no gentleman. I know. But if not that, then what?"

"A rogue, obviously."

Her eyes widened in feigned shock. "Never say so, sir. Had I known that, I wouldn't have agreed to a drive in the first place."

"One might say you are in no position to judge, Miss *Shrew*."

She giggled. "Touché. We are a sorry pair, are we not? A rogue and a shrew."

"I'd say we are a well-matched pair."

"The way two opponents are well matched?" she teased.

"I was thinking more along the lines of my grays."

"Ha," she chortled. "You flatter me yet again, sir."

Ian had to admit, there were probably more flattering things he could have compared them to, like a pair of doves, some matching crystal candlesticks, or even nothing at all. But she didn't seem genuinely offended. In fact, she was still giggling.

"I've landed myself in a pit, haven't I?" he said. "The harder I try to get out, the more I sink."

"Aye, that ye have, Mr. Collum," she said with a sorry attempt at a Scottish accent.

He grinned. "You are a breaker of noses and a murderer of accents, Miss Shrew."

"And there you go, sinking further still."

"In for a penny . . ."

She erupted in laughter and grabbed hold of the

123

pommel with both hands as she doubled over. The horse slowed to a stop as she continued to laugh and laugh. With her wild and frizzy hair half falling out of her knot, she looked tipsy. It was a sight to behold, and he couldn't tear his gaze away.

"I do believe you just snorted, Miss Meacham." He tried not to chuckle, but his voice quivered with amusement.

She clamped a hand over her mouth and muffled her laughter while shaking her head vigorously. More untamed hair fell around her shoulders. Soon there would be no knot left at all.

"I did no such thing, sir," she finally managed to say.

"If not you, then who?" he asked. "I distinctly heard a snort."

She sat up straight, cleared her throat, and promptly said, "The horse, obviously."

Ian shook his head. "Goliath would never snort."

"Shashi would—and did," she said, naming the mare she rode. "Perhaps she has a case of the sniffles."

The conversation had taken a turn towards the ridiculous, but Ian didn't care. In fact, he couldn't remember the last time he'd laughed or smiled as much in one day. Miss Meacham was every bit as charming as she was beautiful.

"Shashi is such a unique name. How did she come by it, and what does it mean?"

"Banjeet gave it to her. It means moonlight."

"It's beautiful, just like his horse," she said, reaching forward to comb her fingers through its mane. "I have to admit, she's taken the fear out of riding for me."

"Perhaps we can go for a ride instead of a drive next time." He held his breath, wondering how she'd answer. That morning, outside the library, she had behaved like a skittish colt—so hesitant to place her trust in him. Now, however, he didn't exactly know where he stood.

"I'd like that," she said at last, and he exhaled in relief.

When they arrived at her house, Ian dismounted and looped his reins around a post. Unlike Miss Meacham's earlier mishap, she slid gracefully down from her horse and into his arms. He held her slim waist for a wee longer than necessary as he looked into her greenish-blue, expressive eyes. Mashed bonnet and wild hair aside, the lass was stunning. High cheekbones, flushed cheeks, and the most kissable lips he'd seen in a while. He couldn't resist teasing her one last time.

"I admire your restraint, Miss Meacham."

Her brow furrowed in confusion, but she made no move to extract herself from his hold. "Restraint?"

"I thought for sure you'd bungle your dismount so you could try to kiss me again."

Her eyes narrowed, and she opened her mouth to say something when a throat cleared nearby. The moment she spied her father, she was out of his arms in a wink.

"Papa." Her face flamed, and she smoothed her hair self-consciously.

"What's this about a kiss?" her father said. Up until that moment, Ian would have never called the man intimidating, but his eyes now flashed dangerously, and Ian worried his harmless teasing might result in pistols at dawn.

"He was only jesting, Papa. Earlier, I tripped when climbing down from his carriage, and our faces collided. It was more painful than romantic, I assure you, and my honor is still very much intact."

Her father didn't appear convinced, likely because of his daughter's current state of dishevelment. In truth, she had the look of a woman who'd just been passionately kissed.

Ian scratched his head. "Pray forgive my poor manners. As I explained in my note, we were caught in a downpour and sought refuge at my place of business. Another man in my employ was with us as well."

The two explanations seemed to appease her father somewhat, though he still looked concerned. "Were you seen traveling back in this state?"

"I made sure we were not," Ian answered. "If anyone spied us, it would have been from afar."

"You needn't worry, Papa," Miss Meacham added dryly. "I'm still merely a shrew."

Mr. Meacham looked from one to the other, probably assessing whether or not he could believe them. After an uncomfortable moment, he shoved his hands into his pockets and sighed.

"Thank you, Mr. Collum, for keeping my daughter safe. I'm certain it has been a long day for you. Would you do us the honor of staying for dinner?"

Movement from a nearby window distracted Ian from answering. A curtain pulled aside and a face appeared. Miss Bethia, he presumed. She took in the scene quickly, caught Ian's eye, and let the curtain fall closed.

It was Miss Meacham who answered her father. "Perhaps another time, Papa. I've kept Mr. Collum from his duties long enough. He must return to Shoreham posthaste."

"Can you not spare an hour, sir?" Mr. Meacham persisted as the door opened behind him. The lass from the window emerged from the house, smiling in an oddly triumphant way. She rushed forward and took hold of Miss Meacham's hands.

"Sarah, where have you been? We've been dreadfully worried about you." Her words were completely at odds with the look of excitement on her face.

"Yes, you appear most worried," Miss Meacham said wryly.

Ian coughed to mask his chuckle.

"Mr. Collum, this is my sister, Miss Bethia. You are already acquainted with my father, I believe."

"Aye. 'Tis a pleasure, Miss Bethia." So, this was the lass who'd stolen Mr. Gyles's heart and inadvertently complicated Ian's life. She had the same high cheekbones as her sister's, the same large round eyes, only hers were a bright blue instead of hazel.

"Do I detect some Scottish in your voice?" Her blonde curls bounced as she cocked her head at him.

"Aye, Miss. I was born in Scotland."

"How interesting." She hooked her arm through her sister's and smiled. "I would very much like to hear how you came to be in Brighton. Do say you will stay for dinner."

"As I was just telling Papa," Miss Meacham said firmly, "Mr. Collum cannot spare the time today."

Ian was sorely tempted to stay, but alas, he was also needed back at his warehouse. "As much as I would love to accept, Miss Bethia, your sister is correct. We recently had a shipment arrive at port, and my presence is required at the docks. Another time, perhaps?"

Miss Bethia wasn't one to give up easily. "Very well. Tomorrow evening then?"

Miss Meacham rolled her eyes, and Ian grinned. "I'm afraid I've already committed to a game of cricket tomorrow afternoon, and they usually last three or four—"

"Cricket, you say?" interrupted their father. "You play cricket?"

"Aye, sir. We are amateurs, but those in my employ and I enjoy the occasional game."

"Who are your opponents, or do you employ so many?" asked Mr. Meacham.

"We play against other crews. Just a way to break up the drudgery of the docks. Those of us involved think it a blessed escape."

"I can well imagine. Are there many spectators?"

"A few."

Mr. Meacham seemed intrigued, perhaps even excited, at the prospect of an amateur game of cricket. Perhaps he, too, felt drudgery of a different sort.

"You cannot be thinking of attending the game, Papa," said Miss Meacham.

"I am," defended her father. "Cricket is a lively sport, and I could use a distraction."

"We are engaged to picnic with Mr. and Mrs. Woolrich on the morrow," Miss Meacham reminded him.

Her father made a face, then waved his hand in a dismissive fashion. "Yes, and so are fifty others. Chelle is to accompany you, is she not? Please offer my condolences. They will not miss me."

From the way Miss Meacham pressed her lips together, Ian guessed that she chose to swallow whatever argument she might have made.

"We should all send our condolences," Miss Bethia added. "I would very much like to see this cricket game as well. We can inform Mrs. Woolrich that Papa has fallen ill and needs our assistance."

"We will do no such thing," Miss Meacham said.

It wasn't hard to discern how each woman felt. They were both expressive, but there was a maturity in Miss Meacham that the younger, more spontaneous sister hadn't yet developed. Miss Bethia seemed driven more by emotion than reason.

Ian shouldn't have mentioned the game at all. He'd stirred a pot and had placed Miss Meacham in a difficult position between her father and sister. He felt compelled to help her out.

"You flatter me, Miss Bethia, but our games can get a wee rowdy at times—not a place for a well-bred lass such as yourself."

Fire sparked in young Miss Bethia's eyes, and too late, Ian realized she'd taken his words as a challenge, rather than a warning.

She patted Miss Meacham's arm. "As long as my father and sister are with me, I will come to no harm."

Ian looked helplessly at Miss Meacham, but it was their father's stern voice that got the young girl's attention.

"Bethia."

Her brow puckered, and she sighed. "Oh, very well. But I have never been to a cricket game before, and I would like to see one."

"Another time," promised her older sister. "Thank you, Mr. Collum, for an unforgettable day and for seeing me home safely."

Ian nodded, knowing he needed to return. But there was something about this family that made him want to linger. Even though they were absent a mother, it felt more complete than anything he'd experienced in a long while. It had been nice to confide in Miss Meacham and speak to her about Banjeet. It would be nice to see her father on the outskirts of the cricket match, cheering for his team.

Dangerous thoughts, he told himself. While he couldn't deny his growing attachment to Miss Meacham, he needed to keep it in check. Despite her father's apparent acceptance of him, Miss Meacham was a gentlewoman. She deserved a man who could take her to balls and parties and give her the life she'd been raised to expect.

Hopefully, she'd figure that out on her own—preferably

after her father gave his consent to Mr. Gyles and before she became too attached.

Not for the first time, Ian cursed Mr. Gyles for tossing him into such a precarious position. Now that he was beginning to get to know the lass, there was a high probability it would not end well.

Ian gathered up the reins of the horse Miss Meacham had ridden and offered them to her father. "If you're interested in watching our game tomorrow, I'd be happy to leave you with Shashi, assuming you can manage to ride her with a side saddle. It's awkward, but doable. I can drive you home in my carriage afterwards."

"Very considerate of you," her father answered as he accepted the reins. "Thank you."

"Miss Bethia, while I cannot condone the cricket game, I can extend an invitation that I've already extended to your sister—that you and your father join me for a sailing excursion on Sunday."

As he'd hoped, Miss Bethia's eyes widened, and she clapped her hands in delight. "How exciting! Please say we may go, Papa."

He hesitated before nodding. "We appear to be in your debt, Mr. Collum. Will you allow us to convey our thanks by joining us for dinner Saturday evening? If you're free, that is."

"Banjeet is welcome as well," Miss Meacham added.

At her inclusion of Banjeet, gratitude overwhelmed his heart. She'd removed her damp gloves and now clutched them in one hand, so he took hold of the other and lifted it to his lips. He tried not to react at the shock of cold he felt, and he quickly sandwiched her fingers between his.

"'Twas a pleasure, Miss Meacham. Now go inside and warm yourself. You are freezing."

She stared at their hands for a moment before pulling free. "Good day, Mr. Collum."

Not wanting to keep her from the warmth of her home any longer, he swung up on his horse and tipped his hat.

KISS FOUR

·· 12 ··

WORRY PRODDED AND poked as Sarah watched Mr. Collum ride away. The anticipation, excitement, and longing he conjured within her were reminiscent of feelings she'd once had for the odious Mr. Hatch. Only with Mr. Collum, they were more potent. For years, she'd fought to protect her heart from ever getting trampled on again, but one drive, one conversation, one afternoon cowering from the rain, and it had all been for naught.

Here she was, as vulnerable and idiotic as she'd ever been.

Stupid, stupid girl.

Sarah turned to walk inside, wanting nothing more than to sink into a hot, lavender-scented bath and drown her worries in the shallow depths of the water. How good would it feel, at least for a time, to forget all about Mr. Collum, his hold on her emotions, and the complexities surrounding their differing stations and circumstances.

Bethia must have had other thoughts, however. Before Sarah could take more than a step or two, her sister grabbed hold of her wrist.

"Crags, Sarah, you look dreadful!"

Sarah might have cared if she didn't feel so depleted. "Tell me something I don't know, Beth." She pulled her arm free and headed for the house, only to be waylaid a second time by her father.

"Sarah, I would like a word once you have cleaned yourself up. I'll have Suzy heat some water and bring it up."

Sarah nodded and continued inside, already dreading the conversation. He would undoubtedly have a great many questions—questions Sarah would rather not answer.

"Even your bonnet looks a fright," Bethia persisted, her footsteps thumping in hot pursuit.

Sarah tossed a glare over her shoulder as she reached the top. "If I am ever feeling poorly about myself, remind me to avoid you like the plague."

"Don't be so dramatic. Mr. Collum must not have been too put off by your appearance or he would not have accepted our invitation for Saturday night."

"Perhaps he didn't want to offend father."

"Psh." Bethia followed Sarah into her bedchamber and began pacing while Sarah cringed at her reflection in the looking glass. Crags indeed. She looked worse than even *she'd* imagined.

"I'll send a note to Chelle immediately. I'm sure she can make you look stunning for our dinner Saturday evening. Mr. Collum will take one look at you and forget all about your current appearance. Chelle won't mind coming on Saturday, will she? We can invite her to stay for dinner as well if you wish, though our numbers are already mismatched, and hmm . . . that may not do at all."

As Bethia talked, Sarah got the feeling she was forgetting something important. Something to do with Saturday and Chelle.

Enlightenment finally dawned and Sarah sighed, not sure if she should be relieved or disappointed.

"Chelle won't be able to come, Beth. She will have her hands full preparing for her school's benefit that evening. I can't believe it slipped my mind. We'll need to send a note to Mr. Collum and ask if we can postpone our dinner invitation."

Bethia's mouth snapped shut and frown lines appeared. "I'd forgotten as well."

An unusual occurrence. Bethia rarely forgot social engagements, especially when they included a certain gentleman.

"Is Mr. Gyles planning to attend, now that he's back from London?"

She shook her head, looking glum. "He left yesterday to attend to his ailing mother and will not return until Sunday. I am supposed to give his regrets to Chelle."

That explained it. Benefit or not, any entertainment became uneventful for her sister if Mr. Gyles could not attend.

Strange how it suddenly felt uneventful for Sarah as well.

The thought pricked at her nerves. Good grief, what had become of her? No man, no matter how tall, handsome, and charming would ever take priority over her family or friends. Chelle had been fretting about this musicale for months, and the school relied on the money they would raise. All thoughts of Mr. Collum would be pushed aside while Sarah willingly—no, *cheerfully*—supported her dearest friend.

He may have wormed his way into her thoughts, but she refused to let him consume them.

"You could invite Mr. Collum to take Anthony's place."

Bethia plucked at the fringe on Sarah's bed clothes, but her attempt at innocence didn't fool Sarah. Her younger sister would do whatever it took to get exactly what she wanted, and what she wanted was for her sister to be as happily matched as herself. The conniving minx.

It wasn't a terrible idea, though. The school educated girls from both the middle and upper classes and invitations had been issued to gentry and tradesmen alike. But . . . "What of Chelle? Should she not have a say in who we invite to her event?"

Bethia waved aside the concern. "Mr. Collum seems wealthy and will likely donate a large sum. She won't mind in the least."

Sarah sighed, knowing she would never get her warm bath if she did not capitulate. Her sister was resilient, and her head was beginning to throb. Truth be told, she'd likely enjoy the musicale even more if Mr. Collum were in attendance.

"If you will leave me be, Beth, I will visit Chelle in the morning and explain the situation. If she wishes to extend an invitation to Mr. Collum, so be it. Will that appease you?"

Her sister slid from the bed with an expression of triumph. "Chelle will most definitely be in favor of inviting him. I'm sure of it. I'm also sure he will accept."

Sarah wasn't as certain, but the discussion had come to an end at last, and she wasn't about to say anything to prolong it.

With a happy jaunt in her steps, Bethia flounced from the room, nearly colliding with Suzy in the hallway. The overworked maid was hauling two large buckets of steaming water to the adjacent chamber where the tub was kept.

Sarah had never been happier to see anyone in her life.

She rushed to take one of the heavy buckets. "Bless you, Suzy dearest. Your timing is perfect."

The maid stumbled a bit as she caught sight of Sarah. "Egads, Miss! What's 'appened to you? Your 'air looks like somethin' died in there."

From down the hall Bethia began cackling, and Sarah glared in her direction before turning back to their maid. "Not now, Suzy. Please, not now."

$\cdots 13 \cdots$

"CHELLE, WHAT A perfect evening this turned out to be," Sarah said warmly as she dragged a chair from the center of one of the classrooms to the side. It had been an enjoyable, relaxing affair, at least for her. Chelle would undoubtedly disagree. Her poor friend had been frantic much of the night, making sure everything ran smoothly. In addition, she had to now prepare for a new term of school, as her students would begin arriving back the following week.

As it turned out, Bethia's Mr. Gyles, had returned earlier than expected and was able to attend after all. He escorted the family in his carriage, and, at the evening's conclusion, when Sarah had expressed a desire to stay behind and help her friend, gallantly offered to take her father and sister home then return for Sarah at a later time.

The more Sarah came to know Mr. Gyles, the more she respected, even liked him. Always the gentleman, he was enjoyable to be around and genuinely seemed to love her sister. With any luck, their father would soon relent and allow the pair to marry.

Sarah dragged another chair to the side of the small room. The school employed only a few servants, and they were busy elsewhere. Not ones to sit idly around when there was work to be done, the two women began setting the room back to rights.

Actually, it was Chelle's example that had taught Sarah to be more considerate of the help. As a schoolmistress, Chelle understood what it felt like to have a great deal of responsibility placed on her shoulders and was always quick to unburden another, no matter their station. Many frowned on her for doing so, but Sarah thought it an admirable trait.

She'd never forget one night at the Marine Pavilion years earlier, when a footman had backed into a guest, lost his balance, and dropped a tray of apple tarts. Chelle had immediately come to his aid, helping to retrieve the fallen tarts, only to stand back up and find several people gaping at her in astonishment.

Instead of succumbing to embarrassment, as Sarah would have done, Chelle had smiled. "I heard that was the last tray, and I do so love apple tarts." She'd proceeded to pop one of the fallen tarts into her mouth.

Prinny had roared with laughter and continued to tease her for months afterwards, always providing extra trays of apple tarts for Miss Ellington so she needn't scrape them off the floor.

"Do you truly think it went smoothly?" Chelle asked. "It's tricky to host the annual benefit here at the school, mostly because we lack a large room for entertaining. I'll be grateful when the renovations are finished on the pavilion, and we can prey on Prinny's goodwill once more."

Chelle looked striking in her pale-blue gown with a matching ribbon in her hair. Normally, her coiffures drew attention, but not this evening. Chelle had chosen a simple knot with thin braids woven throughout.

"I actually like the system you developed," Sarah confided. "Assigning everyone to a small group and rotating them from room to room made it feel more intimate and interesting."

"It felt crowded to me."

"Isn't that what you want when hosting a benefit?" Sarah teased.

"Yes, and tonight was a wonderful success, thanks in part to your Mr. Collum."

"Oh, he's not *my*—pardon, what's this about Mr. Collum?" Chelle had extended an invitation to him, but he'd sent his regrets with no word of explanation. Had he attended after all, and Sarah had missed him?

"He sent a generous donation to the school," Chelle explained. "He even included a note that said he couldn't think of a more worthy cause than that of education. I found it most agreeable."

Sarah took a moment to digest the news, not sure how she felt about it. If Mr. Collum intended to donate, why not come and see the school for himself? She knew for a fact his evening had been free from commitments, and the benefit was one of those rare engagements that included families of all kinds.

Perhaps it was Sarah he wished to avoid. After seeing her crazed reflection in the mirror, she wouldn't blame him.

"He also invited me to join your family on the morrow," Chelle added, her tone bright. "He heard I was a good friend of yours and thought you'd enjoy having me along. I hope you don't mind. To say I'm excited is an understatement. I've never been sailing before."

Just like that, another person in Sarah's life had been charmed by the mysterious Mr. Collum. It had been thoughtful of him to include her friend, and Sarah found her heart warming towards him a little more.

Are you as good and true as you seem? she thought. If only there was someone who could tell her exactly who she should or should not trust.

Sarah grabbed another chair and mustered a delighted expression. "It *is* exciting, isn't it? I'm glad you are coming." Perhaps once Chelle had spent several hours in Mr. Collum's company, she could give an unbiased appraisal of the man's character.

Chelle bent to pick up a few crumbs from the floor. "When you called on me the other morning, I got the impression that your attitude toward Mr. Collum had changed, but I thought it best not to press you at the time. However, now that my musicale is over and I can breathe again, consider yourself pressed. What are your thoughts concerning him now?"

"I . . ." Sarah paused to think it over, only to shake her head. "There is still so much I don't know about him. But I do think he is a good man. A kind man." To herself, she added, *A charming and irresistibly handsome man.*

Chelle gave her a look that conveyed how unimpressed she was by Sarah's description. "Good and kind? Is that all? *I* could have listed those traits."

Sarah dragged another chair to the side of the room, nearly tripping over the corner of a rug in the process. "What do you wish me to say? That I have fallen madly in love with him after only a few weeks? You, of all people, should know I would never succumb to such a fate. I have learned my lesson well."

"I'm not expecting a confession of love," said Chelle. "I only want more details. Something with a little more feeling than kind and good. I have never met the man and know far less about him than you. Do you think him handsome?"

"Yes." Only a blind woman would not think as much.

"Charming?"

"Definitely."

"Intelligent?"

"He did say he values education above all else."

"Touché," Chelle said as she began closing the drapes. "Does he make your insides squeamish in a good way? Does your pulse quicken when he's about? Do you find it difficult to think clearly?"

Sarah blinked a few times before laughing out loud. "Mr. Collum is merely an acquaintance on the verge of becoming a friend, nothing more."

Chelle raised a skeptical eyebrow. "It sounds as though you are trying to convince yourself of that."

"I . . ." Sarah had no argument to make because it was the truth. But as much as she'd like to toss caution to the wind and see what came of Mr. Collum, the idea scared her spitless.

"Not all men are like Mr. Hatch, you know," Chelle said.

"You sound like my father."

"I always thought him a wise man."

"Would you still think that if you knew Mr. Collum has already won him over? With a cricket match, no less. Papa now sings his praises."

Chelle didn't smile as Sarah expected her to do. Instead, her forehead crinkled, and she drew her lower lip into her mouth. When she spoke again, Sarah was all ears.

"I think you are right in being cautious. But at some point, you will need to decide whether or not you're willing to let him in. I don't think you can truly come to know a person until you open your heart to him."

Sarah gave her friend a pointed look. "Sounds like advice you would do well to take, my friend."

"If I ever found a man who'd inspire such a risk, I might."

"Only might?"

Chelle smiled. "I have always been better at giving advice than taking it, as you well know, but I am a spinster schoolmistress now. A man would have to be daft to pursue me, and I have no intention of marrying a man like that."

"Nonsense," said Sarah. "I see men admiring you all the time. Why, only last week—"

Chelle placed a hand on Sarah's arm and gave it a gentle squeeze. "I know you mean well, but this is not a subject I wish to pursue at this time. I had my chance at love long ago, and it was taken from me. But I've moved on, and now I'm content as I am. Another man will not restore what's been lost."

Sarah didn't know why she'd brought up such a tender subject, other than to divert the conversation away from herself, but she was sorry for it. She covered Chelle's hand with her own.

"Let us talk of other things, shall we? We will be sailing tomorrow, and that is more exciting than anything else. Speaking of which, would you be willing to work your magic with my hair before we go? After my fiasco the other day in the rain, I want something that will stay put no matter the weather. I looked positively disturbing."

"I doubt that, but what you're asking is impossible. Unless you'd like me to slather your hair in beeswax, that is."

Sarah giggled at the picture that made in her mind. "That would be even more disturbing."

"Yes, and so we will make your hair as lovely and secure as we can and let the wind blow where it may.

Chelle began snuffing out candles while Sarah relocated the one remaining chair.

"You disappoint me," Sarah teased. "I was certain no feat was too great for you, especially when it came to hair."

"At last, you see me as I am," Chelle said. Only one candle flickered in the darkenss—the one Chelle carried in her hand. Her face glowed from the light it cast, while shadows crept up the walls behind her.

Sarah smiled. "I only see the dearest of friends."

Chelle's answering laugh nearly blew out the last of the light, and she quickly cupped her hand around the flame to keep it burning. "What would I do without you, Sarah? Now, let us get started on the music room before Mr. Gyles returns to steal away my help."

·· 14 ··

CHELLE PINNED THE majority of Sarah's hair into a knot, leaving only a handful of curls to drape around her face and across the nape of her neck. Her bonnet had been secured in place by a wide strip of blue silk tied artfully into a bow at the side of her chin. It would take a mighty gust of wind to set it askew.

As Sarah inspected her appearance, she smiled wryly at her friend. "It seems we didn't need beeswax after all. My faith in you is restored."

"Your faith is misplaced."

"Hardly."

Chelle had arranged Bethia's hair in a similar fashion, along with her own. There wasn't much else to be done for a sailing excursion. However, the varying colors and styles of their bonnets and gowns gave them each a slightly different look.

As Sarah stepped down from Chelle's carriage near the docks, she wrinkled her nose at the smell and lifted her head to marvel at the height of the masts. The spars and rigging of the ships towered over her like two giant pine trees carrying bundles of sails waiting to be hoisted into the skies.

The sound of boots slapping the docks reached Sarah's ears, and she looked over to see Mr. Collum approach. Wearing a navy coat and buff trousers, he appeared elegant, genteel, and happy to see her.

He took her hand and lifted it to his lips. "Aren't you a fetching sight, Miss Meacham. After our last encounter, you had me worried. I wasn't sure your maid would be able to remove all the tangles from your hair, but alas, you're as bonnie of a lass as the day we met."

Sarah caught Chelle's look of surprise and nearly smiled. Mr. Collum could be embarrassingly forthright at times, which Chelle would come to know quickly. Sarah, on the other hand, had expected as much.

"You flatter me yet again, sir," she said. "But yes, the wild animal you last saw has since been caged or tamed or whatever you want to call it. At least for now. I cannot guarantee it will remain that way should the weather turn foul."

"I cannot imagine that will happen. Those clouds you spy in the west will guarantee us a spectacular sunset, nothing more."

"I will hold you to that, sir." Sarah gestured to Chelle at her side. "I'd like you to meet my dear friend, Miss Ellington."

"A pleasure," he said, bowing politely. "And thank you for the invitation to your school's musicale. I am sorry I could not attend."

Chelle pulled a letter from her reticule and held it out to Mr. Collum. "A note of gratitude from my headmistress. We can't thank you enough for your generous donation. And I can't thank you enough for thinking to include me in your sailing excursion. I am very much looking forward to it."

He nodded. "I am glad you could join us. Is it only the two of you then? Did your father and sister decide not to come?"

"My sister would rather die than miss this." Sarah squinted through the sunlight to the road just past the docks, where a barouche rattled towards them at a slow pace. "Here they are now. We couldn't fit into one carriage, so I rode with Chelle. Papa and Bethia are coming with Mr. Gyles."

The news seemed to catch Mr. Collum off guard, and his voice took on a wary note. "Mr. Gyles?"

Oh dear. Had her father misunderstood? "Er, yes. Father said he spoke to you after the cricket game about including one more. Perhaps he was mistaken?"

Mr. Collum recovered quickly. "Nae, I told him he could invite whomever he wished. Mr. Gyles is more than welcome. We have plenty of room aboard."

"Thank you," said Sarah. "He and Bethia are all but engaged, and she couldn't countenance the thought of leaving him out."

"Engaged?" The question was innocent enough, but the way Mr. Collum said it sounded curious, almost probing.

"Not yet, but soon, I hope. I probably shouldn't have said anything. Best not to mention it."

"Mum's the word."

The latecomers soon joined the others on the dock, but when Sarah introduced Mr. Gyles to Mr. Collum, a strange, uncomfortable look passed between the two men. No one else seemed to notice, but Sarah looked from one to the other, wondering what silent conversation was happening between them.

Mr. Gyles caught her eye for a second, then quickly smiled and extended a hand to Mr. Collum. "A pleasure to meet you, sir."

"Pleasure's all mine," Mr. Collum murmured in a way that didn't sound the least bit pleasurable. There was a hardness to his jaw that had not been there before, and his chilly tone seemed to convey some sort of warning.

How very odd. It was as though they already knew each other. But if that was the case, why pretend otherwise? Perhaps they had done some business together in the past and it had not ended well. Or perhaps they only knew of each other by reputation. Or . . . she couldn't fathom what else it might be and made a mental note to ask Mr. Collum about it later.

Mr. Gyles cleared his throat and rubbed his hands together, no doubt trying to dispel the tension. "Which ship is yours, sir?"

"That one, yonder. We call her Barnacle." Mr. Collum gestured at a two-mast schooner near the end of the dock. Sure enough, "Barnacle" had been painted across the side in bold, white lettering.

"How did she earn that particular title?" Chelle asked, sounding amused.

"She was originally christened *Impregnable* by the Royal Navy during the war. After one particular skirmish, however, she took some heavy gunfire and had to be limped back into Bristol, where she underwent extensive repairs to keep her afloat. There she sat until the end of the war, when she was decommissioned and eventually sold to me. By that time, she was covered in barnacles and looked far from impregnable. We cleaned her up, rebuilt her, and gave her a new name."

Sarah's father shifted his weight and grunted. "Interesting you choose a name that reminds you of her lowest point."

"Nae," Mr. Collum said. "It actually reminds me of how far she's come."

Sarah examined the smaller, two-masted ship and decided it was the most regal vessel in the harbor, name and all.

"I like it," she said, earning her a warm look and a smile from Mr. Collum. Strange how such a simple exchange could make her insides tumble about.

He offered her his arm and looked over the small group. "Everyone ready to sail?"

"Oh, yes, please," Bethia said excitedly. "You simply must introduce us to this *Barnacle* of yours."

Mr. Collum led Sarah to the end of the dock and helped her and the others board. He introduced everyone to Captain James, then pointed out the other men, who were scattered around the deck, checking the rigging and preparing the sails.

"You are in good hands, I assure you," Mr. Collum finally promised.

"Nice to see you again, Captain," said Sarah to the shipmaster.

He gave her a confused look of surprise, as though he had no idea who she might be.

She had to smile at that. "You probably don't recognize me without frizzy hair, but we met the other day in Mr. Collum's place of business."

"Ah, yes, of course," he rushed to say. "You appear as beautiful now as you did then, Miss Meacham."

"I hope not," Sarah answered with a laugh. "My maid told me that my hair looked like the nest of a bird after a fierce windstorm."

Mr. Collum chuckled while Bethia was quick to agree. "That's the truth of it. Come now, Captain, you can admit it."

The man cleared his throat and tried again. "What I should have said, Miss Meacham, is that you look even more beautiful than I remember, if that is possible."

Sarah laughed. "Should you decide that sea life is not for you, Captain, you ought to try politics."

"I will keep that in mind."

Mr. Collum proceeded to give them a quick rundown of the schooner, beginning with the uppermost deck at the stern. He showed them the pulley system and tiller used to steer the boat, explaining how it all worked.

Sarah thought it fascinating, as did her father.

"Would a wheel not be easier to steer than a tiller?" he asked.

"Aye," Mr. Collum said, "but on a boat of this size, the pulley system required to operate a wheel is too large, so a tiller is the only option. I have two larger coasters, however, both of which are steered by wheels."

"I see." A curious man by nature, her father had several more questions, all of which Mr. Collum answered with patience and cordiality.

They learned that the schooner consisted of four decks, each a step or two down from the other. Once on the main deck, Mr. Collum told them where they could sit or stand before excusing himself to speak with his shipmaster.

Rapid footsteps pounded up from below, and Banjeet's head appeared from a hatched opening not far away. He leapt up on deck, beaming with pride.

"Miss Meacham!" He grinned, practically skipping towards her. "Have you come to sail with us?"

"Indeed I have, Banjeet," she replied warmly. "And I've brought my father, sister, and some friends as well." Sarah introduced them before adding, "I'm very glad to know you are on board, young shipmaster. We are counting on you to keep us safe."

Banjeet grinned. "I'm no shipmaster yet, Miss, but I will be someday, make no mistake 'bout that."

"I have every confidence in you."

He gave her a cheeky salute before rushing off to speak to Mr. Collum and Captain James. Bethia, Mr. Gyles, and her father wandered over to the side of the foredeck while Sarah settled down next to Chelle on a wooden bench.

"He's a charming boy," Chelle commented.

"The more I know him, the more I like him."

"His guardian is charming as well, however unorthodox his methods."

A few men pushed the boat from the dock, and the workers began using tall oars to propel the boat forward. Sarah breathed in the scents of fish and other unpleasant odors, happy to be leaving them behind.

"Mr. Collum is still a mystery to me," she finally said. "I worry that I am wrong to like him as I do."

"Does it bother you that he owns a shipping business?"

"I . . ." Sarah paused to consider the question. It would definitely uncomplicate matters if Mr. Collum were a gentleman. But then, if he had been born into that sort of life, perhaps he would be more like Mr. Peter Hatch and less like himself.

"I find I value character over status," she finally said.

"Bold words," answered Chelle with a wary look.

"I mean them."

Chelle gave Sarah a sidelong glance and arched a brow. "The fact that he is excessively handsome has nothing to do with it, does it?"

"I used to think Mr. Hatch was handsome. Now I think him a scoundrel."

"You and me both," Chelle agreed. "But would you truly consider attaching yourself to a man who's so obviously beneath you? It would mean severing your connection to the polite world, Prinny's inner circle included, once he returns."

Sarah traced her finger along the grains of the wood at her side. If she was being honest, it *had* been gratifying to bask in the popularity associated with Prinny. She had lived in obscurity for so long that it had felt like stepping out of darkness and into light. But they were not close by any means, nor did she miss his absence. She'd likely not see him again until the renovations were complete on his pavilion. Would he even remember her by that point? Possibly. Probably. The memory of her attacking Mr. Hatch was not easily forgotten.

Which made her an amusement to him, nothing more.

Other than Chelle, Sarah really had no close friends among the ton. Her family was still welcome in many circles, but Sarah was growing weary of people who said one thing to her face and another behind her back. If not for Bethia's comeout and Chelle's need for a companion, she'd likely avoid social gatherings altogether.

"One would think you are trying to be rid of me," Sarah said at last. "Attached already? Honestly. Mr. Collum and I are friends, nothing more."

"You are only kidding yourself if you think that," Chelle said. "The way you look at each other could cause this ship to ignite."

"You are in need of spectacles."

"I am not wrong, and you know it," Chelle insisted, but she didn't press Sarah further. Instead, she sat up straighter and looked off to the side. "I cannot wait to get away from these foul smells. How do seamen stand it?"

"Portsmouth is far worse," a deep, Scottish voice sounded from behind.

Sarah spun to see Mr. Collum towering over them. Her face grew warm, and her body froze. Exactly how much of their conversation had he overheard?

"Mr. Collum," she asked in a too-bright voice, "have you been there long?"

His lips lifted into a wry grin. "Long enough to be grateful that we have a ready supply of water should this ship ignite."

If Sarah's face wasn't burning before, it certainly was now. Curse Chelle for speaking so plainly and Mr. Collum for doing the same. A true gentleman would have never confessed to hearing such things.

He's no gentleman, she reminded herself, wishing she could sink beneath the floorboards to the lower deck.

Chelle rose to her feet and pulled Sarah up as well, giving Mr. Collum a chiding look. "Sir, you ought to be ashamed of yourself, eavesdropping on a conversation that was not meant for your ears."

"Do you intend to box them?" He grinned, making Sarah want to do exactly that. "Better my ears than this excessively handsome face."

Chelle opened her mouth only to close it again. The look of complete shock on her face nearly caused Sarah to giggle. She couldn't recall a time when her friend had ever been at a loss for words.

"I should have warned you, Chelle, that Mr. Collum may look like a gentleman, but he does not act like one. Don't let him put you to the blush. It'll only encourage him."

Chelle blinked a few times before finding her tongue. "Perhaps we *should* box his ears."

"Or slap that excessively handsome face," Sarah added.

"Only slap?" asked Chelle.

"If you are implying that I ought to strike him, you should know that I have mended my ways. Why people continue to think of me as Miss Shrew is a mystery. Miss Charity would be far more appropriate."

157

Mr. Collum's expression became an adorable mixture of disbelief and amusement. He slung an arm around the large mast at his side and leaned against it. "May I remind you, Miss Meacham, that you only just discussed the possibility of striking me."

"I also mentioned you were excessively handsome," she pointed out.

His lips puckered for a moment and he shook his head slowly. "Nae, I believe it was Miss Ellington who said that. You were only parroting her. Or do you agree and think me excessively handsome as well?"

"I think you excessively arrogant, sir."

His responding laughter tickled her insides, or perhaps it was the sway of the boat. Regardless, she liked the sound of it. She also liked the way his eyes crinkled at the corners and his mouth quirked up higher on one side, revealing pristine white teeth that were almost perfectly straight.

Excessively handsome was putting it mildly.

A tall and lanky seaman approached. "The shipmaster says we're approachin' rougher waters and will be 'oistin' the sails soon. Probably best to 'old tight to something solid and move away from this 'ere boon."

Chelle picked up her reticule and nodded towards the others at the side of the ship. "Will that railing suffice?"

He nodded.

She made a hasty retreat, no doubt anxious to get away from Mr. Collum and his unorthodox teasing.

Sarah was about to follow when he captured her hand with his.

"The best view is next to the bow. Come." He nodded in that direction with a smile impossible to resist. Sarah told herself she only wanted to have the best view, but in reality, she was more like a puppy being led along by a leash, happy to follow wherever he led.

Pathetic.

He kept her hand in his until they reached the edge, at which point, she pulled free, taking hold of the railing instead. Her iron-like grip had very little to do with the bumpy sea they were nearing and everything to do with the fact that her knees suddenly felt weak and wobbly. The warmth of his gaze, along with the touch of his hand—through gloves, no less—had disrupted her equilibrium.

Incredibly pathetic.

"Any moment now and you will feel like you are flying," Mr. Collum said.

A flurry of activity sounded behind Sarah, but she didn't turn to look. She was mesmerized by the huge expanse of water opening up before her, a deeper blue than she had ever beheld. Footsteps pounded against the deck, voices called out instructions, sails whooshed in the wind, and the schooner surged forward. The brim of Sarah's bonnet batted around her head, and the smell of saltwater pervaded her nostrils. The boat rose and fell with each wave and trough, exhilarating Sarah like never before.

It truly did feel as though they'd taken flight.

Sarah raised her voice to be heard above the water and wind. "How do you not wish to be out here all the time, like Banjeet?"

He removed his hat to keep it from blowing away and tucked it under one arm, his dark hair whipping around his face. "I enjoy a leisurely jaunt like this, but after journeying to and from the East Indies for months on end, I've come to prefer solid ground beneath my feet and the ability to come and go as I please. Too much time on board, and I begin to feel trapped."

"Do you think Banjeet will grow weary of it as well?"

He shrugged. "Some men are born with a love of the sea that never seems to wane. They feel about the sea the way I feel about my freedom. Banjeet seems to be one of those. He loved every day of our journey from the East Indies."

"He's blessed to have you for a guardian then. Not many could give him so many opportunities to sail," Sarah said.

"I just hope he learns to see other things as opportunities as well, such as his education."

Sarah looked over her shoulder to see Banjeet jump to do the shipmaster's bidding. Eyes bright. Grin wide. He certainly did love the sea. "Have you asked Captain James to emphasize the importance of keeping up with his lessons? Banjeet seems to admire the man a great deal. Perhaps he can have a positive influence."

"I wish he would. Instead, he's constantly telling the lad—and me—that experience is the only education one needs. To some extent, I agree. No amount of reading could prepare Banjeet to captain a ship. But I want the lad to be equipped with more skills than that. I want him to be able to write, communicate, and understand French and possibly Italian. I want him to be able to make his own calculations, and comprehend the science behind the tide, the weather, and the stars."

"You want what's best for him," Sarah supplied, hoping he could hear the admiration in her voice.

"Banjeet doesn't see it that way," he said. "We get on well, but he often thinks I'm trying to curtail him, not help him."

"He's still young and naïve. In time, he'll come to see your intentions for what they are."

"I hope so."

The sound of Chelle's laughter floated their way, and an idea sparked in Sarah's mind. "Perhaps you're looking for tutors in the wrong place, sir. I wonder if Chelle knows of a young lady at her school who could instruct him. A bright and bonnie lass, as you'd say—someone who could make him *want* to spend some time in a classroom."

Mr. Collum snickered. "She'd have to be bonnie indeed."

"Never underestimate the power of a pretty face, sir, especially when combined with a keen mind."

Silence, and then, "'Tis a potent combination, to be sure."

Something in his tone caused Sarah to look up at him. She found him watching her intently. Her pulse quickened, and her breath caught. He seemed to take in every line and curvature of her face before his gaze dropped to her mouth.

Without meaning to, Sarah licked her lips, wondering what it would feel like to kiss him. Her mouth went dry, and she found herself leaning toward him a little.

The look in his eye made her feel as though she wielded some unseen power over him, but then the boat crashed down over a larger wave, and the spell was broken.

He grabbed the railing with one hand and her arm with the other, as though worried she'd lose her balance. It was a valid concern, considering the alarming effect he was having on her. But his touch was not helping matters, nor would it save her from buckling knees.

Have a care, Sarah. Don't let him—

Who was she kidding? Sarah had already done what she'd sworn she wouldn't. She'd opened the door on her heart and practically waved him in.

There was no turning back now, no matter how wise it would be.

"Mr. Collum, is that land I spy in the distance?" Bethia's voice called out.

Bless you, Beth, Sarah thought. She needed a moment to collect her thoughts and unravel the cacophony of emotions raging through her.

"'Tis the shoreline of France," Mr. Collum finally answered. "We have a spyglass on board if you'd like to take a closer look."

Bethia clapped her hands, obviously delighted by the prospect. "Oh yes, can we?"

"Certainly." Mr. Collum raised his voice. "Banjeet, will you bring the spyglass?"

The boy waved from his place next to Captain James. A few moments later, he trotted across the deck of the ship as though on solid ground, looking perfectly at ease. Sarah, on the other hand, still kept one hand on the rail.

He handed the spyglass to Mr. Collum. "Not much fog today. You'll be able to see far."

Mr. Collum lifted the glass to his eye and made some adjustments. "Aye, that I can. I might attribute our good luck to Miss Meacham, if not for the fact that our last excursion didn't turn out so well."

"Aren't you a charmer?" Sarah said dryly, snatching the spyglass from him. She anchored her hip against the rail before lifting the glass to her eye, but only a blurry landscape appeared. She tried to fiddle with it as Mr. Collum had done, to no avail.

"Allow me, Miss," said Banjeet confidently. Sarah exchanged a look of amusement with Mr. Collum while the boy peered through it and made some adjustments.

"Now try," he said.

Sarah lifted it once more and was rewarded with a much clearer view of rolling green hills, rocky cliffs, and pristine beaches.

"So that is France," she murmured. What would it be like to travel to a new country, to surround herself with a different language and culture? Would she like it or would she long for home?

"May I have a look?" Bethia asked from behind, no doubt anxiously awaiting her turn. Sarah passed the spyglass and squinted at the area she had only just examined up close.

"Have you ever been to France, Mr. Collum?" It was a silly question to ask. Of course he had.

"Aye."

"What was it like?"

"It's a beautiful country, but I had a difficult time with the language. Though I studied French in school, I retained very little. 'Tis a shame. Do you speak it?"

"*Oui, assez bien.*" Sarah had always loved the French language. Every now and again, her father encouraged her and Bethia to speak French at the dinner table. Bethia always rolled her eyes, probably because she hadn't become as proficient in the language, but Sarah enjoyed the practice.

Mr. Collum appeared impressed. "Next time, I'll bring you along. You can be my translator."

"You are cruel to tease me, Mr. Collum. France is but a dream to me."

"Ian."

"Pardon?"

"My name is Ian." There was that tone again. Quiet. Serious. Intent.

Sarah didn't reply. She ran her hands along the railing, wondering how close of a connection he wanted with her. There was so much she still didn't know about him, so much she craved to discover.

"Did your father give you that name?"

He stiffened as she expected him to do. "Nae."

A strong gust of wind slammed into her, and she gripped the wooden rail tighter, unwilling to let it distract her. "Where is he now? Or is he . . . gone as well?"

"Nae."

She hesitated before blurting out a question that had been on her mind since their drive. "Why don't you wish to speak of him?"

"I hardly know the man." His jaw tightened as another gust assailed them, blowing his beaver from beneath his arm and sending it flying. Mr. Collum watched it sail out to sea before looking up at the skies with a frown. "If you'll excuse me, I need to speak with my shipmaster."

Sarah gazed across the sea, which was looking a bit more tumultuous. Larger waves formed not far ahead, and the schooner began rising and falling harder than before. A muttered curse sounded from behind, and Sarah twisted to see Mr. Collum pitch sideways, his body hitting the deck before sliding hard into a bench. His head struck first, and he groaned.

Leaving the safety of the railing behind, Sarah rushed towards him, but the ship hit another wave, and she was knocked off balance as well, falling with an *oof* on to her backside. Her legs flew wide, and her skirts tightened around her ankles. She squealed as she slid across the deck, her body colliding with Mr. Collum's.

He grabbed her shoulders to hold her steady. "Are you all right, Sarah?"

Her bonnet had pulled free from some of the pins and now covered her eyes. She craned her neck to look at him, but she could only see his tight, worried lips. Another gust of wind whooshed past, and a chunk of Sarah's hair came free from the knot, whipping her in the face and obscuring what was left of her view.

She could only imagine the sight she made, and the thought made her snicker and then laugh, even as the ship crested another large wave and fell hard. Sarah's bonneted head banged against Mr. Collum, and he groaned again, effectively squashing her giggles.

"I'm dreadfully sorry." She grabbed hold of the bench and tried to move away from him, but another lurch knocked her into him once more. This time, he wrapped an arm around her stomach and held her tight against him.

"Will you please cease moving?"

He didn't have to ask. His close proximity made her body go still. Every part of her was extremely aware of him.

Captain James barked out orders as the boat went up and over another wave. Footsteps pounded as men scrambled to adjust the sails. Sarah might have been frightened by the tumult, but all she could think about was how wonderful it felt to be held by Mr. Collum.

Ian, she corrected in her mind.

The strength of his arms. The hardness of his chest. The warmth of his body. She could remain here forever.

The thought made her shiver, and Ian pulled her closer. "Are you cold?"

"I'm perfectly comfortable," she answered without thinking, then immediately cringed. Could she be any more obvious? What sort of person was perfectly comfortable on the deck of a thrashing ship?

He uttered what sounded like a low laugh, and she closed her eyes in mortification. He knew exactly what had made her *perfectly comfortable.*

Banjeet rushed across the deck, grabbing hold of a rope to keep him steady as they collided with another wave. "Everything good, *Pita?*"

"Aye, attend to your duties and get us out of these waves," Ian said.

The ship began to slow its course but was still rocking with the waves. Sarah righted her bonnet and shoved her hair away from her face, giving herself a better view of the deck.

Bethia and Chelle were clinging to the railing, while Mr. Gyles was doing his best to hold on with one hand while keeping the two women safe. Her father, on the other hand, stood bent over the rail and was currently casting up his accounts. Another wave sent the boat lurching forward, and her father nearly pitched overboard.

"Papa!" Sarah cried, trying to scramble forward to help, but Ian kept her pinned against him.

"What do you intend to do? Knock into him as well? That will certainly send him overboard."

"'Old tight!" boomed a loud voice as the ship began to change directions. Sarah's father turned around and slouched to the ground, grabbing tight to the rail with one hand as he dropped his head between his knees. He looked miserable, but safe, thank heavens.

Bethia was trying to go to him while Mr. Gyles held her back. Chelle simply stood, gripping the rail with both hands and staring at the churning sea with a frightened look on her face.

Once the ship had fully turned, Ian released Sarah and pulled himself to his feet. He lifted her up as well, then gently pressed her down on a bench.

"Stay here and hold on," he said before cautiously making his way to where the others stood. He and Mr. Gyles helped Chelle and Bethia to the benches where Sarah now sat, keeping a firm grip on some ropes tied around the mast. They went to her father next, struggling to keep their balance while the boat rocked and creaked.

"I dropped the spyglass in the sea," Bethia said, her eyes filling with tears. "I thought we were going to die."

Sarah refrained from rolling her eyes, but only just. *Not the time for hysterics, dearest.*

Mr. Gyles was more kind. "There, there, my love," he cooed. "A spyglass is easily replaceable. We have begun our return and will be fine. Can you not feel it? We are going with the waves now, rather than against them, and will be safely back at the dock in no time at all."

Sarah wasn't so sure. She looked at Ian, remembering their conversation from a few days earlier. "Will we be able to pass between the piers without incident?" she asked him. Now that she'd seem them up close, she could understand why he'd been so upset that Captain James had not diverted.

"Aye," he said. "The sea is not that rough, and the schooner is fast and agile. We will be fine."

"Not that rough?" Bethia exclaimed what everyone else was likely thinking. "Do you mean to say ships travel in worse conditions than this?"

Ian's lips twitched, and he nodded. "Aye, Miss Bethia. Far worse, I'm afraid. Mother Nature can be a frightful beast at times."

"I'll never set foot on a boat again," she vowed, making everyone laugh. Well, almost everyone. Their father still looked green and pale.

"Papa, how are you?" asked Sarah.

He said nothing, just stared straight ahead. She opened her mouth to say something more, then clamped it closed when Ian gave her a firm headshake.

"Leave him be," he mouthed, and Mr. Gyles nodded in agreement.

It made little sense to Sarah. She obviously didn't understand the world of men and their silly pride.

Banjeet walked over with a mug of something and tucked it into her father's hand. "Ale will do the trick, sir. Drink some of this and you'll feel better soon enough."

Her father downed the drink as though it would save his

life, only to drop the mug back on the bench and rush to the side of the boat again.

"You were supposed to take small sips," Banjeet called out before looking back to Ian with a guilty expression.

Sarah would have laughed if not for the state of her father. Had he been feeling poorly the entire time? Probably. While she'd been flirting with Ian, he'd likely been fighting back nausea. The sooner they returned to the docks the better.

"Would you like me to fetch another cup?" Banjeet called out, and her father responded with a vigorous shake of his head.

Ian leaned in close to Sarah's ear, his breath tickling her neck. "I did bring a picnic to enjoy while we watched the sun go down, but I think I'd best not bring it out at the moment."

Sarah couldn't help but groan. "I really am bad luck. First rain and now wind. What will be next? Fire?"

He chuckled. "I was present both times as well. Perhaps I am to blame. Regardless, I will make sure our next excursion does not include fire of any sort. 'Tis a pity though. Gathering around a campfire would have been entertaining."

"It would be vastly entertaining!" Bethia said, making it obvious she'd been eavesdropping. She must have overcome her distress because she looked positively giddy at the suggestion. How she bounced from one emotion to another would always be a mystery, but Sarah was glad she was feeling better. If only her father would regain his color.

"What does one do around a campfire?" Chelle mused.

"When I was young," Ian said, "my mother would make small balls of dough, and we'd roast them on the end of sticks. We called them cannonballs. Over the years, I've learned they taste even better dipped in butter and sprinkled with cinnamon and sugar."

168

"That sounds heavenly," Bethia said. "Anthony, do say we can have a fire and roast cannonballs sometime soon. I would dearly love to try that."

Sarah's father groaned from his position at the side of the ship. With his head buried between his knees, his voice came out muffled. "Please refrain from speaking of food at this moment, I beg you."

Bethia looked immediately remorseful. "Forgive us, Papa."

"If it helps," said Sarah, "I can see the piers up ahead. We are getting closer." To Ian, she lowered her voice and asked, "Is there nothing we can do for him?"

"If we were on a long voyage, he would eventually find his sea legs within a week or two, but that is not the case with a short jaunt like this. Not to worry, though. He'll start to feel better as soon as we get him back on solid ground."

"I hope you are right."

"And I hope he'll forgive yet another disaster," Ian said wryly, and Sarah realized she liked thinking of him as Ian. She liked thinking of him in general.

"Oh, Papa is not one to hold a grudge. He is a better person than me in that respect. I've yet to forgive the man whose nose I broke."

Ian smiled a little, but it seemed strained, as though something in her words had bothered him. What, Sarah couldn't say. Perhaps his mind was on other matters, like the poor state of her father.

They sat in silence the rest of the way, and as the ship rollicked its way between the piers, Sarah's gaze drifted across the wide expanse of sea to where the sun had begun to drop in the sky. The clouds were tinged with different hues of pinks and purples, promising a spectacular display if one exercised a little more patience.

Sarah sighed. How lovely it would have been to enjoy

the view from calm waters. But alas, the moment Sarah had crossed paths with the mysterious Ian Collum, her life had been the opposite of calm.

Strange how a run of bad luck actually felt enjoyable.

··15··

IAN ADJUSTED HIS cravat as he followed a petite maid into the salon at Haven House, home of the Meachams. Apparently, the family didn't employ a butler. The last time he'd come, it was Sarah's father who'd answered the door.

It had been two days since the sailing fiasco. Ian hoped it had been enough time for everyone to fully recover, namely Mr. Meacham. The poor chap hadn't been able to get off the ship fast enough.

As they'd parted ways, the look Mr. Gyles had given Ian didn't help matters. He may as well have said, *Do something to fix this soon, man, or that house is but a dream.*

So here he was, attempting to remedy whatever damage had been done, all the while thinking he should leave the house and the bonnie Sarah Meacham well enough alone. Why her family and Mr. Gyles didn't view him as an unworthy suitor was beyond him. Ian *was* unworthy. He was but a coxswain attempting to insert himself into a world of lieutenants and captains.

But that wasn't even the crux of the problem. Nae. The more time he spent in Sarah's company, the more time he wanted to spend with her. Her untamed curls, pert nose, and lovely curves continually enticed him. Her eyes seemed to change colors depending on what she wore. That day on the ship, they'd been a bonnie, seafoam green. Other times they looked like stormy clouds or a clear morning sky. Always bright, always intelligent, and always mesmerizing.

She tested and intrigued him, keeping him on his toes. He liked that she didn't take on airs, that she spoke her mind, and that she maintained a sense of humor regardless of the circumstances.

With each new day, it became more and more laborious to remember that he didn't belong with her. He shouldn't be thinking about her, calling on her, or inviting her to ride. And he shouldn't be thinking of her by her Christian name. But here he was, doing just that, with two horses and a groom waiting just outside, hoping she'd agree to ride with him again.

Why? It had all begun because he'd wanted a house. But now . . .

"Miss Meacham, there's a—" The maid began to announce his arrival before cutting herself off and rushing ahead of Ian into the room. "What are you doin', Miss? You're goin' to 'urt yourself!"

Sarah stood on a pile of books that sat precariously atop a chair, while adjusting a large picture frame above the mantle. Her steel blue skirts lifted, revealing a trim, stocking-clad ankle as she rose on to her tiptoes and pushed the picture to the left.

Ian didn't dare speak, for fear the sound of his voice would startle her and send her toppling to the ground. Rather, he remained just outside the room, hoping the pile of books would stay put.

"Do stop fretting, Suzy," Sarah said as she released the

frame. "I'm perfectly stable. What do you think, Beth? Will that do?"

Miss Bethia stood in the middle of the room with her back to Ian, her blonde curls bobbing as she cocked her head to the side.

"It's still a bit crooked. A little more to the left, I think."

The painting they were positioning was an odd choice. Within the outline of a three-mast schooner, the artist had painted a clear blue sky and peaceful ocean waves. The rest of the painting was not nearly as serene. Scattered haphazardly across the background were planks of wood, sails, and rigging. It brought to mind a shipwreck and cluttered an otherwise pleasing image.

"Yes, that's better," said Bethia, while the maid wrung her hands at Sarah's side. Ian had apparently been forgotten.

Slowly, he walked silently into the room, holding a finger to his lips as he passed a startled Miss Bethia. He stopped directly behind Sarah, who was now examining the painting with her hands on her hips.

"I still don't like it," she said. "Why Mr. Gyles gave you such an obscure painting and why you think it necessary to hang it in the salon is a mystery. The moment you wed is the moment it goes with you to your new home."

"I've already resigned myself to that," said Bethia with a sigh, though her eyes twinkled in delighted expectation at Ian.

Sarah continued to regard the painting, her hair piled in a mass of curls at the top of her head. "It's like the artist painted the ship while in a happy, peaceful state, then experienced an episode of madness and ruined it." She shook her head and sighed wistfully. "It could have been so lovely."

"Agreed," Ian said.

Sarah gasped and spun around, upsetting the pile of

books in the process. Her arms flailed, and she squealed as she fell to the side. Ian was quick to grab her around the waist and set her safely back on the floor, though it took a great deal of effort not to pull her into his arms. The lass had teased and tempted his resolve since he'd met her.

He held onto her for longer than necessary, unable to look away from the stormy blue that were her eyes today.

"You realize books are for reading and not for standing upon, don't you?" he managed to say. "One would think *you* experience episodes of madness."

She quickly stepped away from him, nearly tripping over one of the spilled books in the process. "When did you arrive, Ian? I was not expecting you."

He mentally congratulated himself at the sound of his name on her lips.

A throat cleared nearby, followed by the maid's voice. "Miss Meacham, Mr. Collum's 'ere to see you."

Sarah rolled her eyes. "Why, thank you, Suzy. Do show him in."

The maid bobbed a quick curtsy. "I'll fetch some tea," she blurted before darting from the room.

Ian hid a smile as he crouched to retrieve the fallen books on the floor. After examining the titles, he set them on a side table. "At least they are not copies of the bible this time. I should commend you for that, though I do think there are better alternatives than books when one needs to reach high places. A ladder, for example. Tall stool, even."

Sarah attempted a glare before a snicker escaped. She shook her head as she dropped down on the chair next to her sister. "To what do we owe the pleasure of your company this morning, sir? After our last misadventure, I was certain you'd learned to stay far away from me."

He sat down opposite her and shrugged. "It seems I experience episodes of madness as well."

Miss Bethia laughed while Sarah's lips twitched charmingly. "Considering I just willingly hung a dreadful painting, I would have to say that my madness extends beyond yours."

Miss Bethia's smile became a pout as she folded her hands in her lap. "It is not as bad as that, Sarah. I'll wager Mr. Collum thinks it more interesting than dreadful."

Both women looked at him expectantly, and Ian shifted in his seat before choosing a noncommittal answer. "I've never been a good judge of art, but I can say the outline of the schooner was very well done."

To his amusement, Sarah mouthed the word, "Coward."

"You are quite right, Mr. Collum," said Miss Bethia. "It is well done, as I believe Sarah will come to see in time. I told her to wait until Papa could hang the picture, but she insisted we needn't bother him and could just as easily do the task ourselves."

"Had you asked Papa," Sarah countered, "he wouldn't have allowed us to make the switch. Unlike Mr. Gyles, he has respectable taste in art."

Miss Bethia frowned at her sister. "Anthony only wanted to give me a memento of our sailing excursion. You cannot fault him for that."

"I can and I do, or have you forgotten the excursion did not end well, especially for Papa? He'll not appreciate the reminder, I promise you that. It's a good thing he's not overly observant or he'll insist we take it down immediately."

Bethia leaned back in her chair with a smug look. "I hope he *does* make such a demand. I will tell him that he need only allow Anthony and me to wed and the painting will go away."

"Yes, I'm sure that will do the trick. Papa is definitely the sort to be swayed by an ultimatum, especially coming from his youngest daughter."

Miss Bethia pouted again, and Ian settled back in his seat, enjoying the banter, intrigued by the turn the conversation had taken. He managed a curious, conversational tone. "Am I to assume your father is opposed to the match, Miss Bethia?"

"Yes," she said with a huff.

Ian pressed on, thinking that if he could get Miss Bethia to tell him what he already knew, he wouldn't need to continually feign ignorance of the matter. It would be one less lie to carry around. "That surprises me, considering how amiable they appeared on board the ship."

"It's not a matter of amiability," Bethia explained. "Papa will simply not allow me to marry until—"

"She is another year or two older," Sarah interrupted. She cast her sister a warning glance before adding, "He thinks she is still too young."

Miss Bethia met her sister's look with one of defiance. "In truth, I cannot marry until Sarah does, or until I reach my majority, whichever comes first."

Sarah's jaw clenched as she looked away. Miss Bethia's concession had obviously angered or embarrassed her. Probably both.

"I see," Ian said slowly, an idea forming in his mind— one that could solve his current dilemma quite nicely if he approached it in the right way.

He ran a hand along the arm of the sofa and tried for a light, casual tone. "Would it take an actual marriage to sway him, or would an interested suitor do the trick?"

Sarah continued to glare at nothing in particular while Miss Bethia considered him thoughtfully, nae *delightedly*. "A suitor could do the trick quite nicely, sir. Why do you ask?"

The tone of her voice told him she knew precisely why he had asked. He went along with it anyway. "I'm merely wondering if I could be of assistance in that quarter. I realize I am not a worthy candidate, but—"

"Oh, Papa does not care who she marries, only that she does," blurted Miss Bethia.

Sarah gaped at her sister in horrified disbelief, and only then did Miss Bethia seem to realize what she'd said. She had the grace to look chagrined.

"What I meant to say was—"

"I think your words were clear enough," Sarah snapped. "Perhaps I should go in search of a gypsy to marry. With any luck, the few qualities I possess might turn his head. If that doesn't work, I'm certain old Mr. Winters would take me. He is nearly blind, after all."

In a wise move, Miss Bethia remained silent.

Sarah turned her glare on Ian. "You are not going to court me, sir."

"But he is *already* courting you," Miss Bethia unwisely broke her silence. "Why else would he invite you driving and sailing and call upon you this morning? That is your intent, is it not, Mr. Collum?"

Her inquisitive eyes peered at him, encouraging him to agree, while Sarah closed her eyes in mortification.

Ian took pity on her. "That's a discussion your sister and I should have, Miss Bethia. Miss Meacham, I have brought a spare horse and groom with me this morning. Would you do me the honor of a ride?"

Sarah's eyes flew open, and she practically jumped to her feet. "No, thank you, sir. I am feeling suddenly unwell." She strode from the room, angry footsteps echoing in her wake.

Och, that did not go well, Ian mused to himself. Not only had his plan gone awry, but he'd just taken two steps back in whatever progress he'd made with Sarah.

Jibes and crivens. He'd certainly made a mull of things, not that he was solely to blame. Miss Bethia had been in the wrong as well.

It was time to fall back and regroup, it seemed.

Ian stood and brushed a piece of lint from his sleeve. "It seems my errand has come to naught this morning, Miss Bethia. Pray forgive my intrusion."

"You're leaving?" she asked in surprise. "Oh no, you mustn't. Not yet. Not before you've set things to rights."

He stared at her blankly. What did she expect him to do, follow Sarah up to her bedchamber and insist she hear him out? Had Miss Bethia not seen the sparks practically flying off her sister? In his experience, 'twas best to let a lass calm down first.

"You must go after her, sir. Well, not this minute per se. Wait for her ire to cool first—about ten minutes, I'd say— then you'll likely find her in the garden. It's her favorite spot to pace and think."

"And if her ire has not cooled by then?" he asked.

"Oh, it will. Sarah never stays angry for long."

For some reason, that assurance did nothing to comfort Ian. Ten minutes did not seem nearly long enough to staunch the fire he'd spied in her eyes.

· • **.** • ·

THE PATHETIC SOUND Sarah's slippers made against the garden stones was not at all satisfying. She stomped harder, causing the soles of her feet to sting, which only angered her further.

Papa does not care who she marries, only that she does marry.

The words echoed through Sarah's mind, causing her to

forget all about her throbbing feet. How dare Bethia utter such thoughtless and untruthful words, especially to Ian? Papa cared who she married. It wasn't as though he'd really let her exchange vows with a peddler on the road.

Would he?

Not a peddler, perhaps, but a tradesman hadn't been out of the question. Sarah exhaled a frustrated breath. Perhaps she'd given Ian too much credit. She'd thought of him as a miracle worker, the way he'd won over her father and sister so easily. But what if that hadn't been the case? What if her father was willing to give any respectable-looking man permission to drive his daughter about town and pay court to her? Had he even looked into Ian's circumstances the way he'd looked into Mr. Gyles's? If so, he'd never mentioned it.

Perhaps there was something to Bethia's words after all.

Sarah stopped pacing and sank down on a bench. She planted her palms on the cold stone and leaned forward, staring at a small weed that had poked its way through a crack.

"Is it safe to approach?" The low, Scottish lilt caused Sarah's pulse to quicken.

She despised the way her body instantly reacted, like walking from the cool shade into the sun. Her skin prickled and warmed, craving more.

Curse the man.

"No," Sarah answered, wishing he'd go away but also wanting him to stay. The oddest of conundrums, really.

He probably thought she'd overreacted, and perhaps she had, but between his suggestion and her sister's humiliating words, her heart now wrenched and twisted painfully.

If given the choice, she'd get out of her sister's way in an instant. Sarah despised the position their father had placed them in just as much as Bethia did, and she was doing everything she could to change his mind. But agreeing to let Ian court her for her sister's sake? Sarah couldn't do it, not when the mere suggestion had brought on so much turmoil.

He stepped into the clearing, looking far too handsome. His hands were tucked behind his back as he took one cautious step towards her, then another.

"Should I have brought my sparring gloves?" he asked in a teasing tone.

Sarah wasn't in the mood to be teased, nor did she want to spar with anyone, either verbally or physically. What she wanted most, much to her horror, was to have a good cry. Her eyes stung with unshed tears, and she quickly blinked them away, keeping her gaze locked on the little weed that suddenly appeared to be defying all odds.

Keep fighting to grow, she thought.

It was a silly command, considering she, herself, often weeded the grounds surrounding their home. This weed, however, would be left alone for the time being.

Ian came around the back of the bench and sat down next to her, facing the opposite direction. The way he watched her in such close proximity was disconcerting, and she angled her face to avoid his gaze.

"A picturesque afternoon, is it not? The perfect weather for a ride."

She clenched her jaw in frustration. He did not get to act as though everything was right in the world, as though he hadn't just made her feel like a means to an end.

"Why did you come today, Ian?" Sarah said.

"I thought I made that clear. To ask you for a ride."

"Yes, but why? Why make the effort to seek me out? Why send me books or invite me driving, sailing, or riding? Why follow me out here now?"

A moment of silence, and then, "I should think that obvious."

Sarah continued to look at the ground, refusing to let him see her shining eyes. "Has this just been a game to you? Winning over the eccentric Miss Shrew?"

"Nae, Sarah."

"Then why suggest turning it into a game now?" Her voice cracked, and she had to sniff to keep her nose from running. Drat it all. She turned her body away from him, battling for control. Why couldn't he have taken his horse and groom and gone on his way? She hated that he was seeing her so broken and vulnerable.

He shifted, and she felt his hand rest lightly on her shoulder. He probably meant to comfort her, but it wasn't comfortable. The sensations he evoked, the warmth of each and every finger, her burning desire to scoot closer to him— it made her want to scream and yank her arm away.

"Sarah, I—" His gentle tone made her name sound like an endearment. But then he cut himself off with a muttered curse, and she felt his hand clench a little before it fell away. "Forgive me. You have not given me permission to call you that, nor should you."

More than a little confused, Sarah frowned at the weed, somewhat jealous. If only her life could be as simple.

"*Miss Meacham*," he corrected with a heavy sigh, "I'm not your equal and never will be. Aside from sullying my hands in trade, you should also know that I'm the illegitimate son of a Scottish actress and an English nobleman."

Sarah looked at him then, surprised and not surprised at the same time. Like an answer to a long-awaited riddle, it made sense. Scotland. England. Shrewsbury. His dislike of his father.

He continued. "My mother was on tour in London with

an opera company when they met. They had a torrid affair that lasted only until she found herself increasing. My father, if he can be called such, put an immediate end to their relationship, leaving my mother to deal with the consequences on her own. She lost her position with the opera company and was forced to return to Scotland, ruined."

Sarah watched him, urging him to continue by saying nothing.

"He purchased a small cottage for her and offered a monthly allowance if she promised to keep quiet about me. For my sake, she accepted the cottage but refused the allowance, choosing instead to make a meager living as a seamstress.

"When I became old enough for school, she wrote to my father and threatened to reveal my true identity unless he arranged for me to attend Shrewsbury. She used the same tactic when I became of age to manipulate him into securing me a position with the East India Company."

Ian's eyes were strained, jaw taut, voice pained. "By that point in my life, accepting aid from my father was the last thing I wanted to do. But my mother was a fiery woman who refused to back down when she wanted something. More than anything, she wanted me to be educated, successful, and have the sort of independent life that had been cut short for her. The only times she ever lowered her pride was for my benefit, and I could not find it in my heart to cross her. She loved me fiercely, and I loved her, so I accepted the position, intending to earn as much as I could in as little time as possible, then return and care for her. The worst day of my life was the day I received word of her passing."

He stared straight ahead, his gaze fixed on something behind Sarah. Despite his large size, he looked small and raw. She wanted to take his hand, tell him he was a better man than his father, and offer what comfort she could, but even in her head, the words sounded trite.

"I should not be here now, sitting at your side," he said quietly. "I keep telling myself to leave you be, to stop seeking you out and be content with my life as it is, but I can't seem to do that. *Crivens*, Sar—Miss Meacham—it was not my intention to turn anything into a game. My suggestion to court you was not made for your sister's benefit, but for my own. If you had agreed to my scheme, I could continue to see you under the guise of helping your sister. I could have a respectable reason for arriving at your doorstep instead of appearing as I am—a presumptuous cad."

His words were like a balm to her aching soul, soothing, mending, lifting. In the space of a moment or two, she went from feeling thoroughly downtrodden to . . . well, quite the opposite actually. She felt wanted. Trusted. He'd confided facts about himself that he wouldn't tell to just anyone, and it meant the world.

She was growing weary of fighting her feelings for him. It was a losing battle anyway—one that had been made apparent to her that very afternoon. If Ian had not come to call, if he had decided to abandon his pursuit of her following their sailing fiasco, she would have been done in. Goodness, his suggestion of a feigned courtship had nearly done her in.

At some point between their chance encounter in the library and now, Sarah had grown to care for the man— *really* care for him. Regardless of his past, she wanted him in her life.

Unable to resist the impulse any longer, she slid her hand beneath his and curled her fingers around it.

"The man whose nose I broke?" Sarah began. "His family name goes back five generations. He is esteemed by the ton because of his heritage and connections. But in my eyes, he is the cad, and you are the gentleman. The way you cared for Banjeet's mother and now care for him, the kindness you showed a flower girl on the street, how you won over the cantankerous Mrs. Wright, and the respect I see in the eyes of those you employ—you are a good man, Ian Collum. I could never think of you as beneath me," she said firmly, then added with a smile, "You are too tall for that."

As she spoke, something in his expression changed. The heaviness dissipated, and a new emotion took its place. Hope, perhaps? A half-grin crinkled his eyes, and a tiny dimple to the left side of his lips emerged. Odd that she'd never noticed that before.

His fingers brushed against her cheek in a tantalizing, feather-like touch. He had removed his gloves at some point, and his palm felt heavenly and soft against her skin. She tilted her face into it and breathed in his familiar, exotic scent.

His gaze seemed to take in every part of her face as his fingers continued to caress her cheek. She closed her eyes, relishing the way his touch made her feel. Beautiful, wanted, and so very much alive.

She felt his breath on her cheek before his mouth grazed her ear, sending a happy shiver down her spine.

"I might kiss you," he murmured in that soft, Scottish brogue.

"I might let you."

A moment later, his hands framed her face, and his lips brushed across hers. She sat perfectly still, afraid that if she moved, he would stop. She'd never kissed a man before and had no idea how to go about it, but she wanted to learn, and she wanted Ian to teach her.

Gradually, his lips began to move with a little more

184

fervency, prodding her to respond. She did so tentatively at first, then with more vigor, meeting his passion with equal amounts of her own. Almost of their own accord, her hands traveled up his chest and around to the back of his neck, pulling him closer. He ignited feelings and sensations within her that she hadn't known existed. Spinning one moment and falling the next—she was a clumsy oaf in the hands of a master.

And oh, was Ian masterful.

His mouth caressed hers while his hands moved to her waist. A moment later, she was pulled onto his lap as he held her close. When he began trailing kisses along her jaw and neck, she sighed, thinking there was nothing more pleasurable than being kissed by Ian Collum. Her entire body trembled and trilled, singing a new, blissful song.

His mouth returned to hers for another idyllic minute or two, and all too soon, he pulled back. His forehead came to rest against hers, and his hands gripped her upper arms in a strong and painless hold.

Sarah gulped in deep breaths, eyes still closed, body on fire.

"Och, lassie, what are you doing to me?"

Still happily ensconced on his lap, she ran her fingers across his smooth cheek. "Something good, I hope."

He chuckled as he gently slid her from his lap and stood, pulling her up as well. Then he pulled her into a snug embrace and dropped a kiss on her forehead. "Aye, something very good."

Sarah liked the sound of that. She liked the sound of a lot of things now, even a not-so-feigned courtship with Ian.

"Ride with me?" he asked. "I brought Shashi."

"Aye," she answered in a terrible imitation of a Scottish accent, earning her another chuckle.

He released her at last, promising to wait while she changed. Sarah scampered upstairs and had to do some digging to find her mother's old riding habit. It was sadly out of fashion, but she didn't care, and she doubted Ian would either. Even though it didn't fit perfectly, it felt good wearing something of her mother's. Sarah hugged herself before rushing back down to meet him.

They spent the remainder of the afternoon riding, walking, laughing, and exchanging amusing stories from their youth, like the time Ian stashed some extra biscuits under his bed, only to forget about them until he discovered a colony of ants. Or the time Sarah had been chased along the beach by a flock of herring gulls intent on stealing her sandwich.

Later that evening, as Sarah flopped down on her bed in contented exhaustion, she smiled at the ceiling.

What am I doing to you? she thought. *Nae, what are you doing to* me, *Ian Collum?*

She closed her eyes and imagined his arms around her, his breath on her cheek, and his lips pressed to hers.

A tap on the door interrupted her reverie, and Bethia slipped into the room, a worried look on her face.

She wrung her hands. "Sarah, about what I said earlier. Can you forgive me?"

Sarah rolled to her side and searched her sister's penitent expression. In truth, she hadn't thought about Bethia's words since Ian had given her a reason to forget, but that didn't mean they'd stay forgotten. It was something they needed to discuss, and apparently now was the time.

"I want you to be happy, Beth. Truly, I do. But when you said what you did, it made me feel like you don't want the same for me—that your own happiness is worth the expense of mine. It injured me to hear you say that."

Bethia rushed to the bed, looking stricken, and grabbed

hold of Sarah's hand. "I do care about your happiness, Sarah. How could I not? You are my sister, and I adore you. I just want you to have what I have with Anthony, and when I see the way you look at Mr. Collum, and he at you—well, my only intention was to encourage him."

Bethia crawled onto the bed, tucking her knees beneath her. "You must believe me. I never meant to imply that just anyone would do for you because that isn't true. You deserve only the best. It came out all wrong, and I'm dreadfully sorry. Say you'll forgive me, Sarah. I cannot live with you thinking ill of me, nor can I live with you believing that I think poorly of you."

Sarah traced her finger along the floral pattern of her quilt. "What about Papa? Was what you said true? Does he not care who I marry?"

Bethia winced. "Of course he cares. We both want to see you happily settled. If he didn't think Mr. Collum a good, honorable man, he never would have encouraged him."

"But how do you know he is good and honorable?" Sarah asked. "How well do you know him, Beth? Has father even looked into his circumstances like he did Mr. Gyles's?"

At this, Bethia's confidence faltered. Sarah could see it in the clouding of her eyes, the shifting of her positions. "I'm sure he has."

If that was the case, was he aware of Ian's illegitimacy? Somehow, she didn't think so, nor did she think it would alter his opinion.

Sarah inhaled deeply and sighed. What did it matter, anyway? The knowledge hadn't altered *her* opinion. She was merely hurting and wanted a father who cared enough about his daughter to care about the man she chose to wed. And Bethia—well, Bethia would always be Bethia—dramatic, spontaneous, and a little self-centered. But she was also thoughtful, penitent, and the dearest of sisters. Sarah could never stay cross with her for long.

"All is forgiven, Beth," Sarah finally allowed. "Pray do not let it bother you one minute more."

Bethia's entire body sagged in relief, and she flopped onto her back, as though her worry had drained all the energy from her. "I don't deserve your forgiveness, but I'll take it nonetheless."

"I wouldn't expect otherwise."

Bethia giggled while Sarah's thoughts strayed back to Ian and what it had felt like to be held by him. Pure and utter ecstasy. The remainder of the afternoon had been magical as well. Like a tree with shallow roots in a fierce windstorm, she had fallen hard.

From the corner of her eye, Sarah noticed her sister watching her with a suspicious look.

Before Sarah could check her own expression, Bethia said, "You're glowing."

"I am not," Sarah countered, even though it was probably an accurate description. Her entire body felt radiant.

Bethia scooted back to her knees and grinned widely. "I thought you had gone for a long walk this afternoon, but you've been with Mr. Collum, haven't you?"

"Er . . . no?" Sarah's lie didn't sound even remotely believable. Perhaps if she'd said it with a bit more decisiveness and without twitching lips, it would have been more convincing. Try as she might, however, she could not hide the happiness that threatened to burst.

"Crags, Sarah! Cease fibbing and tell me everything."

"Everything?"

"Yes, everything!"

"In that case," Sarah said, turning on her side, "there is a weed growing up through a crack in the garden. It is a sorry, diminutive thing, but I think—"

"Sarah Rosemary Meacham!" Bethia snatched a pillow and playfully hit her sister with it. "Stop teasing me this instant, or I'll . . . I'll . . ."

"You'll what?" Sarah prodded, wanting to hear whatever silly threat her sister would come up with.

"I shall never let you borrow my white shawl again."

Hmm . . . Perhaps she'd given her sister too little credit. That particular white shawl was a favorite of Sarah's, and Bethia knew it, probably because Sarah borrowed it at least once a week.

"You should just give me that shawl," Sarah finally said. "You rarely wear it."

"Perhaps I will if you'll tell me what I wish to know."

"Do you mean it?"

"As you pointed out, I rarely wear it and would be willing to part with it for a price."

It wasn't a difficult bargain to make, since Sarah would have told her sister anyway—she'd actually been dying to share the news. "Very well then. Your shawl in exchange for my happy tale. Though I believe I'm getting the better deal."

"If you have found love at last, sister dearest, then I strongly disagree."

Love.

Am I in love?

She mulled the word over in her head, even tried it out once or twice, but in the end, she couldn't admit to being fully in love. Not yet, anyway. She needed more time, more assurance, more information.

She was, however, on her way.

KISS FIVE

··16··

COURTING IAN WAS like standing at the helm of his ship as it soared across the ocean waters. Exciting. Unpredictable. Thrilling. No day was ever the same.

Sarah became a quick study when it came to riding. They cantered horses across the beach, splashing water and sand in their wake. He took her out in a dinghy across the River Adur, where they picnicked, fished, and tossed leftover breadcrumbs at a small flock of ducks swimming past. One evening after Sarah and her family had attended an amateur musicale, Ian spread several quilts across the grass, and he and Banjeet, along with Sarah and her family, all settled down to gaze at the stars. Ian held her hand while he and Banjeet pointed out the constellations Polaris, Cassiopeia, Pegasus, Cepheus, and a few others Sarah couldn't remember.

At Bethia's continued encouragement, or rather nagging, Ian planned an evening of roasting what he called cannonballs over the fire. The small group of Ian, Chelle, Banjeet, and the Meachams sat on uncomfortable logs surrounding a large, crackling fire. They each held long sticks with little balls of dough on the end in various stages of doneness. Ian had already eaten several, all slathered in cinnamon and sugar or apricot preserves.

Sarah smiled at the dab of preserves on the corner of his mouth, glistening in the firelight. What would he do if she cleaned it off with a kiss? Of course she'd never do such a thing, especially with her father and sister present. But if they'd been alone, she would have been sorely tempted. It had been too long since she'd felt the softness of those lips.

Ian hadn't kissed her again, hadn't even *tried* to kiss her. He'd been the perfect gentleman. The picture of respectability.

Sarah didn't like it one wit.

Did he regret kissing her?

No, she refused to let any such thoughts dampen her mood. It was too beautiful of a night for that.

"Is something amiss?" he asked quietly. "You seem more contemplative than usual this evening."

The dab of preserves was no longer on his lip, which meant he must have licked it off himself. Still, Sarah's gaze was drawn to that spot.

I'm wondering why you haven't kissed me again. Don't you want to? Was I that terrible at it?

His kissable mouth lifted into a knowing smile, and Sarah felt her cheeks heat as her eyes lifted to his. Drat the man. Apparently, she didn't have to say it out loud. He'd known exactly what she'd been thinking.

Hopefully the dim light of the fire masked her blush.

"I'm perfectly well, thank you," she answered. "Is anything amiss with you?"

He leaned in close enough that their shoulders touched, and his gaze also traveled from her eyes to her lips and back to her eyes. In a hushed voice that only she could hear, he said, "Nae, Sarah, I—"

"Oh, Anthony, you have come at last!" Bethia exclaimed. "I have saved you a spot here on this log beside me. Do sit and try one of these delicious cannonballs."

Sarah looked up to find Mr. Gyles watching her and Ian, a troubled expression on his face. Ian stiffened at her side, causing Sarah to wonder, yet again, about the strange connection they had. It was apparent they shared some sort of history. She had tried to ask Ian about it a few times, but he'd circumvented the questions and turned the conversation to other things.

It was maddening.

Mr. Gyles must have realized the discomfort he'd caused because he turned his attention to Bethia and lowered himself to the log at her side. He smiled and spoke as though nothing were amiss. "You must forgive my tardiness, my dear. I was waylaid by a pressing matter with one of my tenants."

"Oh? Which tenant?" she asked. "Never say Mr. Galveston has fallen ill again. That poor man."

"This time, it was Mr. Hominy, Mr. Sheffield, and a certain troublesome goat. I shall tell you about it later."

Chelle turned her stick over the fire. "Do not refrain on our account, sir. I, for one, would love to hear about this goat."

"Oh, yes," Bethia agreed, lacing her arm through his. "Do tell."

He capitulated, as Sarah suspected he often did with Bethia, and told the group an amusing tale about an escapist goat who'd dined in his neighbor's garden.

While he spoke, Sarah admired the camaraderie and easiness the pair shared. They were mad for each other, but there was also a strong bond of friendship and trust. Sarah found herself hoping that her tentative romance with Ian would develop into such a bond one day.

195

She couldn't shake the feeling that he was keeping something from her—something important. Whether it was the underlying dissension with Mr. Gyles or something else, she didn't know.

Perhaps it was only her imagination.

Bethia laughed at something Sarah had missed. "Stop bamming us, Anthony. I'll wager my favorite lavender ribbon that you did not truly say that."

"Not out loud, perhaps, but I thought it. Why people come to me with such problems is a curiosity. They could—and very well should—work it out between themselves. But apparently it takes a third party to explain that they must compromise."

"You are a dear for helping them," said Bethia with pride. "Now let us make you a few cannonballs, which will surely rid your mind of the goat dispute."

Ian leaned in close and dropped his voice. "It doesn't take much to please Miss Bethia, does it?"

Sarah smiled. "She is easily pleased and easily displeased. An emotional creature, to be sure, but also lovable. She is the best sort of sister there is."

"I don't know what it's like to have a sibling, so I envy you that," came his reply.

"You have Banjeet," Sarah pointed out.

"He's more like a son than a brother," said Ian wryly, "a worrisome one at that."

"Well, I don't have a daughter, so there you are."

He chuckled. "It seems we are even then."

"We're different. You have your men and Banjeet. And I have my father, sister, and Chelle." Sarah wanted to add that she had him as well, but she didn't dare. It was still too soon for that sort of declaration.

"Aye, can't argue with that. My men have become a

family, of sorts, though a tad more disreputable than your own."

Sarah blew on the cannonball she'd just removed from the fire, watching the smoke rise and then disappear. "I wouldn't be so sure. Bethia has been known to discard her bonnet when out of doors, Chelle exchanges letters with men, and you already know about my reputation."

He chuckled. "I'll wager the letters you speak of are merely communications regarding school matters."

"Perhaps." Sarah should have known he'd figure her out.

He shook his head. "'Tis no wonder you and she are friends, with such sordid pasts. Davie was merely a thief who spent several years in prison, and Captain James, a former smuggler."

Sarah stared at him, unable to tell whether or not he was in earnest. "You're joking."

"I speak the truth. I found Davie sleeping on the streets of Portsmouth, begging for food because he was unable to find work after his release. Captain James, on the other hand, fell in love with a bonnie lass who wouldn't consent to marry a man involved with smuggling. He came to me, wanting to reform."

"He's married then?" Sarah asked in surprise. He'd never mentioned a wife, not that she knew much about him.

"Aye. She lives in a small cottage not far from the docks and is expecting their first child in a few months."

Still unsure if he was bamming her or not, Sarah watched him closely. The amusing glint in his eye challenged her to believe him.

At last she shrugged. "A former convict and smuggler are nothing. As I mentioned before, Bethia goes *bonnetless*."

He laughed loudly, drawing the notice of the others.

"What's so amusing, sir?" Bethia asked. "You must share. I dearly love a good laugh."

"Your sister was just telling me how lucky you are not to have a great many freckles," he said.

Bethia's face reddened, and she looked somewhat abashed. "You have found me out, sir. I don't care for bonnets in the least. They rarely favor my face shape and bring ruin to Chelle's pretty creations with my hair."

Ian's lips twitched, but to his credit, he did not laugh. Instead, he deadpanned, "I have never been more shocked in my life."

"I told you," Sarah replied, making him chuckle yet again.

They continued talking, laughing, and eating cannon-balls until late into the evening. As the skies darkened and the temperature dropped, Sarah pulled her blanket tighter across her shoulders, wishing the cold away. She wasn't ready for the night to end. It had all been too perfect.

Well, nearly perfect, anyway. Complete perfection would have included sharing a quilt with Ian while he wrapped an arm around her and she rested her head on his shoulder. Snuggled next to him, she wouldn't feel cold in the least.

Sadly, Ian was the first to stand and gather his blanket. "I'm afraid Banjeet and I must be off. I have an early shipment arriving in the morning and Banjeet has his first lesson with Lady Ariana."

Banjeet made a face until Chelle spoke up, "Remember what we discussed, little man. I will uphold my end of the bargain if you uphold yours."

"Yes, Miss Ellington," he responded. "But it don't mean I have to like it. Or her."

"Doesn't," she corrected. "And no, you don't have to like your lessons, but I'll wager you a new looking glass that you'll adore Lady Ariana. She's witty, kind-hearted, and has an excellent grasp of science and mathematics—two subjects you'll need to master if you wish to be the most sought-after captain in England."

Sarah exchanged a smile with Ian. Now that Chelle was involved, Banjeet would get the education he needed whether he wanted it or not. Chelle took education very seriously and was nothing if not determined.

Ian set his blanket at Sarah's side and said quietly, "I must thank you again for recommending that I speak to Chelle. She's been most helpful."

"I'm glad to hear it."

Sarah's father yawned, then seemed to drag himself to his feet. "It is probably time we all say our goodbyes. The hour is late."

"But Papa," Bethia protested. "Anthony only just arrived."

"I have been here for over an hour, my sweet," said Mr. Gyles gently. "Your father is correct. I should go."

Bethia opened her mouth to argue, but the stern look her father gave her had her clamping it closed and not looking at all happy about it.

Ian picked up a shovel and began tossing dirt onto the dying embers of the fire while Banjeet tried to hide a yawn.

"I can see to the fire," said Mr. Gyles, holding out a hand for the shovel. "You have a longer ride home, and Banjeet appears done in."

Ian hesitated only a moment before nodding. "Much appreciated."

Mr. Gyles nodded curtly and accepted the shovel.

Sarah rose to her feet and stood awkwardly at Ian's side, wondering if the chill she suddenly felt had more to do with Ian leaving than the doused flames. Goodness, he hadn't even left and already she missed him. Love was such a strange emotion.

Her heart stuttered at the thought. There was that word again. Love. Was she truly growing to love this man? There was so much about him *to* love that it was easy to believe herself *in* love.

He reached for her hand and raised it to his lips, setting her pulse to racing. "It seems our luck is improving, Miss Meacham. Only the designated wood caught fire, and your coiffure is still intact."

She smiled, wishing he'd call her Sarah, but he did so only when they were alone. It was something Sarah envied about her sister and Mr. Gyles. He spoke her name easily and even used endearments on occasion.

"Thank you for introducing us to cannonballs and giving us yet another memorable evening."

His fingers threaded through hers as he continued to hold her hand. "I'll be busy all day tomorrow, but are you free on Sunday?"

"I believe so," Sarah answered.

"You'll be hearing from me then." He gave her hand a squeeze before releasing it.

Sarah's stomach fluttered, and she had to fist her hands to keep from reaching out and begging him to stay.

For pity's sake, she told herself firmly. *He is not going off to war. You'll see him again in only two days.*

Two very long days.

"I'll show you to your horses, Mr. Collum," Sarah's father said. "Chelle, would you like me to have your carriage readied as well?"

Sarah answered before her friend had the chance. "We've already arranged for her to stay the night with us, Papa. Her coachman will return for her on the morrow."

"Good, good," said Sarah's father. "I never like you

traveling alone, especially in the dark. Bethia, my dear, will you join me in my study in a minute or two? I'd like a word with you before I retire."

Bethia gave Mr. Gyles a mournful look before accepting her fate. "Yes, Papa." Her downcast tone was almost laughable. Even Mr. Gyles dipped his head to try and mask his grin.

Bethia waited for her father, Ian, and Banjeet to walk away before she rose to her tiptoes and brazenly kissed her beau on the cheek. "Will I see you tomorrow, my love?"

"Indeed, you shall."

"Good." The light of the moon gave Bethia the look of a tortured soul as she tore her gaze from Mr. Gyles and began picking her way towards the house.

Sarah hugged her arms to her chest and smiled at Mr. Gyles. "She has eyes only for you. I think she's forgotten all about Chelle and me."

His gaze still fixed on Bethia, Mr. Gyles murmured, "I'd marry her tomorrow if your father would allow it."

Sarah exchanged a look with Chelle. The poor man sounded as tortured as Bethia had appeared. It could not be easy for either of them to live with such a frustration.

"If it helps, Mr. Gyles, I believe my father is softening on that subject. I wouldn't be surprised if he gave you his consent by the month's end."

Hope flared in the man's eyes. "Truly?"

"Truly." At least Sarah hoped that was the case. If not, she would have some stern words for her father. It was wrong to keep them from marrying. Surely he could see that, regardless of what happened between her and Ian.

Sarah's thoughts flitted to another matter—a matter that could be settled if Mr. Gyles chose to be more forthcoming than Ian.

Sarah hesitated, wondering how to phrase her question. "Mr. Gyles, can I ask you something?"

"Please, call me Anthony, especially if we are to be brother and sister soon." He tossed another shovelful of dirt onto the dying embers, then gave them a stir before heaping on more dirt.

"As my future brother-in-law, I hope you will be direct with me."

Her words seemed to make him nervous. He paused in his efforts to douse the fire and looked warily at her. "What is it you wish to know, Miss Meacham?"

"Sarah."

"Sarah then."

"I wish to know how you came to be acquainted with Mr. Collum." He opened his mouth to reply, but Sarah cut him off. "Don't tell me you met that day on the ship, because I won't believe you. It's apparent the two of you have a history."

For a split second she spied panic in his expression, but he dropped his gaze back to the fire, shielding his eyes from her.

Sarah forged on, determined not to give him time to invent an excuse.

"Anthony, please. The two of you are hiding something, and I must know what it is."

He didn't bother to conceal his panic any longer. He looked like a skittish colt, ready to bolt at any moment.

"What she means to say," inserted Chelle, "is that she's been trifled with before and has no desire to go through that again. If you know something about Mr. Collum that she should be aware of, we would very much like to know what that is."

Anthony's gaze drifted from one woman to the other before he sighed and dropped his head—in guilt or defeat, Sarah couldn't tell.

"There is something you should know," he said at last.

· · 17 · ·

SARAH STOOD FROZEN in place, feeling everything and nothing at the same time. She was surprised and not surprised, believing and disbelieving, hurt, numb, angry, ambivalent, and . . . cold. So very cold. The chill in the air penetrated through her entire being. Even her bones felt cold.

A house. Ian had done it all for a house.

The so-called chance encounter at the library hadn't been chance at all, but a calculated move on his part. The notes, the books, the teasing, his efforts to know her better had all been an orchestrated plan meant to convince her father to let Bethia and Anthony marry. And like a naïve animal, she'd taken the bait and stepped directly into his trap. Nae, she'd *fallen* into his trap.

Blast it all, she was even thinking like him now.

"Sarah," Mr. Gyles said, "I can't begin to express the self-loathing I feel for my part in this charade. I had no thought beyond Bethia and the desperation I felt. I honestly didn't think you would—no, that is no excuse. I—"

"Thank you for your honesty, Mr. Gyles," Chelle interrupted firmly, "but I believe the fire is sufficiently put out. You may go."

Sarah didn't see his expression, didn't really see anything beyond charred wood covered in dirt. She only heard the scraping of boots against earth as he walked away.

A fierce shivering overtook her. She tried to tug the blanket back over her shoulders, but it kept slipping from her grasp.

Gentle, purposeful hands lifted the blanket and tucked it around her.

"Come," Chelle said. "Let us get you inside before you take a chill."

Those same hands guided Sarah inside and up the stairs to her bedchamber. They helped her out of her frigid gown and into a slightly warmer nightdress. They removed the pins from her hair, brushed and braided it, and finally tucked her into bed.

Sarah immediately rolled to her side and curled into the softness of her bedclothes, wishing her emotions would sort themselves out enough to let her sleep.

"Rest," Chelle said in a soothing tone.

Not a minute later, the door flew open, and Bethia's excited voice jarred Sarah from her daze.

"Oh, Sarah, Chelle, you'll never guess. I've just had the most exhilarating news! Papa has consented to let me marry Anthony at last! Can you believe it? Oh, I shall not sleep a wink this night."

Chelle gave Sarah's hand a fortifying squeeze before her calm and quiet voice responded to Bethia.

"How exciting, dearest. Let us go to your chamber, and you can tell me all about it."

"But—"

"Sarah wasn't feeling well and has already fallen asleep. We should let her rest," said Chelle.

Bethia's voice dropped to a whisper, much to Sarah's relief. "Oh no, has she taken ill? Shall I fetch Papa?"

"I don't think it's anything that a good night's sleep won't mend. She'll feel better on the morrow, I'm sure."

If only Sarah shared her friend's confidence. For now, she was just grateful for her interference.

The room fell into darkness as Chelle snuffed out the candle, and footsteps shuffled across the room before a creak signaled the closing of the door.

Blessed silence at last. Only it didn't feel blessed. It felt more like a curse. On the same night her sister's hopes had finally come to fruition, Sarah's had fallen to pieces.

Find the good, came her mother's voice, along with the memory of all the good her mother had found despite life's setbacks.

Sarah needed to be more like her mother—her sweet, courageous, optimistic mother.

At least Bethia would finally be able to wed. Papa could not go back on his word at this point. That was something.

At least she finally knew the truth.

And at least . . . surely there were more positives to be had.

Think, Sarah, think.

But her brain was so very tired, and she ached with an old wound that suddenly felt fresh and raw. Like a fool, she'd opened herself up to a man who didn't truly care for her. She'd given him her trust, her first real kiss, and her heart. Only this time, the pain ran deeper. So much deeper.

If Sarah hadn't known before, she did now. She was in love with Mr. Ian Collum. And he was in love with a house.

She closed her eyes, but not before a tear escaped and splashed onto her pillow.

· · • · · ·

SARAH AWOKE WITH an achy head and dry, scratchy eyes. The morning light bled through the cracks in her curtains, taunting her with a bright and beautiful day.

What rot, she thought sourly, rolling away from the sight. *Even the weather won't sympathize.*

She pulled a pillow over her face and squeezed her eyes shut, wishing she could return to the painless oblivion of sleep. Only, had it been painless? She had a vague recollection of sailing across the sea with Ian, only to fall overboard and sink to the bottom when he didn't jump in to save her.

She groaned into her pillow, knowing sleep would elude her. Her mind buzzed, and her body pulsed with a restless energy that would not be stilled.

Sarah flung her bedclothes back and scooted to the side of her bed. She would go outside and take a long walk in the fresh air. And she'd continue to walk until her mind quieted and her body begged for more sleep.

She dressed quickly then trotted down the stairs. Just as her foot landed on the bottom step, the door opened, and her father walked in from outside. He was dressed in buff-colored trousers and a chestnut coat with a rumpled cravat. His hair had a disheveled look to it, as though wind or nervous fingers had rearranged it. More likely, though, he hadn't taken the time to tame it that morning.

"Good morning, Sarah," he said cheerfully. "I'm glad to see you up and about. I thought I'd have to wake you. This missive has only just arrived for you. Banjeet is holding his horse out front, waiting for a response."

Sarah didn't dare speak for fear her voice would sound

as scratchy as her throat felt. She merely nodded and cracked open the seal.

> *Sarah,*
> *I would be honored if you would join me for a ride on Sunday afternoon. There is something I would like to show you.*
> *Yours, Ian*

Sarah nearly scoffed at the word *Yours*. Ian was certainly not hers and never would be. It was past time for this charade to end.

She grabbed a pencil from a nearby drawer and scribbled a reply.

> *Mr. Collum,*
> *I appreciate the invitation, but I am otherwise engaged on Sunday afternoon.*

She was tempted to add *Not yours* but signed only her name instead.

As luck would have it, Suzy happened by, so Sarah gave her the note and asked if she'd return it to Banjeet. Then she looked back to her father, who continued to stand awkwardly in the foyer, waiting for her to finish.

Hands behind his back, he swayed and scuffed at the floor with his boot.

"Is there something else, Papa?" Sarah asked as she tugged on her gloves, ready to bolt out the doors. Why hadn't her father kept at least one horse? Now that she'd grown comfortable riding Shashi, Sarah would give anything for a good gallop. Perhaps then she could outpace the fidgety pain that clawed away at her.

"You're dressed for walking," her father finally said.

"Yes."

"Might I join you? I could use some fresh air."

Sarah furrowed her brow, not wanting his company but not wanting to be rude either. "Were you not just outside?"

"I had only just left the house when Banjeet happened by. The weather is delightful, and a walk sounds equally so, assuming my daughter will join me."

There had been numerous times during the past several years that Sarah would have been thrilled by such an invitation. Why now? Why today? The morning was indeed cursed.

"I would love your company," she lied. "But I don't wish to go far. A quick jaunt about the grounds is all the exercise I require this morning." She prayed she could mask her distress for the duration of their walk. Already it felt laborious.

"Is something the matter, my dear?" he asked, as though really noticing her for the first time.

She pasted a smile on her face. "Not at all. Shall we be off then?" Without waiting for an answer, she strode towards the door. He would have to step lively if he wanted to keep up.

He did. He matched her pace step for step.

The moment the rays of the sun touched her skin and the fresh air filled her lungs, Sarah felt some relief. It didn't remove her restlessness and certainly didn't do much for her pain but it eased something inside. Gave her hope. Reminded her that life's overcast skies and storms did not last forever. Eventually, the sun would return to her life.

"What did Mr. Collum have to say this morning?" her father asked, bringing up the one topic Sarah wished to avoid the most.

She gritted her teeth and forced a response. "He invited me for a ride on Sunday afternoon."

"You're becoming quite the horsewoman, I hear."

"I enjoy it, but I still have much to learn."

"You always were a quick study."

The ensuing silence was awkward to say the least. Her father had never been adept at small talk, which made her wonder why he'd wished to join her.

He cleared his throat. "I'm sure you're aware that I spoke with Bethia last evening. I informed her that I'll no longer stand in the way of her marriage."

"You made her the happiest of women."

"She mentioned that I may have given you the impression that I, er . . . do not care—or rather, would be willing to accept anyone's suit for you."

Merciful heavens, Sarah thought. *Not this, not now.* She couldn't handle another layer of hurt on her already towering pile.

"You should know that I believe Mr. Collum to be a decent sort of fellow."

Believe? Decent? The words were enough to push Sarah over the edge. Perhaps if her father had taken the time to really know Mr. Collum and uncover his true intentions, she wouldn't be in this position now.

Her voice held a note of sarcasm as she answered. "How comforting it is to know that the appearance of decency is all a man needs to recommend himself to me."

His steps faltered for a moment, and he was quick to say, "Forgive me, Sarah. I did not intend it to come across like that. I only meant that—"

"Papa, it no longer matters. I have come to the realization that Mr. Collum and I will not suit. I'll not be seeing him any longer." She probably should have filtered her words a little more, but they'd practically shot from her mouth—a product of her ever-growing restlessness, no doubt.

Her father ceased walking, but Sarah continued forward—at least until his commanding voice insisted she stop. She paused where she stood but didn't turn around.

"When did you decide this?" He stepped in front of her, replacing her view of the meadow with a brown jacket and rumpled cravat. She should have remained silent.

Her gaze fell to her feet as she admitted, "Last night."

"After I had changed my mind regarding your sister?"

"Yes, but that was not the reason I changed my mind about Mr. Collum."

"Please explain."

"I'd rather not." She turned her head, despising the tears that threatened to spill. Blast it all. She didn't want to cry.

"Does his profession have anything to do with it?"

"No."

"I don't understand."

"Perhaps if you'd looked into his situation like you did with Mr. Gyles, you would." Her tone hadn't been sharp or angry, merely wooden. Hollow. Sad.

She blinked fiercely, wishing her tears to the devil. "Why do you want to marry me off so badly that you don't care who the man is or what his true reasons are for courting me? Am I that much of an inconvenience to you?"

Her voice broke, and she clamped her mouth shut, hating her weak emotions. "Please, Papa," she pled. "I only want to walk in peace."

After a long moment, he slowly stepped aside.

A surge of relief filled her, and she moved past him. Not two steps later, his quiet, but firm voice pierced her ears. "Sarah, I have only ever seen you as my beautiful, intelligent, strong-willed daughter. If Mr. Collum sees something else, he is a fool. When you have cleared your head, please find me in my study. There are some things we need to discuss."

He left her, and Sarah's feet carried her only as far as a wooden stump. She sank down on it and peered up at the bright blue of the skies, missing her mother so much it ached.

"You shouldn't have left us, Mama," Sarah said. "We still need you. *I* need you."

She frantically searched the skies, but the heavens didn't open, nor did her mother magically appear. Her head dropped to her hands and the sobs finally came, yielding to the overwhelming pain, frustration, and sorrow. She cried for her lost mother, for all the humiliations she'd endured, and for the man who'd finally captured her heart but didn't really want it.

Gradually, the throbbing ache in her chest began to dissipate and a tentative calm entered her mind.

Have faith, my dear. The sun will rise again. Her mother's voice came quietly, but it sounded almost real, as though she could be sitting nearby.

Sarah lifted her head, and her breath caught in her throat when she spied a hummingbird hovering over a flower, its wings flapping ferociously. Despite her wretchedness, a warm, peaceful feeling wrapped around her like a quilt.

Her mother had always loved hummingbirds.

·· 18 ··

THREE HOURS AFTER Sarah had been left alone in the meadow, she returned home having achieved her goal: total exhaustion. Her lack of sleep coupled with an empty stomach and endless hours of walking had brought her home dead on her feet.

She went first to the blessedly empty kitchen, where she found some bread and cheese to stave off the worst of her hunger pains. Then she sought out her father as promised, finding him ensconced in his favorite chair, reading a book.

He looked up when she entered, then closed his book and removed his spectacles, gesturing for her to sit in the chair next to him.

Sarah gratefully sank down, wishing she could kick off her boots and stretch her toes. Oh, how her feet ached.

"Feeling better?" he asked.

"Less emotional, yes, but more tired," Sarah admitted. "I did not sleep well last night."

He steepled his fingers under his chin and watched her for a moment before lowering his hands to his lap. His face looked haggard and worn. Burdened.

Guilt nibbled at Sarah's insides. Her earlier outburst was probably to blame.

"There will never be a good time to tell you this, Sarah," her father said, "but after our conversation this morning, I've realized there are some things you need to know—things I have been wrong to keep from you."

The haunted look on his face was a familiar one. Sarah had been introduced to it following the death of her mother, and it had accompanied him for more than a year before gradually giving way to moments of peace and contentment. This past month, however, it had subsided completely. Or so she'd thought.

"When it came to your mother's health, I was willing to try anything and everything to make her better. It did not matter the cost. But in the end, the cost took a heavy toll on our finances. I have tried to economize as much as possible, but it has only postponed the inevitable. I now have very little to my name, and within the year, I will have no other choice than to sell the house."

Sarah gasped and leaned forward, her fatigue forgotten. "Papa!"

He rubbed his temples and sighed. "I would never push you into a match with just any man, but I hope you can now understand why I have been so insistent that you at least try. You will be left with nothing, my dear, and I'd like to see both of my daughters happily settled, not just Bethia. Mr. Gyles has assured me that there will always be a place for you in their household, but I don't think you will be happy there. You are far too independent."

"Oh, Papa," Sarah said. "I am not worried for myself. I am worried about you. What will you do?"

He shrugged. "I'll need to seek employment and find a small flat somewhere, possibly in Hove. I have resisted doing so for as long as possible because of how it will affect you and Bethia. But the time is coming that I will no longer have a choice in the matter."

Sarah looked around the small study, trying to picture someone else in her father's favorite chair. An uneasy feeling settled in her stomach. This was her father's room. Everything attested to it. The portrait of her mother that hung above the fireplace. The books piled on the bookshelves in an orderly fashion. The large, grandfather clock that stood majestically against the wall. The pillow her mother had embroidered. The smell of paper and leather.

No. He couldn't sell this house. It was his home. Hers. Bethia's. Too many memories were stashed here.

"Why did you not tell me before now? I could have found work somewhere. I could have—"

"That is precisely the reason I didn't tell you," he said. "I knew you would have sought out a position as a companion or governess or something or other. But they are my debts, not yours, and that is not the life I want for you."

"They are *our* debts, Papa. It's not as though you squandered our money or gambled it away. You spent it trying to help Mama, and we wouldn't have had it any other way."

"Yes, but it didn't save her, and now my daughters must suffer because of it."

Sarah let out a long breath and leaned forward, feeling ill all of a sudden. One would think she'd be accustomed to loss by now, but the thought of walking away from this house and all of its memories made her nauseous.

"I shall speak to Chelle at once. Perhaps there is an opening at her school."

He shook his head and even smiled a little. "I have no doubt you would make an admirable instructor, my dear, but I fear your reputation would disqualify you. What mama would wish her daughter to be schooled by the infamous Miss Shrew?"

Sarah scowled at her father but couldn't argue his point. Blast the unforgiving nature of the ton.

"Is there no other option than to sell?"

"I could take up piracy."

"Papa."

"No, my dear. I can see no other way." His gaze flicked to hers for a moment, and his jaw worked back and forth. Sarah recognized that look. There was something more he wanted to say but he wasn't sure how to say it or even if he should.

She braced herself for more distressing news. "What is it?"

He pressed his lips together briefly before speaking. "Will you tell me what has occurred between you and Mr. Collum? I cannot fathom what it might be. You say his intentions are not what they appear, and I find that most troublesome. I've always considered myself a good judge of character and truly believed him to be a fine man."

Sarah squirmed in her seat. She should have expected the question, but she was unprepared how to answer. If she fully explained the situation, it would cast Mr. Gyles in a bad light, and she couldn't do that to him or Bethia. Mr. Gyles may have behaved thoughtlessly, but he'd done so out of desperation to be with her sister and not because he was a bad man.

"The way Mr. Collum looks and speaks to you has me convinced he's in love with you, Sarah. What other motives can he have for pursuing you the way he has done?" Her father's brow furrowed in confusion. "I cannot understand it."

At his words, Sarah's heart ached all over again. Tears

stung her eyes, and she pinched herself hard to keep them at bay. *I will not cry for you again, Ian. I will not.*

She stood abruptly. "Forgive me Papa, but I cannot speak of Mr. Collum at present. Perhaps in time I can be more forthcoming, but . . ." Her voice faltered as she rapidly blinked the tears away, wishing them to the devil.

He nodded gravely. He may not like her answer but he understood.

Sarah dipped into a brief curtsy before making her escape, her fingers balling into fists as she went. Whatever benefit she'd gained from her walk that morning—whether it was some semblance of peace or merely exhaustion—was gone in a flash. She wanted to scream out in frustration and smash everything around her.

Instead, she strode out into the sunshine for another long walk.

··19··

FOR THE SECOND night in a row, Sarah slept fitfully. Ian had again invaded her thoughts and her dreams, bouncing her back and forth between happy memories and the painful knowledge that there would be no more of them. Added to that was the disturbing matter of losing their home.

As with the morning before, Sarah dressed quickly, almost frantically. Her calf muscles ached abominably from her lengthy walks the day before, but if she stayed in her room a moment longer, she'd go mad. What she needed was a distraction.

Something.

Anything.

She thought briefly about the pianoforte, but the noise would certainly wake her father and sister, and the last thing she wanted was company.

As luck would have it, Sarah had been able to avoid her sister all day yesterday. She'd returned from her second, lengthier walk to discover that Bethia had gone to Mr. Gyles's home for dinner. When she'd burst into her room later that night, Sarah had once again pretended to be asleep.

While her emotions were still so close to the surface, Sarah couldn't bring herself to face her sister.

In a quiet, almost sad voice, Bethia had said, "Why must you be asleep or out for a walk when I wish to speak to you most? I am sorely tempted to wake you, but . . . I will not. In spite of everything, I hope you are having sweet dreams, sister dearest."

The door had closed, and Sarah rolled onto her back with a frown. In spite of everything? What had Bethia meant by that? Surely Chelle or Mr. Gyles had not confided in her.

Blast. One more thing to worry over.

And worry she had. All. Night. Long.

What Sarah needed now was a reprieve that didn't involve walking. *But what? Oh, sweet-tempered Shashi, I could really use a ride right now.*

The reminder of the horse reminded Sarah of Ian, which caused her to quicken her steps as she fled her room. She took the stairs gingerly, her muscles protesting each step down.

About midway in her descent, a loud knock startled Sarah, and she had to grab the banister to keep from losing her footing. Who would possibly have come at this hour of the morning?

Surely not Banjeet with another note—he'd come twice yesterday, and twice Sarah had sent her regrets. Could it be Ian? No, he'd never come this early . . . or would he? A sudden nervousness caused her to stiffen and contemplate bolting back up the stairs. She'd rather be trapped in her room than face Ian.

"Was that a knock I 'eard?" Suzy appeared at the foot of the stairs, watching Sarah with a look of confusion. Sarah opened her mouth to shush her maid when another loud rap echoed through the silence, followed by the door opening on its own.

Through the crack in the door, Chelle's lovely face appeared. When her bonnet struck the door frame, she scowled and pushed the door all the way open. Her expression brightened when she spotted Sarah on the stairs.

"Oh good, you are up. I was worried you had shut yourself away and would refuse to come out. Ought to have known you had more sense than that."

Suzy cast Sarah an odd look before dropping into a quick curtsy. "If'n I'm not needed, Miss . . ."

Sarah waved her off, and Suzy darted back down the hallway, nearly colliding with Bethia, who had just rounded the corner with a large tea tray.

Sarah blinked at her sister as she walked painfully down the rest of the stairs. What a strange morning this was turning out to be. First Chelle and now this. Bethia never rose with the sun, choosing instead to keep to her bed until nine at the earliest. But here she was at half past seven, wide awake, her hair tied into a simple knot and carrying a breakfast tray, no less.

Rather than brighten when she spotted Sarah, as Chelle had done, Bethia slowed her steps, looking wary.

"You're up early," Sarah commented.

"I . . ." Bethia's gaze flicked to Chelle's before returning to her sister's. "I brought you breakfast."

She thrust the tray in Sarah's direction, spilling some tea in the process.

Sarah stared at the tray but didn't take it right away. Something odd was afoot. Her sister had made tea and toast, albeit slightly burned toast, and Chelle had the look of a conniving minx.

Not trusting either of them, Sarah cautiously accepted the tray and set it down on a nearby table before folding her arms and raising her brow. "What are the two of you about?"

Chelle grinned while Bethia clasped her hands nervously.

"We have formed a plan," Chelle answered. "A rather brilliant one at that."

Oh dear. A plan formed by Chelle and Bethia could only mean trouble. Sarah suddenly wished she'd stayed in bed with her door bolted tight. She could only assume this had something to do with Ian, and she didn't want to make any plans regarding him, not even nefarious ones. He'd consumed too much of her thoughts already.

Chelle threaded her arm through Sarah's and gave it a pat. "I can see we've made you uneasy, but you mustn't worry. We are going to have such fun today, and doesn't that sound better than wallowing?"

It did sound better. Much better. But no matter how desperate Sarah was for the distraction they offered, in her current mood, she'd likely drag them down with her. She couldn't bring herself to make them suffer as well.

"I have no intention of wallowing, so—"

"That's the spirit," said Chelle. "Once you eat, Beth will help you change into the most hideous frock you own. We can't have you ruining this pretty thing, now, can we?"

Sarah glanced down at the plain, blue gown she wore, thinking it only marginally pretty. Compared to the dresses her sister and friend wore, however, it was lovely. Both of theirs were well-worn and decidedly outdated. Good heavens, what were they thinking to do? Lie in wait for Ian and toss handfuls of mud at him as he passed? Hmm . . . that actually did sound somewhat fun.

"What, exactly, does this plan entail?" Sarah asked, wary and intrigued. She wasn't about to commit to anything without an explanation.

Chelle's grin widened, and she released Sarah's arm to

grab the tray. "You must first eat, change, and come with us. All will be revealed soon enough."

That didn't sound suspicious, Sarah thought dryly. She pushed an errant curl from her face and frowned at the tray. "I'm not hungry, and where are we going?"

Chelle ignored the question and set the tray back on the table. "I suppose you don't need to eat right away if you'd rather not. We have some luncheon packed in my carriage. Beth, take her up to her room and help her change. I'll let the coachman know we're ready to leave. Whatever you do, don't tell her a thing."

Bethia seemed to gain confidence from Chelle. She straightened, nodded, and grabbed Sarah's arm, pulling her up the stairs. "Do you still have that awful brown gown the parson's wife gave you a few years ago?"

Sarah wished she could say no, but that particular dress was hidden away at the very back of her wardrobe where she never had to look upon it. The color of cinnamon with purple flowers and green leaves, the fabric was truly horrid. It wouldn't look good on a rodent, which was the reason Sarah had never given it to anyone else, not even someone in need. Why the parson's wife had thought to gift it to her was still a mystery. Perhaps it was punishment for arriving late to too many Sunday services.

In the bedchamber, Bethia began rifling through her wardrobe. "It must be here somewhere. You never throw anything away."

Sarah couldn't deny it. Tossing out a perfectly service-able gown felt wasteful, even one she'd never worn.

"Beth, tell me what this is about. I beg you."

Golden curls bobbed as her sister shook her head and continued to pull out one gown and then another. "I promised Chelle I wouldn't say a thing, and I'll not go back on my word. We only mean to cheer you up, dearest. Ah, here it is." Bethia frowned as she pulled the dress from the wardrobe. "Goodness me. This is even worse than I remembered."

"I can't possibly see how wearing that will cheer me up. It matches my mood perfectly." Sarah paused, watching her sister closely. "I'm assuming you're aware of what has occurred? Did Chelle confide in you?"

Bethia's jaw immediately tightened, and fire flashed in her eyes. She tossed the gown on the bed and began unfastening Sarah's buttons with angry movements. "Anthony told me all about it yesterday. I cannot believe he would do such a thing to you, Sarah. I'm so angry. I told him not to make our betrothal public since I'm not certain if I still wish to marry him."

Sarah's mouth fell open in surprise. She'd expected Bethia to be cross, but not *that* cross. Then again, her sister was nothing if not dramatic.

"Oh, Beth, that poor man. How could you say as much to him? Of course you wish to marry him still."

"Not if he is willing to sacrifice my sister's happiness for his own. Honestly, what was he thinking?" Bethia helped Sarah out of the blue gown and into the ugly brown one. "I gave him quite the tongue-lashing last evening and demanded he take me straight to Chelle's, refusing to speak another word to him during the entire ride. I'm still so mad I could . . . well, I don't know what I could do precisely. I'm just not sure I can ever forgive him for doing this to you. How could he?"

Sarah waited for Bethia to finish fastening the buttons before throwing her arms around her sister. Her loyalty warmed Sarah's heart. If one good thing had come from the past two days, it was the knowledge that her father and sister loved and cared for her more than she'd realized.

Sarah drew back and smiled. "Thank you for standing up for me, Beth. It means the world, truly. But don't be angry with Anthony forever. He made the mistake of letting his heart rule his head—something we're all guilty of doing. I'm sure if he'd realized what would come of it, he would've never suggested it. What angers *me* is the fact that Ian agreed to the scheme. What was *he* thinking?"

"I haven't the faintest idea, but you can be sure I will be giving him a similar tongue-lashing the moment I see him. Now let me look at you. Yes, truly hideous. It's the perfect gown. Let's be off. It seems we could both use some cheering up, and I believe Chelle has landed on just the thing."

· · • · ·

SARAH STEPPED DOWN from the carriage and eyed the structure before her with misgiving. She didn't need to ask where they'd come. She already knew. This was *the* house. The one that inspired it all.

It wasn't exactly grand. In fact, to most onlookers it probably looked shoddy. Brown brick in various stages of discoloration. A high-pitched roof in desperate need of repair. A garden overrun with weeds. Walls and windows covered in untamed ivy. To say the least, it was a bit of an eyesore.

"Are you certain this is it?" Bethia appeared skeptical and unimpressed. Her thoughts were as obvious as the green in her gown. Ian had gone to such extremes for *this*? Surely Sarah's heart had been worth something bigger and better.

"I'm certain," Chelle responded with a nervous glance in Sarah's direction. She, too, had wondered the same.

Sarah might have been equally offended if not for the fact that she found much to like in the property. The stunning, unobstructed view of the sea. The bowed windows lurking beneath the ivy. The row of understated corbels that ran the length of the roofline. An old wood sign that read, *IVY COTTAGE.*

Once tamed, scrubbed, and repaired, Ivy Cottage would be quite charming. It was also a definite improvement to Ian and Banjeet's current residence.

Which was precisely why she shouldn't have come. Now there would be a picture to accompany the ache and haunt her dreams.

Chelle straightened and lifted her chin. "Why are we standing about? The paint and paintings should already be inside. A few footmen from the school brought them by earlier."

Sarah remained where she stood, giving Chelle a stern look that said, *I'm not stepping foot inside that house until you explain.*

With a shrug, Chelle gestured toward the structure. "I'm sure you agree that Ivy Cottage could use some renovating."

Even though the words caught Sarah off guard, she didn't widen her eyes, frown, or even furrow her brow. Surely, she'd heard wrong. "You want my help improving it?"

A devious grin appeared on Chelle's face. "Not all renovations can be called improvements, especially when they involve ghastly pink paint and the most disturbing artwork you'll ever see. Come, take a look for yourself. Anthony has given his full consent."

"It was the least he could do," Bethia muttered.

Intrigued, Sarah followed Chelle and Bethia inside, only to come face to face with the most revolting pictures she'd ever seen. A man with the head of a goat, a creepy, ghostlike image of a person's bones hovering over a boat. A buxom woman with a long, frizzy beard. There had to be at least a dozen paintings, all ranging from grotesque to bizarre to—as Chelle had said—disturbing.

"Prinny donated these to the school when he began renovating the pavilion. Wasn't that thoughtful of him? Apparently, they'd been stashed away in his attics for years and he needed the extra storage. I was tempted to use them as examples of what not to paint in our art classes, but I couldn't bring myself to show them to innocent young ladies, so they were relegated to *our* attics—until now, that is. Won't they look fabulous on Mr. Collum's newly painted walls? I can't think of any better adornments than these."

Sarah looked around her at the paint-chipped walls, faded wooden banister covered in dust, and a morning room darkened by a mass of ivy-shaped shadows. As with the exterior, it would be an easy thing to see the space for its potential, but Sarah didn't want to see it that way. She wanted to see all of those paintings hung on a backdrop of pink walls.

"Was the paint a gift from Prinny as well?"

Chelle nodded. "He's extremely charitable when it suits his purposes and has instructed Mr. Nash to give any unwanted supplies to our school. Unlike Prinny, however, Mr. Nash asks whether we'd like the donations beforehand, or we would have no attic space left. This paint should have been a vibrant red, but it was tinted incorrectly and was therefore unusable. When Mr. Nash first offered it to me, I politely turned him down. Yesterday morning, however, I sent him a note, inquiring if it was still available. The paint arrived on our doorstep that evening."

"How very accommodating of him." Bethia grinned. "I can't think of a better color to paint the walls of a bachelor's home, can you?"

Chelle slipped her arm through Sarah's and gave it a gentle pat. "If Mr. Collum desires this house enough to injure my friend, we'll see to it that he receives a fitting reception."

"I can already see the look on his face." Bethia molded her features into a dramatic expression of horrified shock. "He'll likely sputter and grow quite red."

Sarah smiled a little, wishing she could be a witness to his reaction. *It doesn't feel good to be duped, does it?* she would say to him. *I hope you enjoy your new home.*

"We must also paint his bedchamber," Bethia added. "I believe we have some old drapes that would look most fitting in that room. They are a rusty orange, which will clash abominably with pink."

Sarah felt a giggle bubble up from somewhere deep inside. Her shoulders shook before the sound escaped, and before long, she was clutching her belly as laughter overcame her. Goodness, it felt good to laugh. So much of the ache, turmoil, and stress erupted along with it, and the day suddenly appeared bright and even hopeful.

She could conquer this.

She *would* conquer it.

With her sister and friend at her side, she could overcome anything. How she loved them both.

Chelle rolled up her sleeves and snatched a paintbrush from the pile on the table. "Let's paint a house pink, shall we? Perhaps we should repaint the sign out front as well and give it a new name. Hmm . . . what about Primrose Cottage or Pinkerton Place?"

"Those are far too sedate," Bethia said. "No. I think we should name it The Blushing Begonia."

This, of course, sent all three of them into peals of laughter.

·· 20 ··

IAN RAPPED ON the door of Haven House and stood back to wait.

Twice now, Sarah had sent her regrets using the same tepid excuse: *I appreciate the invitation, but I am otherwise engaged.*

The first time, he'd been able to dismiss it, but when he'd invited her to picnic with him on the beach Tuesday next something she loved to do on an afternoon she was typically free—and she still turned him down, he could dismiss it no longer. Something was amiss, and he was determined to get to the bottom of it.

After what felt like an interminable amount of time, Mr. Meacham opened the door. Instead of his usual friendly greeting, his eyes darted about in a nervous fashion, as though he suddenly wished he'd bolted the door instead of opening it.

Ian was the first to speak. "Good day to you, sir."

"Er . . . Mr. Collum, how do you do? We were not expecting you this morning. To what do we owe the pleasure?"

Ian had always been welcomed with a wide smile and a hearty handshake. Today, however, he was not.

Aye, something was definitely wrong.

Ian fingered the small posy he'd purchased from the young flower girl in town. "Is Miss Meacham home to visitors this morning? I would like to speak with her if I may."

Mr. Meacham eyed the posy distrustfully, as though they'd sprout thorns at any moment. "I'm afraid she is away currently, but I'd be happy to deliver the flowers upon her return." He sounded so stiff and formal. Not like him at all.

Ian glanced up at a window above, wondering if Sarah was truly gone or merely hiding behind a curtain somewhere. What had happened between the night of the campfire and now? Worry gnawed at him. Could she have learned about the bargain he'd made with Mr. Gyles? Nae, 'twasn't possible. Mr. Gyles would never say anything, not when it had been his idea. There was too much at stake.

It had to be something else. A new rumor in town, perhaps—one that Sarah couldn't easily dismiss?

His hand fell to his side, and the posy along with it. "I'd prefer to give the flowers to her myself. Can you tell me when I might find her at home?"

Mr. Meacham shifted the book he held from one hand to the other. "I can't say for certain." At Ian's raised eyebrow, he added, "Rather, *she* did not say."

It took a great deal of control not to force his way inside and see for himself, but Ian had learned long ago that emotional outbursts rarely brought about desired results.

He inhaled deeply instead. "Are *you* at home to callers, sir, or are you otherwise engaged as well?"

Mr. Meacham's brow furrowed, his feet shuffled, and he appeared hesitant to answer. After an awkward silence, his shoulders sagged, and he took a step back, indicating Ian was free to step inside.

It wasn't the most amiable of welcomes, but it wasn't a closed door in his face either. Ian would take what he could get, along with whatever answers Mr. Meacham would give him.

Ian was led to the study—a slightly cluttered, but cozy room, with a large fireplace, two comfortable looking armchairs, and enough books to keep a man busy for months.

Mr. Meacham gestured to one of the chairs and sat on the other, setting the book he'd been holding on a side table next to a pair of spectacles.

Not sure where to begin, Ian ran his hands along the arms of the burgundy velvet chairs. He wasn't normally at a loss for words, nor had he ever thought of Mr. Meacham as intimidating, but here in this room, with frigid cold eyes staring at him, Ian had to force himself not to squirm.

Best get it over with.

"I wonder, sir, if there is anything I've done to cause offense. It's apparent something is amiss, and I would like to know what that is and how I might make amends. Your family, particularly your daughter, has become dear to me, and . . . well, I would never want to jeopardize our good relations."

Mr. Meacham steepled his fingers under his chin, his gaze diving deep into Ian's soul. "How dear, exactly?"

Not expecting the same directness, Ian fidgeted in his chair, unsure how to answer. He pictured Sarah laughing with Banjeet and nearly toppling out of a boat when a fish yanked on her line. He thought of her standing atop a pile of bibles as she strained to reach a book, riding Shashi across the beach, or trying to come to his aid on an unstable ship's deck only to topple down next to him.

Ian couldn't rid his mind of the lass. Her adventurous

233

spirit, sense of humor, acceptance, good heart, the scent of lavender, the feel of her body pressed to his, and the taste of her lips . . .

Och, he was a glutton.

"Very dear," he said at last. So dear, the thought of losing her scared him as much as the night he'd almost lost Banjeet to a stormy sea.

"I'm falling in love with her," Ian added, wanting her father to understand exactly how much was at stake for him.

More silence followed, and it seemed an age before her father finally said, "I believe you."

Ian sighed, feeling like he'd overcome the first obstacle in a long line of them. It was a start.

"Tell me something, Mr. Collum. Do you, or did you, have some ulterior motive when it came to courting my daughter?"

Ian's cravat suddenly felt tight. His fingers clenched around the arms of the chair as dread took residence in his stomach. "Why do you ask?"

Mr. Meacham rubbed at the back of his neck, and Ian could almost see an internal debate going on in his mind. Out of loyalty to his daughter, should he continue this conversation or leave well enough alone?

"She mentioned that your reasons for pursuing her may not have been as honorable as they appeared," Mr. Meacham finally admitted. "Can you tell me why she'd think such a thing?"

Jibes and crivens, she did know. Mr. Gyles, blast him, must have told her the truth. Why, Ian had no idea, but the deed was done whether he understood it or not.

You should have been the one to tell her, chided an internal voice.

Pain registered between his eyes, and he closed his eyes

and rubbed his forehead to keep it at bay. Sarah might have a kind heart, but she could also be stubborn and unforgiving. The ton didn't call her Miss Shrew for no reason. Ian had seen the hardness in her eyes when she'd spoken of the last man who'd trifled with her affections. It had been years, but she still despised him.

He opened his eyes to find the same frigid look that had met him earlier. Realizing he had no other choice than to confide in Mr. Meacham, Ian sighed. He could only hope Mr. Meacham would be more forgiving than his daughter.

"Aye," Ian finally said. "I can."

·· 21 ··

FOR FIVE STRAIGHT days, Ian stood on the doorstep of Haven House, and for five straight days he was turned away. The lengthy letter he'd written to Sarah had also been returned unopened.

Mr. Meacham had been no help. While he'd conveyed his sympathies and claimed to hold no ill will, he'd also made it clear that he would not interfere in any way. If Ian wanted to earn back Sarah's good opinion and trust, he'd have to do it on his own—a feat that was proving deucedly difficult.

One particular morning, he arrived to find Mr. Gyles already on the doorstep, exchanging words with the Meacham's timid but surprisingly determined maid.

The door closed, Mr. Gyles glowered, and Ian nearly smiled. *Tit for tat*, my friend. *Tit for tat.*

Ian remained on his horse, knowing it would be an exercise in futility to knock on the door as well. He glanced at an adjacent window, where a pair of bonnie blue-green eyes peered at him before a curtain dropped and hid them from view.

Nae, he would definitely not be speaking with Sarah today. Ah, well. At least she knew he'd come. And he'd continue to come for as long as it took to get her to speak with him.

Mr. Gyles sat down on the top step and removed his hat, tossing it back and forth between his hands. As much as Ian wanted to despise the man for causing this debacle, he couldn't. Without the house and the bothersome contingency that had come with it, Ian would have never met Miss Sarah Meacham.

Ian squinted in the sun before looking back at the sorry chap on the Meacham's step. "You have the look of a man who could use a stiff drink. How about a pint? I know a place not far from here."

Mr. Gyles appeared ready to decline, only to change his mind and press his hat back on his head. "Why not? I've nothing better to do."

Thirty minutes later found them seated in a nearly-empty tavern, sipping ale.

Mr. Gyles was the first to broach the subject. He took a long swig before slamming his mug back to the table and spilling some of the liquid. "This is all my doing, I know, but you must find a way to regain Sarah's good opinion. It's the only way Beth will ever forgive me. Think of the house, man. Don't you still want it?"

He looked so downtrodden and hopeless that Ian almost felt sorry for the bloke. But for him to bring up that blasted house at this time was, well, offensive. Ian might not display his emotions as openly as the man seated across from him, but he found much to dislike in their current situation as well.

"You may keep your precious house. I don't want it any longer."

Mr. Gyles was about to take another drink, but he paused, slowly lowering his mug to the table as he stared at Ian. Confusion gave way to realization, and some of the hopelessness faded from his expression.

"You like her," he said hesitantly, as though he didn't dare to believe it. "I mean, *really* like her."

"And you like Miss Bethia," Ian returned.

Mr. Gyles leaned forward, grabbing the edges of the table as though his life depended on it. "I *love* her," he corrected. "Can you not see what this is doing to me? I'm going mad, man. *Mad.*"

He did have a wild, crazed look about him. Ian swirled his drink and watched a small whirlpool form. In truth, he might have a similar mindset if not for his belief that he would, somehow, in some way, win Sarah back. It would take time and certain finesse, but he *would* do it. Now that he'd found her, he wasn't about to let her slip from his life.

"Have you told her how you feel?" Mr. Gyles asked, as if that were the answer to everything.

Ian couldn't keep the dryness from his tone. "Aye, she granted me an audience at half past *never*. In case you hadn't noticed, she'll not speak to me any more than Miss Bethia will speak to you."

"You must *make* her listen." Mr. Gyles's fingers began to turn white.

"How should I do that? Abduct her? Tie her to a tree while I declare myself to her?"

The younger man seemed to think it a valid suggestion. He snapped his fingers and pointed at Ian. "Yes, that's brilliant. We can dress as highwaymen and waylay their carriage. You can spirit her off and—"

"They don't have a carriage," Ian interjected before the man could get too carried away.

"She rides with Chelle often enough. We can nab her then."

Apparently, Ian needed to point out the other, far more fatal flaw in his plan. "If you think holding her captive will somehow ingratiate me, you do not know Sarah at all. It would only serve to fuel the fire of her anger."

Mr. Gyles brooded for a moment more, only to snap his fingers again. "We can hire someone else to do the deed, and you can be her rescuer."

Ian slowly reached across the table and slid Mr. Gyles's drink away from him. "I believe you've had enough."

The younger man didn't seem to mind or even notice. "How did you earn her affections to begin with? Can you not do the same again? Think, man, think!"

Ian considered the suggestion as he gulped down a mouthful of ale. "What worked the first time will not work again. Even if I managed to cross paths with her in town, she wouldn't give me the time of day."

Mr. Gyles sat back, folding his arms and glowering. "At least I'm trying to think of a plan. All you seem capable of doing is finding fault."

'Twas true enough, Ian conceded. But as much as he would like to force Sarah into a conversation, that wasn't the way with her. He'd betrayed her trust, and now he had the difficult task of earning it back.

Mr. Gyles had made a good point, however. Ian had manipulated certain situations and found a way past Sarah's defenses before. He could do so again. He'd just have to approach the situation with more caution and subtlety this go around. If she wouldn't allow him to explain, he'd have to find a way to show her.

Aye, that's precisely what he'd do.

He watched his swirling ale, and the beginnings of a

plan began to form. It needed more thought and tweaking, but . . .

"I have an idea," he said at last. "It'll take time and patience on our part, but I believe it might work. First, however, I need you to do something for me. Do you think Miss Ellington will listen to you?"

"I will make her."

·· 22 ··

SARAH SAT IN the morning room as the clock chimed the hour of noon. She pressed her lips together with a frown. For the past five days, Ian had attempted to call between the hours of ten and eleven. Today, however, he'd not come. Had he at last given up? Was it finally over?

The knowledge should have comforted her, or at the very least eased her mind. It had been a difficult thing to see him ride up on his stallion, looking so handsome she'd wanted to run to the door and throw herself into his arms.

It's the house he's after, not you, she had to remind herself daily.

Yesterday, Chelle had promised to send Mr. Gyles a note, instructing him to sell the house and be done with the whole sorry affair. Apparently, he'd not wasted any time. Ian must have obtained his heart's desire at last and had no reason to visit Haven House any longer.

Sarah closed her eyes against the painful ache and tried to think positively. This was a good thing. He would stop coming around, and she could finally move on.

Trouble was, everywhere she went reminded her of him. The library, the sea, the beach where they'd ridden horses, the river where they'd fished, the garden where he'd—no, she would not think of that kiss anymore, no matter how perfect it had been. But, drat it all, even the ashes in her fireplace reminded her of the night they'd roasted cannonballs.

Perhaps selling their home would be a good thing.

No, not if it meant parting with all the memories of her mother.

A loud rap startled her into dropping the book she held. Could it be Ian? Had he come after all? Part of her soul soared while the other part curled into a corner and hid its face. She tensed, waiting for Suzy to answer the door, but it was Chelle's voice that echoed through to Sarah.

"Good afternoon, Suzy. Is Sarah at home? I've only got a few minutes before I need to be back at the school."

"In here," Sarah called out, wishing she didn't feel so disappointed. Chelle never called on the days she was required to teach. Something must be amiss.

The moment her friend entered the salon, Sarah asked, "Is everything all right?"

Before Chelle could answer, Bethia burst into the room, flushed and out of breath. "I heard the knock and came as soon as I could. Oh, Chelle, what a blessed relief to see you here. This house has felt like a coffin of late."

Sarah frowned at her sister. "That's kind of you to say, Beth."

"Oh, you know what I mean." Bethia waved her hand. "Pray tell, Chelle, have you brought us news of any kind?"

"I have." Chelle took a seat and grabbed a small cake from the tea tray. "Forgive me, but I'm famished. I typically take luncheon at this time, but I've come here instead."

Sarah slid the tray towards her friend. "Have as many as

you'd like. I can tell Suzy to fetch some bread and cheese as well."

"No, these cakes will suffice." She took a bite and chewed while Sarah and her sister waited anxiously for her to swallow.

"I've only come to tell you that Mr. Collum has declined the house. Mr. Gyles came to the school last night explaining that he no longer wishes to purchase it."

Sarah exchanged a look of confusion with her sister. "Why not?"

Chelle shrugged. "He didn't give a reason. Only said he's no longer interested in the property."

Bethia's hand flew to her mouth. "He must have seen what we did to it. It's the only explanation. Was Anthony very cross?"

Another bite of cake disappeared into Chelle's mouth, and she wiped the crumbs from her fingers. She waited until she'd swallowed to answer. "Not cross at all, and I can't imagine how Mr. Collum could know. We made sure the drapes were closed, and the key has remained in Mr. Gyles's possession ever since."

"I don't understand," Bethia said. "Why else would he walk away from it?"

Sarah glanced heavenward, wondering if her sister really thought so poorly of her. Chelle must have had the same thought because she cast Sarah an apologetic look.

"Hmm . . . on matter of principle, perhaps?" Chelle said. "By giving up the house—something Mr. Gyles has assured me is a great sacrifice for him—Mr. Collum is showing exactly how much he cares about Sarah."

"Oh, yes, of course," said Bethia, as if only just considering that point of view. "That must be it. Oh, Sarah, how wonderful."

It might be, if that was indeed the case, but there could be many reasons why Ian walked away. Perhaps her sister had been right, and he'd somehow learned about their recent "renovations." Perhaps he'd just changed his mind. Or perhaps he'd found someplace else he liked better.

As much as Sarah would love to believe Chelle's explanation, she couldn't bring herself to hope for it. After all, he hadn't come to call this morning as he usually did. Wasn't that a sign he'd chosen to walk away from both the house and her?

Chelle gulped down a cup of tea and brushed a few crumbs from her gown. "I must go, but I shall see you both at Mr. and Mrs. Taylor's this evening, correct?"

Sarah groaned inwardly. She'd forgotten all about the musicale.

"Yes," she said with a weary sigh. "We will see you tonight."

"Correction," Bethia said firmly. "Sarah and Papa will see you tonight. Anthony is to attend as well, and I'll not set foot in any house where he is present."

Sarah had to smile at that, as did Chelle. Bethia had taken her self-righteous indignation and run wild with it. Mr. Gyles would have his hands full once they were wed.

Chelle picked up her reticule and stood. "I will come beforehand, and we can get ready together, Sarah."

"Thank you." Once again, Chelle had gone out of her way to try and brighten Sarah's day. From pink paint to a new coiffure to hopeful news, Chelle was always at the ready. There wasn't a truer friend in all the world.

· · • · · ·

THAT EVENING, SARAH sat between her father and Chelle at Mr. and Mrs. Taylor's annual amateur musicale. They'd

never been overly choosy in their choice of musicians—
allowing most anyone to sing or play—and as such, the affair
had become less and less attended over time. It was the
reason Sarah's family had always made a point to attend. She
liked the Taylors and their unstuffy ways.

This evening, however, with her thoughts in constant
turmoil, Sarah found it easy to tune out the noise—at least
until the sound of a fiddle, accordion, and wooden flute
floated into her subconscious.

She looked up to see a small, round man with a bushy
beard grinning widely as he tapped his foot along to the
music. When he joined in with a strong Scottish accent, his
voice was surprisingly pleasant.

The Bonniest Lass in a' the Warld
The bonniest lass in a' the warld,
I've often heard them telling,
She's up the hill, she's down the glen,
She's in yon lonely dwelling.
But nane could bring her to my mind
Wha lives but in the fancy,
Is't Kate, or Susie, Jean, or May,
Is't Effie, Bess, or Sarah?
Now lasses a' keep a gude heart,
Nor e'er envy a comrade,
For be your een black, blue, or gray,
Ye're bonniest aye to some lad.
The tender heart, the charming smile,
The truth that ne'er will falter,
Are charms that never can beguile,
And time can never alter.

Was it Sarah's imagination or had the man paused when
he'd sung the name Sarah? He didn't look her way at all, but

there was something in the twinkle of his eye that teased and taunted.

Good grief, get a hold of yourself. He'd done nothing of the sort.

As people began to clap, Chelle leaned over. "That was an interesting choice of songs and an even more interesting change to the lyrics."

"What do you mean?" Sarah whispered, her hands joining in the applause.

"That song is one we've taught to the girls in our school, so I'm familiar with it. I'm also fairly certain the singer replaced the name *Nancy* with *Sarah*."

"And I'm certain you're only thinking what you wish to think," Sarah replied. "How could you possibly remember all of those names?"

"I don't, really. I'm not the music teacher. But it's a song of rhymes, and *Sarah* does not rhyme with *fancy*."

A strange feeling tickled Sarah's stomach. She couldn't remember hearing the word *fancy* or noticing whether or not *Sarah* had rhymed with anything. Was Chelle correct? Had her name been inserted in the lyrics on purpose? Was Ian somehow behind this?

"I've got to hand it to Mr. Collum," Chelle said quietly. "That was clever of him."

A spark of hope flared inside Sarah, but she was quick to quash it. This was just Chelle's way of attempting to cheer her up again. Ian couldn't possibly have arranged for that artist to come and sing that song. It was too much of a stretch.

Later, however, when she overheard Mrs. Taylor say that the Scottish song had been a last-minute addition, Sarah's hopes rose just a little.

·· 23 ··

NOON CAME AND went with no appearance from either Ian or Anthony. Bethia looked ready to burst into tears, so Sarah had proposed an outing to town. Perhaps the air, crush of people, and change of scenery would help both of their moods.

As Sarah walked alongside her sister, she thought back to the evening before. It now seemed ludicrous to think that Ian had something to do with that song.

Chelle and her theories.

What Sarah needed to do was forget Ian and put her efforts into finding some work. She refused to stand by and watch her family lose their beloved home when she could do something to prevent, or at the very least, postpone it. Perhaps the library was hiring. She could stop in and inquire of Mrs. Wright.

"Oh, Miss," a young feminine voice called out. Sarah turned to see the small flower girl rushing her way with a large, slightly haggard posy. Her dress was also haggard, with its frayed hem and patched holes. She stopped in front of Sarah and dipped into an awkward curtsy.

"For you, Miss." She pushed the posy into Sarah's hands. "That nice, tall gent said I'm to give 'em to you. A bonnie posy for a bonnie lass, he said. Bought me one too, even though I made 'em meself."

She blushed and smiled, and Sarah smiled back. There was no mistaking Ian's handiwork this time. Her spirits lifted as she raised the posy to her nose and breathed in the fragrance of yarrow and purple anemones.

"What's your name?" Sarah asked the young girl.

"Mary, Miss. Mary Mack."

"Well, Miss Mary Mack, this is the loveliest posy I've ever received. Thank you."

The little girl's blush deepened, and she bobbed another curtsy before scurrying back to her stand.

Bethia watched her go, a thoughtful expression on her face. "What a darling child. She's about the same height as me when I was her age. I wonder if some of my old dresses would fit her."

Sarah tried to keep the look of surprise from her face. Bethia had never been one to give much notice to those in need. It wasn't that she was unfeeling or didn't care. She was merely distracted by other, more obvious things.

"What a good idea, Beth," said Sarah, proud of her sister for seeing past her own distress. "We should bring her a few of them and perhaps a loaf of bread or two as well?"

"Yes," Bethia agreed. "Yes, we should."

As they continued walking, Sarah's smile remained. She smelled the flowers again as she searched the street, looking for a high-perched phaeton.

"That was good of Mr. Collum to get you flowers," Bethia said, sounding glum.

Sarah thought it best not to reply.

A bell chimed as she and Bethia walked into the library.

Bethia glanced around, looking unhappy and bored, while Sarah inhaled the familiar scents of leather and paper. Yes, this was a place where she could easily work. She could even look past the snubs and whispers of others if it meant helping her father.

"Ah, Miss Meacham," Mrs. Wright said the moment she spotted Sarah, "how very fortuitous. A book was recently returned that I thought you might enjoy. I set it aside for you. One moment."

Sarah's mouth nearly fell open at her words. Mrs. Wright had willingly held a book for her? It couldn't be.

Mrs. Wright's head disappeared behind the counter, and Sarah slowly approached while the other woman rummaged around.

"Ah, here it is." She popped back up with a wide smile on her face. "The first volume of *Northanger Abbey* and *Persuasion*—two stories published as a four-volume set at the beginning of last year. According to my records, you have yet to borrow any of them. I take it you've not read them?"

"No, I haven't." Sarah accepted the book gratefully, running her fingers along the copper-colored cover. Years ago, she'd read and enjoyed *Pride and Prejudice* and *Sense and Sensibility*, but she hadn't gotten around to reading any of Miss Austen's other tales.

"I'm sure the remaining volumes can be located for you. They are not horror stories, mind you, but I believe you will find them more to your liking than *Frankenstein*."

"Thank you, Mrs. Wright. That was most thoughtful of you."

The woman gave a slight wave of her hand. "Posh, no trouble at all. I hope you enjoy it."

Sarah fingered the rough pages of the book before clutching it to her chest. The proprietress likely had no idea how much her small act of kindness had touched Sarah, but it had. Perhaps the two of them *could* become friends.

Sarah cleared her throat. "I wonder, Mrs. Wright, if you happen to be in need of any help at the moment."

The woman frowned in confusion, obviously not understanding what Sarah was asking.

"What I mean to say is, I am looking for work and am hoping you might have a position available at your lending library."

"Oh." Mrs. Wright's eyes widened. She stared at Sarah for a moment before glancing around in a frantic fashion, as though searching for any odd job she could give Sarah. "I . . . er . . ."

"I don't mean right away, but should you ever find yourself in need of additional help, I'd appreciate it if you would consider me. I love books, you know, and organization. I'm also a quick learner."

The woman's shoulders relaxed, and she gave Sarah a sympathetic smile. "I'm fully staffed at present, Miss Meacham, but should that change in the near future, I will most certainly let you know."

"Thank you." Sarah tried to mask her disappointment as she returned to Bethia's side. Her sister had taken a seat near the door and now thrummed her fingers across the table while staring aimlessly out the window.

"Let's put you out of your misery, sister dear, and continue our jaunt through town."

Bethia straightened and bounced to her feet. "Already? But you haven't even perused the shelves like you always do."

Sarah held up the book she carried. "I have what I came for. We can go."

"Thank heavens." Bethia wrinkled her nose. "It always smells so musty in here."

As they continued their journey up the street, pausing to look at some bonnets in the milliner's windows, Sarah kept an eye out for a certain tall gentleman with dark hair and chestnut eyes. She wasn't sure what she'd say to him if they did cross paths, and a small part of her was relieved when they didn't.

It wasn't until she had returned home and curled up in her favorite chair that she realized the book from Mrs. Wright had really been a gift from Ian. Tucked between the pages of the first chapter, she found a note.

For Miss Sarah Meacham,
> *A woman who has tried my patience, upset my bookshelves, tilted my world, and snagged my heart. May you find this book (or rather this note) as persuasive as the title suggests.*
> *Yours, Ian*

P.S. I have vols II, III, & IV in my possession should you wish to read them. You need only grant me an audience.

Oh, that wretched man. A light, airy happiness bubbled up inside Sarah. She snickered then laughed out loud. Tried his patience and upset his bookshelves indeed. Her favorite part, however, was the word *Yours.*

Was he hers?

"What's so amusing?" Bethia asked from her place on the couch not far away. She squinted at a needle while she jabbed a length of thread through the eye.

Sarah tucked the note back into the book, not wanting to upset her sister again. If Bethia learned that Ian had made another romantic overture, while Anthony had not, there would be no consoling her.

"Only this book. It's vastly entertaining."

"Will you read it to me?" Bethia asked.

"Of course." Sarah hadn't yet read the first line, so she really had no idea if the tale would be as amusing as she'd suggested, but she began reading anyway.

> *No one who had ever seen Catherine Morland in her infancy, would have supposed her born to be an heroine. Her situation in life, the character of her father and mother, her own person and disposition, were all equally against her.*

Bethia looked up from her embroidery with a frown. "This doesn't sound amusing at all."

No, no it didn't. But that didn't keep Sarah from laughing again.

··24··

IAN SLID THE pages of his ledger aside and raked his fingers through his hair. His eyes were bleary, mind numb. He'd go mad if he had to look at another number. How Davie did this all day, Ian couldn't understand. As soon as the man returned from London, he would be given a well-deserved raise.

He stretched and walked to the window overlooking the street, where he squinted, sure he'd just seen a mass of red curls enter the pub down the way.

You're going mad, he muttered to himself. Only yesterday he could have sworn he'd seen Sarah on the beach as he rode past, but it was merely a bonnet with a mass of red feathers.

Had she realized the Scottish song had been for her? Had she received the flowers? Seen the note he'd tucked into that book? Had she been treated to an ice at Carington's Tea Shop, compliments of him? Did she even like ices?

Och, he was behaving like a lovesick fool. What had begun as a subtle attempt to win her back had quickly transitioned into obvious desperation. Would she even reply to his note and request the remaining volumes of *Northanger Abbey* and *Persuasion*? Mrs. Wright had assured him that she would want to finish the tales, but now an entire week had passed with no word from her. For all he knew, she hadn't yet been to town and was still unaware of the lengths he'd gone to win her back.

Perhaps he needed to do something more. Something bigger.

Lovesick fool.

Ian stretched at the waist, twisting his spine back and forth and his shoulders along with it. His body felt tight and sore, as though he'd just spent an afternoon sparring instead of hunching over ledgers.

Footsteps clattered down the stairs, echoing through the small office space—a reminder that he needed to begin looking for another house in which he and Banjeet could live.

The lad burst into the room, his face aglow. "I've lessons today, *Pita*. Must be off."

Banjeet looked downright giddy, and was that cologne Ian smelled? Over the past few weeks, Ian had noticed a significant decrease in complaints about lessons and an increase in excitement.

"Am I to assume you are liking Lady Ariana?"

Banjeet's face flamed, and Ian had to look away to hide his grin. It seemed Banjeet was experiencing his first tendré.

"She must be an interesting instructor," he amended.

Banjeet relaxed, and his grin widened. He swiped the black hair from his forehead and began tugging on his boots. "Did you know the angles of the moon and stars can be used to calculate longitudes?"

Ian nodded. "I did, though chronometers are now used for that purpose."

"Does Captain James have a chronometer?" Banjeet asked, eyes round.

"Aye. He doesn't have much use for it these days—'twould be difficult to get lost along the English Channel—but he'd never make a long voyage without one. You should ask him to teach you how it works when next you sail."

Banjeet finished pulling on his boots and grabbed his jacket from the rack. He whipped it on and smoothed back his hair. "A good captain should know how to calculate angles without a chronometer, just in case it breaks or gets lost. Least that's what Lady Ariana says."

The more Ian learned about Lady Ariana, the more impressed he'd become with her. She'd been able to do what no other tutor had done for Banjeet. Just like Sarah had foretold, she'd made him *want* to learn.

"You should listen to Lady Ariana. She sounds like a wise woman."

"She is that. Says I must practice my letters each day for at least thirty minutes. If someone can't read what I write, or if I spell certain words wrong, it could cause all sorts of problems."

"Indeed." Ian strove for a straight face. How many times had he tried to tell the lad the same thing?

He thought back to that day on the ship when Sarah had first suggested he look for a bonnie tutor with a keen mind. Ian had been desperate enough to try anything, so he'd taken her advice and contacted Miss Ellington even though he hadn't truly believed it would make a difference.

He'd been wrong.

Banjeet pulled a timepiece from his pocket and flipped it open, frowning at the time. "Drat, I'm late." He charged out into the day, slamming the door behind him.

Ian couldn't help himself. He laughed out loud. *Drat?*

'Twas Lady Ariana's influence, no doubt. Och, how Ian would love to see the look on Captain James's face the first time Banjeet used that expression onboard.

He shook his head as he returned to the desk.

'Twould seem there were now two lovesick fools living here.

·　.　•　.　•　.　.　·

Dear Mr. Collum,

I'd like the second volume of Northanger Abbey, please. Would you be willing to call on me at your earliest convenience?

—Miss Meacham

Sarah reread the words with a frown, then crumpled the paper and tossed it next to three other wads in her fireplace. Such waste. She began pacing across the wooden planks of her small bedchamber.

Think, Sarah, think.

It should be an easy note to write. But every word she'd written sounded so bland and . . . well, wince-worthy. Not at all the sort of letter she wished to write.

If only Miss Austen would appear in her room to instruct her. *She'd* undoubtedly come up with something businesslike and clever, yet personal at the same time. But not too personal. Sarah wasn't ready to reveal herself completely, not until she saw for herself the truth of his feelings.

For pity's sake, just write something and be done.

Sarah squared her shoulders, took a seat once more and stretched her fingers, popping a few knuckles in the process. Then she pulled a fresh sheet of paper from the drawer and began anew.

Dear Mr. Collum,

The plight of Catherine Morland has captured my interest completely. The pompous Mr. Thorne only just left town, and though I hope he will stay away forever, I'm certain that will not be the case. He will return, and when he does, he'll stir up trouble for Catherine and somehow keep her from Mr. Tilney, who I cannot help but champion.

But is Mr. Tilney a worthy suitor? Does he care for her in earnest? Can she trust that his motives are genuine? Will he stay true to her no matter the complications that arise?

I'm of the strongest opinion that it would be better to live one's life alone than with someone who does not or cannot love.

I am hopeful that vol 2 will bring answers to these questions. If you are still inclined to loan it to me, you will find me at home on either Tuesday or Thursday morning between the hours of ten and noon.

Sincerely,

Miss Meacham

P.S. If you'd like to bring Mr. Gyles with you, Bethia—or rather I—would be in your debt. She has been most sullen of late, and I believe he is the antidote.

Sarah quickly folded and sealed the note, knowing that if she reread her words, she'd crumple yet another piece of paper. Then she donned her bonnet and pelisse and went in search of Bethia. Ten minutes later, she located her sister in the garden, mournfully plucking the petals from a sunflower.

"Care to walk with me into town?" Sarah asked. "I need to post a letter, and from the looks of things, you would benefit from the exercise as well. We can take a few loaves of bread and those dresses we found in the attic to our new friend, Miss Mary Mack."

Bethia didn't move. She only peered up at Sarah, her large, blue eyes sparkling with unshed tears. "It's been five days since he's even tried to call on me. I'm fearful I've lost him forever."

"Oh, Beth." Sarah took a seat next to her sister and gave her hand a squeeze. "After being turned away several days in a row, can you blame him? A man's pride can only take so much rejection."

"So he's given up on me, just like that? We are still betrothed! At least I think we are. I only asked that he not make it public just yet."

Sarah released Bethia's hand and gave it a pat. "He has not given up. I'll wager my best dress on it. He's probably just giving you the time you need to come to your senses. Speaking of which, have you? Come to your senses, that is."

"I . . ." Bethia's brow furrowed, and her lips pursed. "I don't know. I'm not cross with him any longer, but how can I forgive him when you are still at odds with Mr. Collum?"

Sarah lifted the note she'd just written and pointed at the name and direction on the front. "I'm not at odds with him any longer, or at least I hope not to be very soon."

Bethia's eyes widened, and she grinned. "Was it the flowers?"

Sarah gave a little shrug. "Among a few other things."

"What other things?"

"Oh, I don't know. A certain song at the musicale. A note tucked in a book. The fact that he's willing to walk away from the house."

"What song, and what note? Do you mean to tell me that all this time, Mr. Collum has been romancing you while my Anthony has done nothing at all?" Her eyes flashed with indignation. "I take back everything I just said. I'm most definitely still cross with him. Why, if he were to call on me at this very moment, I'd . . . I'd . . . well, I'd put an official end to our betrothal, that's what!"

Merciful heavens. Sarah rubbed at the spot between her brows, feeling a headache coming on. She drew in a deep breath before grabbing Bethia by the arm and putting a stop to her rampage.

"Beth, dearest, Anthony adores you. You have an entire shelf overflowing with dried flowers from him, and a drawer packed with notes. He has waited ages for your hand and has gone to extreme lengths to obtain Father's permission, only to be turned away day after day when he arrived on our step to apologize. Perhaps now is not the time to be angry and instead plan a romantic overture of your own."

Bethia seemed to consider Sarah's words, at first with a stubborn frown, then with a more thoughtful expression. She twisted a blonde curl around her finger.

"Perhaps you are right," she said at last. "But what can I possibly do? Write a note? Send *him* a posy? What rot. I can't think of a single thing."

Sarah understood completely. Ever since she'd received Ian's note, she'd been at a loss for how to proceed. Other than his place of business, she had no idea where she might stumble upon him. She couldn't exactly walk into the pub near the docks and leave something there for him, nor could she call on him.

In the end, a note was the only thing she could think to do.

"Let's walk to Carington's and get an ice. We can bring

your old dresses and visit Miss Mack, post my letter, and decide on a plan for Anthony along the way. How does that sound?"

"I'll get my pelisse."

Thirty minutes later, they were ensconced at a table in the tea shop, awaiting their order. The moment an ice was placed in front of Sarah, with the words, "Compliments of Mr. Collum, Miss Meacham," Bethia became angry all over again.

Mr. Gyles, it seemed, had some groveling to do.

·· 25 ··

THE HOUR WAS ten minutes to noon on Thursday. Sarah had about lost hope that Ian would come when she spied a large dark horse carrying a tall rider coming up the drive.

Her breath caught. Her pulse quickened. Her fingers fidgeted and shook.

He's here. He's nearly here.

She pinched her cheeks and inhaled deeply, willing her breathing to regulate. The last thing she wanted to do was sound like a nervous ninnyhammer. She smoothed the folds of her favorite morning gown—a light green muslin—and patted her hair. If only Chelle could have worked her magic this morning, but alas, school claimed much of her time these days. Instead, Sarah and Bethia had ministered to each other, producing only marginal results.

Her slippers tapped against the floor in a staccato fashion, and Sarah pressed down on her knees to keep them still. What would Ian say? What would she? She'd had ample time to come up with a plethora of things, but now that he had finally come, the pounding of her heart drowned out all thoughts.

Bethia spied him as well.

"It appears as though Mr. Collum has come," she said petulantly. "I'm beginning to think that Anthony never received my note."

After all of their planning and scheming, the girls came up with several ideas to get Anthony's attention. Some were ridiculous, like feigning a sprained ankle in front of his house, while others were downright laughable, such as Bethia posing as a man to confront Anthony at the alehouse. In the end, however, Bethia had followed Sarah's lead and penned a note.

Still, it had felt good to laugh with her sister.

Now, however, Bethia was no longer laughing. Tears wet her eyes, and her lips trembled. "What if he's changed his mind? No, I will not spoil this day for you. I will be up in my bedchamber if you need me."

She began to rise when Sarah caught sight of another horse and rider coming around the bend.

"Beth," Sarah said.

Her sister froze then raced for the window, her tears clearing as fast as they'd come. "It is. Oh, it is! He's come at last!"

She scurried first to a chair, only to move to the sofa seconds later. She picked up her embroidery and shoved a needle through the fabric, wincing when she stabbed herself.

"Crags!" She shoved the tip of her injured finger into her mouth. "I think I drew blood."

Sarah tried not to giggle, but she wasn't entirely successful, judging by the glare Bethia cast her way. But Sarah was still grateful to her sister. Her frenzied antics had lightened the mood and eased some of Sarah's anxiety—until a loud knock thudded through the room.

Sarah startled, wondering if Suzy had heard or if the

girls would need to answer it themselves. Much to Sarah's surprise, however, it was their father who appeared in the foyer. He gave them a strange look before pulling the door open.

"Ah, Mr. Collum. Mr. Gyles. Come in, come in."

"Thank you, sir." And just like that, Ian stepped into her foyer, his hat in his hands and his dark hair falling across his forehead. He looked over and caught Sarah's gaze.

Her hands shook while her heart reared and bucked like a wild stallion. He searched her face while Anthony raced between them, no doubt anxious to be at Bethia's side.

"My dear, can you forgive me? I was called to London on some urgent business last week and only just returned early this morning." He continued talking, but Sarah paid them no heed after that.

Ian stepped into the room, his eyes still on hers. Sarah tried to rise, but her body felt glued to the chair. She gripped the cushioned arms tightly in an effort to keep her hands from trembling.

"Mr. Meacham, I'd like a private word with your daughter, if I may," Ian said, still watching her.

"Sarah is old enough to speak for herself," her father replied.

Sarah swallowed, then nodded, not trusting her voice.

"Would you care for a stroll in the garden?" He held out his hand, and she stood, slipping her fingers into his.

She noticed then that he carried the second volume of Jane Austen's book in his other hand. He tucked her arm into the crook of his elbow, and she held on tightly, worried her legs would give out. His jaw was freshly shaven, his cravat tied perfectly, and goodness, did he smell good. Sarah swayed a little closer.

How she'd missed him.

He didn't speak again until they were in the garden, at the same spot where he'd kissed her before. Her lips tingled with anticipation. Surely, he intended to kiss her again.

He captured her hand in his, and she reveled in the feel of it. Large and masculine, strong and gentle. And the warmth. Oh, the warmth.

He tossed the book he held onto a nearby stone bench. "Volume two, as requested. You must be anxious to discover Miss Morland's fate."

I'm more anxious to discover my own.

She swallowed, forcing herself to speak. "I am, thank you."

He took both of her hands and threaded his fingers through hers. "Can you forgive me, Sarah? I'll admit, it all began as a means to an end, but it didn't take long to realize that the ending I wanted most was you."

Her heart swelled as she stared at their hands. "That house must be quite charming for you to go to such lengths to obtain it."

"I've always gone after the things I want."

"Even at the expense of someone else?"

To her surprise, he chuckled, then raised her hand to his lips. "After hearing about the wild and untamed Miss Shrew, I was more concerned with the fate of my nose than your feelings. I was sure you'd scoff at my efforts—you, a friend of the prince, and me, a lowly, illegitimate tradesman. You certainly didn't make it easy on me."

Sarah reached up to touch the bump on his nose. "It's been broken before, hasn't it?"

"Aye."

"Another woman?"

He chuckled again and shook his head. "Shrewsbury could be a rough place for a nobody like me." When she frowned, he added, "Not to worry, though, I held my own."

"It's the other boy that concerns me. What did you do to him?"

"Boys," he corrected. "There were two or three of them. And let's just say they learned to stay away from me after an encounter or two."

She laughed and couldn't resist slipping her arms around his waist. "I've a mind to start calling you Mr. Shrew."

Amusement sparked in his eyes, and the tiny dimple she'd recently discovered made an appearance. "Are you proposing to me, Miss Shrew?"

She stiffened and pulled free from his embrace. "You're as pompous as you were when we first met. I'm doing no such thing. I only meant that—"

"That we're a match well made." He reclaimed her hands and pulled her back into his arms. "I completely agree. Just promise that no matter how much I goad you in the coming years, you will leave my nose alone. Wives should not beat their husbands."

Wives. Husbands. Coming years?

He'd spoken the words so effortlessly, as though he'd already asked her to marry him and she'd already said yes. But had he? Had they come to an understanding without her realizing it?

"Nor should husbands beat their wives," she added carefully, not sure what else to say.

He cupped her jaw and stroked her cheek with his thumb, his expression softening. "I would never beat you, Sarah, nor will I intentionally hurt you again. Och, my bonnie lass. Say you forgive me. Say you love me. Say you'll marry me. I've been in a wretched state these past few weeks without you."

Sarah stared at him. She'd expected an apology and a

profession of adoration, perhaps even a kiss. Not a proposal. Heavens. Was she ready for this? It was too soon.

As she searched his dark and penetrating eyes, a sense of calm quieted her fears and spoke peace to her soul. In that instant, she knew.

"I forgive you," she breathed.

"And . . ." he prodded.

"I love you." She felt the truth of it from the tip of her head to the flats of her feet.

He smiled, and his thumb brushed lightly across her lips.

Kiss me, she silently begged.

"You're forgetting one thing," he murmured, his mouth quirked up at one corner.

Out of patience, she rose to her tiptoes and pulled his head down to hers. "Yes," she murmured before pressing her mouth to his.

Ian groaned and pulled her tight against his chest, taking her lips captive with his own. His kiss was commanding and gentle, strong and soft, and utterly intoxicating. This time there was no reticence on her part. She met his passion with equal amounts of her own, kissing him as brazenly as she could.

Ian *loved* her—the wild and unstable Miss Shrew. He'd interrupted her life with his teasing and mysterious ways. He'd instructed her on sailing, riding, and kissing. And he'd shown her a man who was as caring and witty as he was adventurous.

Once upon a time, Sarah had vowed to never trust a man again. She'd erected walls meant to keep them out— solid, large, impenetrable walls—and they had worked admirably until Mr. Ian Collum had come along.

One would think that he'd come at her strategically and

forcefully, tearing down those walls until they were nothing more than piles of rubble. Sarah might have thought the same at one point. But now she knew that hadn't been the case. Her walls were still very much intact—still impenetrable, still secure.

Ian hadn't knocked them down at all. He'd simply found a door, and with it, a key.

BONUS
KISS

·· Epilogue ··

A BLINDFOLD COVERED Sarah's eyes, making it impossible to see anything beyond small slivers of light. The phaeton bounced along, occasionally hitting ruts that threatened to unseat her. If not for her tight grip on her seat, she would have been knocked from her high perch long before.

"Are we nearly there?" Sarah asked, not for the first time.

Ian's arm snaked around her, and he pressed a kiss to her temple. "Patience is not one of your virtues, is it?"

"It wouldn't be one of yours either if you were in my position. It's not easy to stay balanced when I can't see what's coming."

He gave her shoulders a squeeze. "Never fear, my love, I've got you."

Sarah didn't take much comfort in his words, especially when the carriage hit another large rut. Good heavens. Where were they going? He'd distracted her earlier with news of her father, and she'd paid more attention to that than the direction he'd driven.

A little over a fortnight ago, her father had taken a position with Ian's shipping company. He was now responsible for managing his warehouses and keeping track of the inventory. At first, Sarah had been uncomfortable with the situation, but after only a week, her father appeared happier than he had in a long while.

"I enjoy being useful," he'd confided in her the previous evening, "and the compensation I'm receiving will enable me to remain where I am, at least for the time being. Ian even invited me to play cricket with them." He'd chortled, a sound that had been as unfamiliar to Sarah as her late-mother's voice. "Imagine trying to play such a game at my age. What nonsense."

Sarah had smiled and kissed his cheek. "Your new position seems to agree with you, Papa."

"I think it does, my dear. I think it does."

In that moment, Sarah's love for Ian and his goodness had nearly overwhelmed her. He'd given her father a purpose and likely paid him a much higher wage than someone else in a similar position.

Yes, Ian Collum was a good man. And he was hers.

The carriage lurched, and Sarah let out a small squeal as her body slammed against the side of the seat.

Ian was quick to pull her back. "Dreadfully sorry, my love. I should have taken the direct route instead of this longer, less traveled road. I just didn't want you to deduce our direction."

Sarah pressed her boots against the floorboard and her back against the cushions, hoping it would keep her from sliding again. "Tell me we are getting close."

"Aye, nearly there."

"Thank heavens."

A few bumps and jolts later, he finally stopped the

carriage and helped her down. Solid ground had never felt so good.

He led her forward a few paces before removing her blindfold. His arms wrapped around her shoulders from behind while she blinked against the sudden brightness.

As her eyes adjusted, a house came into view—a familiar, brown-bricked house with overgrown ivy, charming corbels, and a high-pitched roof. The moment Sarah realized where he'd brought her, she wanted to jump back onto the phaeton and take her chances with the road.

"What do you think?" he said in her ear.

"I . . . er . . ."

"It's not what you're used to at Haven House, but we can enlarge it at some point. The grounds are extensive and the view, magnificent." He gently turned her around, and a panoramic view of the English Channel filled her vision. It was as lovely today as it had been the last time she'd stood here.

"It's breathtaking," she murmured.

"There's more. Come, let me show you the inside."

He began to pull her along, but Sarah dug in her heels, frantically trying to think of something—anything—that might dissuade him from his errand.

"Ian . . . Is this . . . *the* house?"

It had been the right question to ask. He stopped, hesitated, then eyed her nervously.

"Aye, but before you form any conclusions, this was all Anthony's doing. He insisted we take the house, and at a significant discount from the price we'd originally agreed upon. 'Twas too good of a deal to pass up, Sarah, especially now that we are betrothed. I'll not have you living near the docks, and this property has such potential. Once you see the drawing room, along with the extensive veranda out back, you'll understand."

Of course Anthony had discounted the price. How could he not? What had once been a cozy cottage now looked more like a brothel, not that Sarah really knew what brothels looked like. But if she could imagine such a place, it would look very similar to Ian's future bedchamber.

"You haven't officially purchased it yet, have you?" she asked.

He nodded. "Signed the paperwork last evening. I realize that I should have spoken with you first, but I wanted to surprise you."

Little did he know that he was in for a surprise as well.

A very big surprise.

"I really wish you would have," she said. "Now that we are soon to be married, we should make decisions like this together."

He pressed a kiss to her cheek. "If I promise to consult you on every important matter from now on, will you forgive me?" He grinned, trying to coerce the same reaction from Sarah. When she only stared at him, he added, "If you hate it, we can find another property and sell this one. I would never make you live in a place you despise. But give it a chance. I have the greatest hope that you will love it as much as I do."

Did, she mentally corrected him. *As much as you* did.

He took her hand and began pulling her toward the house once more, her booted feet protesting each and every step.

He paused to frown at the wooden sign that had once read *Ivy Cottage*. The faded white lettering had since been painted over with the words *The Blushing Begonia* in pink lettering.

"That's odd."

In hindsight, Sarah and Chelle should have added *Brothel* to the end, if only to keep the alliteration going.

Good grief. What had seemed so amusing a month ago now felt utterly childish. The Blushing Begonia, indeed. Sarah wanted to take the phaeton and ride away as fast as she could. She'd even go blindfolded if it meant not facing Ian when he saw inside his precious home.

He led her to the door, where he tugged a key from his jacket pocket and made short work of opening the lock. The moment he stepped inside, his hand went slack in hers, and his body stiffened. The expressions that played across his face were almost laughable. Shock, disgust, and finally . . . indignation.

He released her hand and walked slowly into the drawing room, where the painting of the man with the goat's head mocked them from above the mantle.

"*Jibes and crivens,* what's happened here?"

If Sarah had been thinking clearly, she would have remained silent, but her mouth opened of its own accord and words came out. "I didn't know you liked pink so well, my love. Perhaps you should have consulted me after all?"

Silence.

His shoulders tightened before he turned slowly around to face her, brow lifted, eyes narrowed, mouth firm and unyielding.

"You did this."

Sarah swallowed, thinking her betrothal might soon come to an end. The color on the walls was truly awful. And that picture? What sort of artist would paint such a thing? It must have been a joke of some sort.

A pity Ian didn't seem amused by it now.

Sarah lifted her chin and attempted a look of offended outrage. "I don't see how you came to that conclusion. I've no talent for painting."

"Obviously."

She glared. "How would I obtain such . . . a, er . . . masterpiece? Why, that frame alone would cost more than a decade's worth of my pin money. Or were you not attending when Papa told you of our reduced circumstances? He did mention that to you, did he not?"

A change of subject was definitely the way to go, but perhaps not *that* particular subject. She'd just given him yet another reason to put an end to their engagement.

Drat her cursed tongue.

Ian folded his arms, the expression on his face unchanged. "You'll be living here as well, you realize."

"Yes, but I did not know that when—" There she went again, blurting things out that should have stayed in. She bit down hard on her tongue and stepped backward as he moved forward, pointing an accusing finger at her.

"Tell me, *Miss Shrew*, was it you who painted the walls by the stairs? There are splatters of paint all over the floor and banister."

"Er . . . no?" A lie, as Sarah *had* painted those walls— well, most of them, anyway. Bethia had helped a little.

"I don't believe you."

Blast his perceptiveness.

Defeat settled across her shoulders. She had no choice but to give up the ruse or appear an even greater simpleton. He'd have found her out eventually anyway.

She refused to accept all of the blame, however. If not for Ian and Anthony's ridiculous—no, *offensive*—bargain, none of this would have come about. She should tell him that, and she would. Right at this very moment.

Ian stopped in front of her, close enough that his tantalizing cologne tempted her senses. It was a new scent, rich and warm, with a hint of orange, and it drew her to him like a moth to a light.

Unable to stop herself, she closed the gap between them and fiddled with the lapels of his jacket before sliding her hands up his chest and around the back of his neck.

"You did say Anthony discounted the price, did you not? Perhaps we could use that savings to, er . . . redecorate? The walls were in need of a fresh coat of paint anyway."

He looked heavenward, as though pleading for patience, then pulled her close, dropping his forehead to hers. "'Tis a good thing you're a bonnie lass, or I might throttle you."

"You'd never."

"Nae, but I would make you live with it like this for a while, just to teach you a lesson. But that would mean I'd have to do the same."

"A fresh coat of paint it is, then." She grinned and stood on tiptoe to kiss his cheek. "You, my love, are the most kind, forgiving, wonderful man alive." Under her breath, she added, "I hope you'll remember those traits once you see your bedchamber."

He immediately cringed. "Not the bedchamber too."

She pushed her fingers up into his thick, luscious hair. How she loved touching him. She tried to pull his head down so she could kiss him, but when he resisted, a pang of conscience had her saying, "I truly am sorry, but what else was I to do? I thought I'd fallen in love with a man who cared more about four brick walls than me."

"You could have yelled at me or beat my chest with your fists. Perhaps then we could have resolved things sooner, and this"—he gestured around the room—"would have never happened."

"It was Chelle's idea," Sarah tried. "She practically forced me to help."

He sighed and gathered her close, tickling her neck with his stubble. "Did she tie the brush to your hands and threaten to whip you if you didn't comply?"

"Something like that, yes." Goosebumps flooded down her spine as his lips continued to work their magic. Goodness, he was making it difficult to think.

"Liar."

Her mouth fell open in feigned affront, and she pushed against his chest. "You deserve your pink bedchamber, sir. Along with the painting of the bearded woman and those hideous orange curtains."

He closed his eyes with a grimace before opening them again. "Apparently, your decorating skills are no better than your organizational ones. 'Tis a good thing you only reorganized my place of business, or my bookcase would likely be purple or some other putrid color, along with the floor around it. Did you not think to cover the stairs and banister when you painted? We may have to live with pink splatters for years to come."

"How you flatter me, sir. If you find me so sadly lacking, why marry me at all?"

He laughed, then fingered one of her curls, twisting it around his finger and tempting Sarah with his scent, his close proximity, and his tantalizing lips. "I'm counting on you, my bonnie lass, to read horror stories to our children and teach them how to jab properly. I also have high expectations that you'll kiss me whenever you wish."

Sarah stepped up on the bottom stair so she wouldn't have to stand on tiptoe to wind her arms around his neck. "It is my wish to kiss you right now, you impertinent and ridiculous man."

"How you flatter *me*," he said before kissing her in a way that stole her breath and with it, her equilibrium. She clung to him on that bottom stair in a house that would soon be hers.

Odd how it suddenly felt very much like home, pink walls and all.

Someday she would have to thank Mr. Anthony Gyles for devising a plan that had brought Ian into her life. She'd have to thank her father as well, for demanding that she give him a chance. And she'd have to thank Ian, for pursuing her in the most delightful of ways and for teaching her how to kiss.

Dear Reader,

A million thanks for reading! If this story gave you a happy escape from reality for a time, I have accomplished my goal.

If you're interested in being notified of new releases, or want to check out my other books, you can find me online at RachaelReneeAnderson.com. My newsletter is only sent out when I have a new release (or perhaps a really great sale).

If you can spare a few minutes, I'd be incredibly grateful for a review from you on Goodreads or Amazon. They make a huge difference in every aspect of publishing, and I am always so thankful whenever readers take a few minutes to review a book.

Best wishes!

Rachael

ABOUT RACHAEL ANDERSON

RACHAEL ANDERSON is a *USA Today* bestselling author and mother of four crazy and awesome kids. Over the years she's gotten pretty good at breaking up fights or at least sending guilty parties to their rooms. She can't sing, doesn't dance, and despises tragedies, but she recently figured out how yeast works and can now make homemade bread, which she is really good at eating. You can read more about her and her books online at RachaelReneeAnderson.com.

ACKNOWLEDGEMENTS

This is always a difficult section for me to write. No words can convey my gratitude for all the people who have aided, supported, listened, and encouraged. I have been blessed to have so many wonderful people in my life—from friends and family to readers who I've never had the pleasure of meeting. Thank you ALL.

Years ago at a book signing, I met Kathy, a wonderful woman who took a chance on one of my books. She has since become a well-known book reviewer (Bookworm Nation) and supporter of clean romance. After the publication of my Serendipity series, I hit a wall in my writing career. I was out of ideas and motivation and wasn't sure if I had any more stories in me. It was Kathy who shared with me some of the ideas floating around in her head—ideas which eventually inspired the stories in my Brighton series. She yanked me out of my rut and gave me the push I needed to move forward.

When it comes to editors, I have a truly awesome team of helpers. No writer creates the perfect story, no matter how many revisions (least of all me), but if not for Alison, Andrea, & Karey, my stories would have plot holes, incongruent characterizations, and a host of typos/gram-matical errors. More than that, they push me to become a better writer with each story I write. I owe them so much!

I must also thank the world's greatest agent, Meire Dias at Bookcase Literacy. Not only is she the sweetest, most charming woman alive (seriously), she has also managed to get my stories published in the Czech Republic, Hungary, France, Italy, Germany, & Brazil. I am in awe of her talents, connections, and poise.

My greatest supporter also happens to be my husband, Jeff. Even though stories written by Brandon Sanderson and Clive Cussler are more up his alley, he always reads each of my stories. In addition, he willingly takes over the cooking, cleaning, and parenting whenever I have deadline looming or just need a break. I love him loads and think everyone should have a spouse like him.

I can't end this section without also thanking my Heavenly Father. I have strong beliefs about who I am, where I come from, and the direction I want to go with my life. That knowledge and inspiration has helped me with each and every one of my stories.

Milton Keynes UK
Ingram Content Group UK Ltd.
UKHW021315070823
426454UK00022B/759

9 781941 363290